Nipa Wu ◎著

哈佛高材生的

英語寫作

學習其實有捷徑 只要用對方法
讓哈佛高材生 **Show You How** !!!

三大高分絕招

成功地在**學測**、**指考**、**新多益**中三試三贏

① **命中率百分百**
獨創「必考字彙」和「就是這樣寫」單元，善用零碎時間，
每日十分鐘點滴累積滿分實力!!!

② **文法最易學**
由「必考文法概念」單元，結合日常生活題材，擺脫長篇式文法學習!!!

③ **培養思考力**
從「必考句型與解析」單元，構思句子組成，
靈活搭配所學文法，學習成效更滿分!!!

作者序

　　在教英文的過程中，發現低分考生的困境，是很難寫出完整的句子，這時候，學生需要的是學習「句型」！從反覆熟悉句型中，抓到文法的訣竅，再代換不同的單字，進而學會造句，表達出自己的意思。

　　本書以50個常用句型為基礎，從比較級、最高級等基本句型，到時態，再到常用的連接詞、轉承詞等，每個句型都搭配歷年指考、學測、多益考題中的常用單字造句，提供28個例句，讓學生在學習句型的過程中，也能背誦精選單字。

　　每個例句，都是依據情境精心設想，每個句型並有解析與文法概念擴充，詳細說明一個句子從無到有的結構，並釋疑文法概念，列舉句型變化，反覆記誦與熟背，不但能幫助低分考生突破寫作的困境，學會造句，對於英文已有基礎的學生，相信也有所助益，在平鋪直敘的表達方法外，以各種轉折、連接、片語句型表達更複雜的文意！

Nipa Wu

編者序

　　學生的英文寫作能力並未因為英語教學提前至小學一年級，或是背了許多字彙而有所改善。此外，許多學校老師在評估學生程度或進度後，大多於高三才開始讓學生接觸英文寫作，學生急急忙忙寫了幾篇，緊接著模擬考試，還要準備其他科目轉眼間就要考學測了。只有少數程度較好的考生能在英文非選題部分應答自如，甚至有不少考生拿到了英文作文零分。追根究柢英文寫作並非短時間就能速成的，加上老師負責的班級數跟學生人數不太可能給予每個考生在英文寫作上有更多的協助。

　　本書精選了學測、指考和新多益三大測驗中出現過的常考字，考生能由這些常考的動詞等搭配句型，並善用零碎時間，如每節下課造一句，從高一開始持之以恆，並搭配文法學習跟課堂英語課程等，於高二或升高三時，相信有更多時間能準備其他科目，在其他同學都還在煩惱如何準備時，相信你已經暗中領先了其他考生許多。

編輯部 敬上

目　次

學測篇

Contents

指考篇

新多益篇

學測篇

【句型1】 Unable to + V...，S + V...

103學測 必考字彙表 V1～V28

1. dissect	8. depart	15. cancel	22. assure
2. obtain	9. reduce	16. collect	23. realize
3. settle	10. finish	17. gather	24. devote
4. offer	11. approach	18. harvest	25. quit
5. prevent	12. neglect	19. generate	26. recommend
6. impress	13. replace	20. prohibit	27. explore
7. stir	14. represent	21. recall	28. conquer

必考 句型與解析

【句型 1】Unable to + V..., S + V...（無法…）

【結構】 Unable to "dissect" +（解剖）+（解剖的物），S（執行動作的人）+
V（所執行的動作）…. Dissect ⇨（所解剖的東西）frogs ⇨（解剖的
場合）in the biology class。Unable to + V1 (dissect) + ...。

【句子】 Unable to dissect frogs in the biology class, John turns to his lab
partner for help.

【中譯】 無法在生物課上解剖青蛙，約翰轉向他的實驗夥伴尋求幫助。

解　析

由句型一【Unable to + V1..., S + V....】可以得知，其後所加上的動詞有所變化時，可延伸出不同的多樣式句子，由 dissect 試想所解剖的東西為何，進一步作出推想，例句中為 frogs，進而可以推想解剖青蛙的所在地為何？，若想到為在生物課時其後加上 in the biology class，完成了前面的部分。之後試著推想解剖的人是誰，若為 John，John 當主詞，其後加上所解剖的動作為何，若句意為轉向 turns to 加上轉向誰…，turns to his lab partner for help 轉向他的實驗夥伴求救。而以下的其他例句也會因為動詞的變化可以延伸出許多不同的句子，讀者可以藉由自身經驗造句，推想並藉由表格上的動詞造出各式不同變化的句子。

必考文法概念

【1】 當兩個句子「主詞相同」時，而兩個句子又有因果關係、條件關係時，為精簡句子就可使用「分詞構句」，常用於閱讀與寫作時，因此有必要好好認識它。如本例句中，原本由以下兩個句子組成：

(1)John is unable to dissect frogs in the biology class.

(2)John turns to his lab partner for help.

兩句有因果關係，所以本可以用連接詞合併為一句：

Because John is unable to dissect frogs in the biology class, he turns to his lab partner for help.

【2】 所謂的分詞構句，就是為了精簡句子、變化句型，將連接詞 Because 去掉，並將代表原因句子的主詞 John 去掉，整合起來，就變成：

Unable to dissect frogs in the biology class, John turns to his lab partner for help.

【3】 分詞構句放句首時，與第二句以逗號隔開。

一般分詞構句有主動與被動，若去掉的主詞主動執行該句的動作，則改成「Ving」分詞構句，代表主動進行。如：

Having enough food, Martha stopped eating.

因為已經吃了足夠的食物，瑪莎停止吃東西。

若去掉的主詞無法執行該句的動作，則改成「p.p.」分詞構句，帶表「被動」進行。如：

Overloaded with work, Jeff decided to cancel the trip.

因工作負荷過量，傑夫決定取消這趟旅行。

【4】 在分詞構句中的否定，Not 須提到句首，如：

(1)Martha did not have enough food.

(2)Martha ordered another hamburger.

可 合 併 為 ⇨ Not having enough food, Martha ordered another hamburger.

沒有吃到足夠的食物，瑪莎點了另一個漢堡。Not 提到句首，代表否定。

【5】 分詞構句中，第一個句子也可以被簡化為分詞片語，如用 to 帶領的片語，代表計劃、目的要達成的事項：To see the Helen's face clearly, Jack turned on the lights. 為了清楚地看見海倫的臉，傑克打開燈。而在句型一的範例中，是以 unable to 開頭之分詞構句，代表「無法進行、從事某項動作」。

就是這樣寫

2. Unable to obtain an agreement with the United Kingdom, American colonies declared independence in 1776.

無法跟大英帝國取得協議，美國殖民地在 1776 年宣布獨立。

3. Unable to settle the dispute, Maggie finally decided to give up her inheritance.

由於無法平息紛爭，梅姬終於決定放棄她繼承的財產。

4. Unable to offer the guest any food, the poor woman gave him a cup of hot tea.

無法給客人任何食物，這位貧窮的女人給他一杯熱茶。

5. Unable to prevent the disaster, what we can do is to run away.

無法預防災難，我們所能做的只有逃跑。

6. Unable to impress the interviewer, John failed to get the job.

無法讓面試官印象深刻，約翰沒有得到那項工作。

7. Unable to stir the passion in his students' hearts, the teacher was frustrated about his teaching experience.

無法激起他學生心中的熱情，這位老師對於他的教學經驗感到很挫折。

8. Unable to find any morning flight, I had to depart at midnight.

因為找不到任何早上的班機，所以我得在半夜離開。

9. Unable to reduce any weight, Joyce was going to give up her diet program.

無法減輕任何的體重，喬伊絲即將放棄她的節食計劃。

10. Unable to finish the project on time, Frank finally allowed us to help him.

無法準時完成這個計劃，法蘭克終於准許我們幫助他。

11. Unable to do this alone, he approached us to get some help.

無法一個人做這件事，他向我們尋求一些幫助。

12. Unable to get enough sleep, David neglects his health due to his busy work.

無法獲得足夠的睡眠，大衛因為他忙碌的工作忽略了健康。

13. Unable to turn on the air conditioner, I think I should replace the battery in the remote control.

無法開啟冷氣機，我想我應該更換遙控器裡的電池了。

14. Unable to find a better gift, I gave my mom a banquet of flowers to represent my love for her.

找不到更好的禮物，我送我媽媽一束花以代表我對她的愛。

15. Unable to find someone to fill in my work, I cancelled my trip to Europe.

找不到人替補我的工作，我取消了我去歐洲的旅行。

16. Unable to turn on the gas stove, we had better collect some wood to boil some hot water.

無法點燃瓦斯爐，我們最好收集一些木柴以燒一些熱水。

17. Unable to find a proper shelter, people gathered in the local school after the hurricane.

找不到適當的避難處，在颶風後人們聚集在當地學校。

18. Unable to find enough labor, we had to harvest the rice by ourselves.

找不到足夠的勞力，我們必須自己收成稻米。

19. Unable to generate enough electricity, the solar panels failed to work in the rainy days.

無法產生足夠的電力，太陽能板在雨天無法運作。

20. Unable to prohibit people from polluting the river, the government

decided to close off the area from visitors.

無法阻止人們污染河流，政府決定將這個區域關閉，謝絕訪客。

21. Unable to recall his name, I could only smile at him.

無法記起他的名字，我只能對他微笑。

22. Unable to catch the thief, the police could only assure the family that they would continue to monitor the area.

無法抓到小偷，警察只能跟這家人保證他們會繼續偵查這個地區。

23. Unable to finish the job, I realized that I need some partners to reach my goal.

無法完成這項工作，我理解到我需要一些夥伴以達成我的目標。

24. Unable to run for the race anymore due to the injury, Victor devoted his love towards sports in coaching runners.

因為受傷而無法再參加跑步競賽了，維克多把他對運動的熱愛投入在培訓跑者上。

25. Unable to change his boss's mind, Paul quit his job last month.

無法改變他老闆的心意，保羅在上週辭職了。

26. Unable to show her around Taipei myself, I can only recommend a few places for her to go.

我無法自己帶她逛台北，只能建議一些地方讓她去。

27. Unable to find a guide, I explored the area by myself.

找不到嚮導，我自己一個人探索這個區域。

28. Unable to conquer China, Japan lost more and more manpower toward the end of the Second World War.

由於無法征服中國，日本在第二次世界大戰失去越來越多的人力。

【句型 2】To + V... , S + V...

29. adopt	36. participate	43. question	50. discover
30. reduce	37. impose	44. describe	51. inspire
31. reward	38. disturb	45. wander	52. convey
32. disguise	39. receive	46. experiment	53. represent
33. defend	40. notice	47. ignore	54. collect
34. interact	41. warn	48. respect	55. bend
35. negotiate	42. preserve	49. associate	56. erect

必考　句型與解析

【句型 2】To + V... , S + V...（為了達成…目的）

【結構】　To rescue stray dogs（為了拯救流浪狗的目的）⇨ John ⇨（執行動作的人／主詞）adopt ⇨（所執行的動作）stray dogs ⇨（所領養的事物）。

【句子】　To save stray dogs from suffering, John adopted twelve dogs at home.

【中譯】　為了拯救流浪狗免於受苦，約翰在家裡領養了十二隻狗。

解　析

句型 2【To + V..., S + V... 】可以得知，其後所加上的動詞有所變化時，可衍伸出不同的多樣式句子，由 save 試想所解救的東西為何，進一步作出推想，例句中為拯救狗 stray dogs，進而可以推想解救流浪狗免除的狀況為何？若想到是為了解救流浪狗免於受苦後，其後加上 from suffering，完成了前面的部分。

之後試著推想解救流浪狗的人是誰，若為 John，John 當主詞，其後加上他所從事的行動為何，以達成解救流浪狗的目的，因而提出：adopted twelve dogs at home 在家領養了十二隻狗，此句的前因後果因而完整。當一個動詞是目的時，可以用不定詞 to V 作為開頭，可依表格上的動詞造出各式不同變化的句子，原形動詞前加 to，置於句首，先說明想要達到的目的，再寫出主詞為達成此目的所執行的動作，依動詞的變化延伸出許多不同的句子。

必考文法概念

To + V，不定詞置於句首表目的，修飾全句，置於句首，表示加強語氣的意思，之後須以逗號隔開。To V... (In order to V...)，S + V...

【1】 To see more clearly, Bob put on his glasses.
為了看得更清楚，鮑伯戴上他的眼鏡。
此句等同於

In order to see more clearly, Bob put on his glasses.

本句型內所有的 To + V..., S + V... 都可以置換為 In order to + V，S + V...。

【2】 請注意當不定詞片語置於句首時，to 之後所從事行為必須要與主詞一致才行。

如：To lose weight, exercise is necessary. (X)

這句是錯的，因為不符合分詞構句。當兩個句子「主詞相同」時，而兩個句子又有因果關係、條件關係時，才能省略第一個主詞的原則。

To lose weight, Jane exercises everyday. (O)

為了減輕體重，珍每天運動。

這才是正確用法，因為 Jane 在兩個子句都是主詞，故可在第一個子句省略。本句等同於：

Jane exercises everyday in order to lose way.

就是這樣寫

30. To reduce traffic congestion, the city allows the citizens to drive cars in the old town only during the weekdays.

為了減少交通阻塞，市政府只容許市民在週間開汽車進舊城區。

31. To encourage the students to speak out, the teacher rewarded each student who asked a question with a candy.

為了鼓勵學生發言，老師獎勵每個問問題的學生一顆糖果。

32. To get away from the police, the criminal disguised himself with paints on his face.

為了躲避警察，這個罪犯在他的臉上塗上油彩偽裝。

33. To seek justice, Jane defended her innocence at the court.

為了尋求正義，珍妮在法庭上捍衛她的清白。

34. To be a more personable boss, Jeff interacted with his employees like friends.

為了成為一個更可親的老闆，傑夫像朋友一樣跟他的員工互動。

35. To get the best deal, Karen negotiated with the seller for a long time.

為了得到最好的價格，凱倫跟賣家商議了很久。

36. To get as much experience as possible, the team participated in more than ten baseball games last semester.

為了盡可能地得到經驗，球隊在上學期參加了超過十場棒球比賽。

37. To maintain order in the class, the teacher imposes a lot of rules on us.

為了保持班上秩序，老師對我們強加了許多規定。

38. To borrow the key for car, Kevin had no choice but to disturb his father from napping.

為了借車鑰匙，凱文別無選擇只好打擾他爸爸的午睡。

39. To be able to send her children to school as a single mom, Mary received many help from the social welfare.

為了能把她的孩子送去上學，作為一個單親媽媽，瑪麗接受了許多來自社會福利的幫助。

40. To get a close-up photo of the vase, Louie noticed the it had a little crack on the surface.

為了為這花瓶取得一張特寫，路易注意到它的表面有一個小裂痕。

41. To create a safer green economy, the experts warned the country not to rely on nuclear power in the future.

為了創造更安全的綠色經濟，專家警告國家未來不要再依賴核能。

42. To maintain their culture, the indigenous tribes are working on preserving their languages for the next generation.

為了保持他們的文化，原住民部落正努力為下一代保存他們的語言。

43. To be independent thinkers, students should learn to question everything.

為了成為獨立思考者，學生應該學習對一切事物質疑。

44. To attract tourists to come, the journalist described the scenic site with many excessive adjectives.

為了吸引遊客來，記者用很多誇張的形容詞描述這個觀光景點。

45. To find the most ideal place to live, Jennifer wandered around the country in the past two years.

為了找到最理想的居住地，珍妮佛在過去的兩年在國境裡到處遊蕩。

46. To find the best solution, scientists experimented with different methods.

為了找到最好的解決方案，科學家以不同的方式加以實驗。

47. To show her dissatisfaction toward Tom, Eva ignored him throughout the party.

為了顯示對湯姆的不滿，艾娃在整個派對上都忽略他。

48. To keep the tradition, we should respect the elderly no matter how.

為了保持傳統，我們應該無論如何都尊敬長輩。

49. To memorize the vocabulary more quickly, we can associate the words with different images.

為了更快的記好字彙，我們可以將字聯想到不同的圖像。

50. To overcome the cultural barrier, Harry discovered a new way to market his business in Africa.

為了克服文化障礙，哈利發現了一種在非洲行銷他生意的新方式。

51. To encourage the students to realize their potential, teachers need to inspire the students to follow their dreams.

為了鼓勵學生實現潛力，老師需要激發學生追求他們的夢想。

52. To avoid negative response from the employees, the manager conveyed the company's new policy in a very careful way.

為了避免員工的負面反應，經理以一種非常小心的方式傳達公司的新政策。

53. To get more business, the company designed a new logo to represent its image.

為了得到更多的生意，公司設計了一個新的商標以代表它的形象。

54. To build the house with second hand materials, Joe collected a large number of used wood and bricks over the years.

為了用二手材料蓋房屋，喬在過去的幾年裡收集了大量的用過的木材和磚塊。

55. To make the structure for an arcade roof, Bill bent the steel frame slightly.

為了做拱形屋頂的結構，比爾將鋼架稍微彎曲。

56. To make his house look more prominently, David erected a bamboo pole in the front yard.

為了讓房子看起來更顯眼，大衛在前院樹立了一根竹竿。

【句型3】 連接詞 Because

1. dismiss	8. advise	15. relieve	22. expand
2. manage	9. consult	16. eliminate	23. recover
3. march	10. motivate	17. project	24. vanish
4. connect	11. predict	18. depart	25. examine
5. produce	12. require	19. jail	26. solve
6. loosen	13. display	20. capture	27. imply
7. impress	14. target	21. operate	28. impact

必考 句型與解析

【句型3】連接詞 Because。

【結構】 Because + S + V..., S + V... I am angry ⇨ 一個宣言（statement）⇨ because ⇨ 因為，Dismiss ⇨ 忽略，My opinion ⇨ 我的意見，in the conference ⇨ 會議中。

【句子】 I am angry because he dismissed my opinion in the conference.

【中譯】 我很生氣因為在會議中他忽略了我的意見。

解　析

由【句型 3】Because + S + V..., S + V... 可得知當 because 前後句意有所變化時，可衍伸出不同的多樣式句子，第一句主詞為 I，I am angry 我很生氣，因為什麼原因呢？ because 因為 he dissmissed my opinion，便推想生氣的原因是因為他忽略了我的意見，又補充是在什麼情況下，於是寫 in the conference 在會議中，如果想要更加詳細，可以再增加時間如 last week 上週或 last month 上個月等等，讓本句有更多細節。

之後，可按照表格內的不同動詞，試想是因為發生了什麼原因，造成主詞產生什麼反應，這個 " 結果 "+ because +" 原因 " 的結構，就是本句型的造句要素，可依不同動詞變換出不同的句意。

必考文法概念

【1】 because 的意思是 " 因為 "，是表明因果的連接詞，用來連接兩個子句，可以放在句中說明原因，順序是 " 描述結果的子句 "+ because + " 說明原因的子句 " 也可放在句首，一開始就說明因為什麼樣的原因，導致什麼樣的結果。

如：Because the baby cried so much, I did not get much sleep last night. 等同於 I did not get much sleep last night because the baby cried so much. 我昨晚沒有睡太多因為嬰兒哭得很兇。because 所引導的子句放在前時，注意之後要加逗點。

【2】 because 也可以跟 so 替換，變換位置後使用於句子中，如：Because I didn't have dinner, I was very hungry. 等同於 I didn't have dinner, so I was very hungry. 我沒有吃晚餐，所以我很餓。So 代表的是原因的意思，唯需注意 because 跟 so 不可以同樣放在一個句子中，如：

Because I didn't have dinner, so I was very hungry (X)

因為 (Because) 與所以 (so) 不能於同一句子中使用。

【3】 因為英文要求主從分明，一個句子只能有一個主要子句，其餘為從屬子句，因此如果兩個子句都有連接詞開頭，會分不清哪一個為主要子句、哪一個為從屬子句，不合英文文法。

【4】 because 和 because of 的分別：

because 是連接詞，帶出一個副詞子句，作為修飾語。

because of 是介系詞片語，帶出一個名詞或名詞片語，作為修飾語。

如：I am very tired because of my lack of sleep last night.

我很累因為我昨晚缺乏睡眠。because of 在此連成一起使用為片語，帶出 my lack of sleep last night 為名詞片語，表達原因。或者，可將 my lack of sleep last night 改成子句，則可如下表示：

I am very tired because I was lack of sleep last night.

就是這樣寫

2. The passengers were safe because the pilot managed to glide down to land on the riverbank.
   乘客都平安因為駕駛員設法使飛機滑行降落在河岸。

3. The soldiers are very tired because they have been marching throughout night.
   士兵們很疲累因為他們整夜都在行軍。

4. The trip takes less time because now the highway connects the two towns.
   旅程的時間減短了，因為現在高速公路連接了兩個城鎮。

5. We can be sure the wine is organic because we produce the grapes ourselves.
   我們可以確定這酒是有機的，因為我們自己生產葡萄。

6. The boat would not move because he forgets to loosen the rope.
   船沒有辦法動因為他忘記鬆開繩索了。

7. Freddie receives a promotion because his presentation really impressed the manger.
   佛萊迪得到了晉升，因為他的簡報實在使經理印象深刻。

8. I lost my way because you have advised me to go the wrong way.
   我迷路了因為你指導我走了一條錯的路。

9. The kid's behavior improves because his parents have consulted with an education expert.
   這個孩子的行為有所改善，因為他的家長有向教育專家諮詢。

10. The team performs well because the coach always motivates the kids to do their best.
    這個團隊表現很好，因為教練一直激勵這些孩子們盡力做到最好。

11. I am going to bring an umbrella because the forecast predicts that it is going to rain in the evening.

我要帶一把雨傘，因為預報預測傍晚即將下雨。

12. Please bring an ID with you because the bouncer will require you to show an ID at the door.

請帶一張證件，因為警衛在門口會要求你拿 ID 給他看。

13. The vendor attracts a lot of business because he displays the items beautifully.

這個小販吸引許多生意，因為他把商品展示得很美麗。

14. The campaign was successful because it targeted at the right audience.

這次宣傳很成功，因為有針對正確的聽眾。

15. She feels much better because the medicine relieves her pain.

她覺得好多了因為這個藥紓解了她的疼痛。

16. He feels being treated unfairly because the teacher eliminates him from joining the game.

他覺得被不公平對待，因為他的老師排除他參加這個遊戲。

17. The room will be beautiful because the lights projected on the wall in the night.

這個房間會很漂亮，因為在晚上燈光會投影在牆上。

18. We need to hurry up because we have to depart within ten minutes.

我們必須趕快，因為我們必須在十分鐘內出發。

19. He cannot find a job anywhere because he has been jailed for five years.

他到哪裡都找不到工作，因為他曾經被關進監獄五年。

20. Nobody wants to go to bed because the film really captures their attention.

沒有人想要睡覺，因為這電影真的抓住他們的注意力。

21. He is a dangerous co-worker to work with because he operates the machine dangerously.

他是個與他一起工作會很危險的同事，因為他操作機器非常危險。

22. The company's revenue goes up because it expands into a new market.

公司的利潤上升，因為它擴展到新的市場。

23. She recovered from her cold quickly because she drank a lot of lemon juice.

她感冒恢復得很快，因為她喝很多的檸檬汁。

24. We cannot catch the thief because he just vanishes from the street.

我們抓不到那位小偷，因為他就像是從街上消失了。

25. I feel ensured by the doctor because he has examined me thoroughly.

醫生讓我覺得很安心，因為他很周全的為我做檢查。

26. The teacher gave him the grand prize because he had solved the most difficult problem.

老師給他最大獎，因為他解決了這最困難的問題。

27. The poem is very difficult to understand because it implies a lot of meanings.

這首詩很難理解，因為它指涉很多意義。

28. Steve Jobs was said to be the most influential IT industry leader because he impacted the way we related to technology.

史提夫賈伯斯被稱為是具有影響的科技業領袖，因為他影響我們跟科技連結的方式。

【句型4】 If 假設句

1. warm	8. vicious	15. prestigious	22.complex
2. flexible	9. horrible	16. unrealistic	23. remote
3. splendid	10. ordinary	17. basic	24. deep
4. primitive	11. unusual	18. enormous	25. famous
5. friendly	12. massive	19. limited	26. lucky
6. generous	13. interactive	20. distinctive	27. excellent
7. warm-hearted	14. striking	21. unique	28. radical

必考 句型與解析

【句型4】If 假設句

【結構】 If 假設句：If（假設）+ the weather is warm in the region（A 條件）, you can grow tobacco here（可做某件事，某情況可以發生）。

If ⇨ 如果，The weather is warm ⇨ 條件，You ⇨ 主詞，Warm ⇨ 溫暖，Grow ⇨ 種植（V），Tabacco ⇨ 煙草。

【句子】 If the weather is warm in the region, you can grow tobacco here.

【中譯】 如果這個區域天氣溫暖，你可以在這裡種植煙草。

解 析

由句型 4【If 假設句】可以得知，當 If 的假設條件變化時，之後會產生不同的結果，可衍伸出不同的多樣式句子。第一句 If 開頭後，說明假設條件為 the weather is warm in the region 如果當地氣候溫暖，the weather 是假設子句的主詞，warm 是溫暖 in the region 是進一步修飾，代表這個區域的氣候溫暖，因此完成了前面的假設子句。那麼如果當地的氣候溫暖會發生什麼事呢？You can grow tobacco here. 你可以在此種植煙草。

You 是主要子句的主詞，代表假設氣候溫暖的條件滿足了，主詞就可以執行、從事某種動作。因為種植煙草需要有當地氣候溫暖的條件，所以可以想見，如果主人翁 You 可以驗證氣候夠溫暖的話，就可以種植煙草了，因此完成了整個句子。這就是本句型的造句要素，可依不同動詞變換出不同的句意。

必考文法概念

假設語氣是用以表達假設、猜想、或非事實的情況，之後的子句代表當此假設條件發生後的情況。

【1】 在本範例中，介紹 if 假設句的最基本用法，if 是針對「未來」做假設，if 後方的動詞需用「現在式」。

If 主詞 1 + 動詞 1（現在式），主詞 2 + 動詞 2（助動詞）.

If she comes to my party tomorrow, I will be very happy.

如果她明天來我的派對，我會很高興。

comes 為現在式，而 I will be very happy 則採用為未來式，代表我明天會很高興。

【2】 If 後也有 will, would, can, could, may, might 等各種情態助動詞，利用主、從句時態的不一致，產生各種基本句型。如：

If you study hard, you will pass the exam. 你將通過考試

You might pass the exam. 你有可能通過考試

【3】 If there is... 代表如果有這種情況發生了，如：

If there is storm tomorrow, we will cancel the trip.

如果明天有暴風雨，我們會取消旅程。

If there is any mistake, I will correct it immediately.

如果有任何錯誤，我會立即修正。

【4】 If 之後的子句也可以用祈使句，代表如果某樣情況發生了，請對方立刻做這樣的事情。例如：If there is something unusual, report to the security guard immediately. 如果有不尋常的事情發生了，馬上向警衛報告。

✎ **就是這樣寫** ❜

2. If you are flexible, you can play basketball much better than other people.

   如果你的身體靈活，你籃球會比其他人打得好很多。

3. If your idea is splendid, it will be adopted by the company.

   如果你的點子很精彩，就會被公司採用。

4. If people can survive without electricity in the primitive society, I think we can learn to reduce the use of energy in our modern world.

   如果原始社會的人可以不用電而生活，我想我們可以學習在現代世界中學習減少能源的使用。

5. If we are friendly to the new student, she will not feel so alone anymore.

   如果我們對新來的學生友善，她就不會感到那麼孤單了。

6. If you are generous, you will be liked by people around you.

   如果你很慷慨，你會受身邊的人喜愛。

7. If Lisa becomes warm-hearted, she will learn to appreciate everything people have done for her.

   如果麗莎能變得心胸溫暖的話，她就會學習感謝人們為她所做的一切。

8. If his intention is vicious, you must protect yourself.

   如果他的意圖是惡意的，你一定要保護自己。

9. If the weather is horrible tomorrow, we will cancel the trip.

   如果明天天氣很糟糕，我們會取消這次旅行。

10. If that is just an ordinary exhibition, I would not want to waste my time to see it.

    如果那只是一場平凡的展覽，我不會想浪費我的時間去看。

11. If there is something unusual, report to the security guard immediately.

如果有什麼不尋常的事情發生了，立刻向安全警衛報告。

12. If there is a massive wave coming, evacuate from the beach right away.

如果出現巨浪，立刻從海灘上撤離。

13. If the class is interactive, students would not feel bored easily.

如果課程是互動的，學生們不會輕易感到無聊。

14. If there is a striking news, Tom is often the first one to know.

如果有令人震驚的消息，湯姆通常都是第一個知道的。

15. If she goes to a prestigious college, it will make her parents very proud.

如果她去念一個地位尊貴的大學，會讓她父母很驕傲。

16. If your plan is unrealistic, it will be rejected by the manager.

如果你的計劃不實際，會被經理否決。

17. If the course is too basic, students would not find it too interesting.

如果課程太基本的話，學生們不會覺得太有趣。

18. If you cannot pay off previously enormous debt previously, how can I lend you more money?

如果你不能付清你之前巨大的債務，我怎麼能借你更多錢？

19. If we only have limited funding this year, we must tighten up our budget.

如果我們今年的經費是有限的，我們一定要緊縮我們的預算。

20. If his performance is distinctive, he will get a scholarship to study abroad.

如果他的表演很傑出的話，他會得到一筆海外留學的獎學金。

21. If your style is unique in fashion design, it will be recognized by the media very quickly.

如果在時尚設計上你的風格獨一無二的話,很快就會被媒體辨識出來。

22. If the issue is complex, it may take us more than three months to solve it.

如果這個議題很複雜的話,也許我們會花超過三個月的時間解決它。

23. If the place is remote, we might need to rent a four-wheel drive in order to reach there.

如果這個地點非常偏僻的話,我們也許需要租一輛四輪傳動車以抵達那裡。

24. If he is in deep trouble, he will definitely call his mother.

如果他深陷麻煩的話,他一定會打電話給他的母親。

25. If you become rich and famous one day, will we still be friends?

如果有一天你變得有錢又有名,我們還會是朋友嗎?

26. If I am lucky, I might get a promotion this year.

如果我幸運的話,我今年可能會獲得升遷。

27. If you receive an excellent result for your test, you will be admitted into a good school.

如果你的考試有很優秀的結果,你就能夠被好學校所錄取。

28. If his opinion is too radical, it will not be accepted by the general public.

如果他的意見太激進的話,將不容易被大眾所接受。

【句型 5】 S + V..., S + V + O

1. surrender	8. commend	15. discount	22. contribute
2. postpone	9. collapse	16. frustrate	23. break
3. abandon	10. dismiss	17. represent	24. escape
4. oppose	11. rebel	18. assemble	25. carry
5. book	12. withdraw	19. invest	26. issue
6. observe	13. relieve	20. disappear	27. emphasize
7. demand	14. suspect	21. kill	28. damage

必考 句型與解析

【句型 5】 S + V..., S + V + O

【結構】 S + V..., S + V + O... ，I ⇨ 主詞，Surrender ⇨ 動詞。

【句子】 I surrender.

【中譯】 我投降。

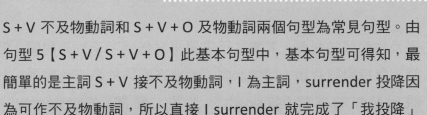

S + V 不及物動詞和 S + V + O 及物動詞兩個句型為常見句型。由句型 5【S + V／S + V + O】此基本句型中，基本句型可得知，最簡單的是主詞 S + V 接不及物動詞，I 為主詞，surrender 投降因為可作不及物動詞，所以直接 I surrender 就完成了「我投降」的句子，之後不一定需要加受詞，句意已完成表達。

補充說明，surrender 也可作及物動詞，是放棄的意思，之後可以接受詞，因此 I surrender my gun. 我放棄我的槍，槍是受詞，這就是 S + V + O 的句型。可依表格上的動詞造出各式不同變化的句子，可以推想主詞要執行什麼動作，該動詞為及物動詞或不及物動詞，然後再選擇是否加上受詞，依動詞的變化延伸出許多不同的句子。

必考文法概念

【1】 不及物動詞指動詞的動作止於行為者的身上，後面不需要受詞。

S + V 句型的動詞為不及物動詞，如：stop、fly、walk、run 等等。

My watch stopped.

我的錶停了。

The bird flies away.

鳥飛走了。

He walks slowly.

他走得很慢。

I ran yesterday.

我昨天跑步了。

【2】 不及物動詞的後面，其實並不需要再寫任何字來補充說明。但必要時，會接副詞片語，如情狀副詞、地方副詞片語或時間副詞片語，說明發生的狀態（如 slowly）、地點、時間（如 yesterday、three months ago）等等，在句型結構上屬於修飾語，不會影響句型結構的，主要接在不及物動詞後面說明的。

【3】 及物動詞是指動詞後面直接接名詞，也就是受詞 (O)

S + V + O 及物動詞，如 love 是及物動詞，之後需要加受詞 I love you. 我愛你，you 為受詞。

或者 He gave me a book. 他給我一本書，give 為及物動詞，me 為受詞。用中文的概念來說，在中文裡面，如「他打我」，打是及物動詞，必須要接受詞我，此句才完整，否則，他打，則不知打了誰、何物。而「錶停了」，停則是自己停下來，為不及物動詞，並不需要受詞，本身就是完整的句子。然而要注意，在英文裡許多動詞其實是既可作及物動詞，也可作不及物動詞，如範例中的 surrender 就為此類。學習的目的並不是去記憶區分及物動詞或不及物動詞，而是在多讀句子、培養語感後，能夠利用及物動詞與不及物動詞的原理分析句型，了解句子的結構。

就是這樣寫

2. He postponed the meeting until next week.

他將會議延期到下禮拜。

3. The mother abandoned her son when he was very young.

這個母親在兒子很小的時候就遺棄他。

4. John opposes my opinion all the time.

約翰總是反對我的意見。

5. She booked the flight ticket for Christmas three months ago.

她在三個月前就訂了聖誕節的飛機票。

6. The sailor observes the sky to look for signs of the hurricane.

水手觀察天空，尋找颶風的徵兆。

7. I demand you to repay all the debt you have owed me by tomorrow.

我要求你在明天之前還清你所欠我的一切債務。

8. I commend her to you without reservations.

我毫無保留的向你推薦她。

9. The house collapsed after the typhoon.

房子在颱風之後崩垮了。

10. He always dismisses my opinion which really annoys me.

他總是忽視我的意見，這真讓我惱怒。

11. Mike rebels against his father by choosing music as his career.

麥克以選擇音樂作為職志來抗逆他的父親。

12. He withdrew his trust after he found out that Kevin had been lying to him.

他收回他的信任，當他發現凱文過去曾欺騙他。

13. The nurse relieved the patient's pain by giving him some pills.

護士給病人一些藥丸,緩解了他的疼痛。

14. I suspect his true intention.

我懷疑他真正的意圖。

15. She discounted all the rumors because she only believed in what she saw.

她忽視所有的流言,因為她只相信自己眼睛所見的。

16. The news frustrated him greatly.

這個新聞讓他大大的沮喪。

17. The Queen represents the Great Britain and should be respected.

女王代表大英帝國,因此必須被受尊重。

18. The technician assembled the car quickly.

技師很快的組裝了這台車。

19. I invested more than a million in this company.

我在這個公司投資超過一百萬。

20. She disappeared without saying goodbye.

她沒有說再見就消失了。

21. The criminal killed three men and ran away.

這個罪犯殺了三個人然後逃走了。

22. Gandhi contributed to the founding of modern India greatly.

甘地對現代印度的建立貢獻良多。

23. My boyfriend broke up with me last month.

我的男朋友上個月跟我分手。

24. The wolf escaped from the trap and ran back to the woods.

狼從陷阱裡逃走,跑回樹林裡。

25. She carried a big bag of books with her all the time.

　　她總是隨身攜帶一大袋的書。

26. The police issued him a ticket for his speeding.

　　警察因為他的超速開給他一張罰單。

27. She emphasized her own importance throughout the speech.

　　她在整個演講裡強調她自己的重要性。

28. The strong wind in the night damaged the roof.

　　晚上強烈的風損壞了屋頂。

【句型6】S + be 動詞 + Adj

102學測 必考字彙表 Adj1～Adj28

1. tolerable	8. dense	15. popular	22. positive
2. sensitive	9. harsh	16. humble	23. standard
3. reluctant	10. stiff	17. common	24. religious
4. modest	11. concrete	18. tiny	25. decorative
5. singular	12. rare	19. major	26. alcoholic
6. prompt	13. intelligent	20. huge	27. cooperative
7. expensive	14. serious	21. ancient	28. heavy

必考 句型與解析

【句型6】S + be 動詞 + Adj。

【結構】 S + be 動詞 + Adj。My job ⇨ 主詞，Is ⇨ 動詞，Tolerable ⇨ 形容詞。

【句子】 My job is tolerable but not very good.

【中譯】 我的工作還可以忍受，但並不是很好。

解　析

由句型 6【S + be 動詞 + Adj】此句型可得知，主詞是 My job 我的工作，在有主詞後，設想出一個能描述主詞的形容詞，在本例中為 tolerable 可忍受的，如果需要補充說明，則加上 but not very good. 代表我的工作可忍受，但不是非常好，完成了句子。可依表格上的形容詞造出各式不同變化的句子，設想不同的主詞，配搭以不同的形容詞，從而完成 S + be 動詞 + Adjective 形容詞的基本句型。

必考文法概念

【1】 S + be 動詞 + Adj：主詞 + be 動詞 + 形容詞是基本五大句型之一，最簡單的用法如：

She is tall.

她很高。

The sky is blue.

天空是藍色的。

He is handsome.

他是英俊的。

The tree is green.

樹是綠色的。

This flight attendant is considerate.

這位空服員是體貼的。

The tea is hot.

茶是燙的。

【2】 用來描述主詞具有某種特質或特徵。在寫作上，主詞可以是簡單的 he、she、人名或是名詞，或也可以是一串比較複雜的名詞子句作為主詞，如：

The book you are reading is very interesting.
你在讀的那本書很有趣。

【3】 其中 the book you are reading 就是名詞子句，整個可以當作主詞，而 interesting 修飾該主詞，所以整體而言，還是符合 "S + be 動詞 + 形容詞" 的句型原則。

【4】 常見形容詞詞尾一

意義	字尾	例字
充滿…的	-ful	beautiful 美麗的
	-ous	courteous 客氣的
意義	字尾	例字
有…性質的	-ish	selfish 自私的
	-ive	competitive 有競爭力的
	-ly	timely 適時的
	-some	quarrelsome 喜歡爭吵的
意義	字尾	例字
有…的	-ed	surprised 驚訝的
	-ing	increasing 增加的

【5】 常見形容詞詞尾二

意義	字尾	例字
可 / 能…	-able	fashionable 流行的
…的	-ible	irresistible 難抵抗的

意義	字尾	例字
…的	-al	logical 邏輯的
	-ic	economic 經濟的
	-ical	economical 節省的
	-ial	essential 必要的
	-ous	various 不同的

意義	字尾	例字
無…的	-less	jobless 無業的 childless 無子女的

就是這樣寫

2. He is sensitive to the noise.

   他對噪音很敏感。

3. Mary is reluctant to accept Tom's proposal.

   瑪麗很遲疑是否接受湯姆的求婚。

4. Kevin is a modest person although he is extremely successful.

   即便凱文極度成功，他仍然很簡樸。

5. The young pianist's taste for music is singular.

   這個年輕鋼琴家對於音樂鑒賞力非凡。

6. The receptionist is always prompt to answer the calls.

   接線生永遠及時回應電話。

7. Big houses are expensive to maintain.

   大房子的維護很昂貴。

8. The smell of the odor was so dense that everyone rushed to leave the room.

   這股臭氣的味道非常濃烈，以至每個人都急忙離開房間。

9. John is a harsh teacher, he barely smiles to his students.

   約翰是個很嚴厲的老師，他幾乎不對他的學生微笑。

10. His body is very stiff; therefore, this yoga class is too difficult for him.

    他的身體很僵硬，所以這堂瑜珈課對他太困難了。

11. His idea is very concrete, but I do not see we have the financial resources to do it.

    他的想法很具體，但我看不出來我們有財務資源去執行它。

12. The collections in the museum are very rare.

    這座博物館的收藏很罕見。

13. The boy's response was so intelligent that delighted his teacher.

    這位男孩的回應如此聰慧，讓他的老師很高興。

14. The patient's injury is so serious that he needs immediate operation.

    這位病患的傷勢非常嚴重，他需要立即的手術。

15. That song was popular with people from my mother's generation.

    這首歌在我母親那一輩如此受歡迎。

16. He is very humble about his achievement.

    他對於他的成就很謙虛。

17. The family name "Chen" is very common in Taiwan.

    「陳」這個姓在台灣很常見。

18. Her room is very tiny. You can barely put a desk in it.

她的房間很小，你幾乎無法在裡面放進一張書桌。

19. The mistake he made this time was major, nobody can ignored it anymore.

這次他犯的錯誤很重大，沒有人可以再度忽略它了。

20. The house is so huge that it takes me three days to swipe the floor.

這間房子很巨大，要花我三天時間才能把地板掃完。

21. The computer is ancient, why don't you throw it away?

這台電腦好古老，你為什麼不把它丟掉？

22. His response is always so positive and encouraging.

他的回應永遠是正面和鼓勵的。

23. The pianist's performance was standard but nothing surprising.

這位鋼琴手的表現很標準，但沒有令人驚奇之處。

24. My father is a very religious person. He never misses going to the church on Sundays.

我的父親是很虔誠的人，他從來不會錯過在星期天去上教堂。

25. This column in the room is purely decorative; it does not have a real function.

房間裡的這根柱子純粹是裝飾性的，它沒有任何真正作用。

26. The drink is alcoholic, please do not serve it to people under 18.

這個飲料含有酒精，請不要把它提供給 18 歲以下的人飲用。

27. The suspect is very cooperative in answering the police's questions.

嫌犯很合作的回答警方的問題。

28. The box is very heavy, please do not move it by yourself.

這個盒子很重，請你不要自己搬它。

【句型7】 被動語態

101學測 必考字彙表 V1～V28

1. occupy	8. increase	15. tailor	22. develop
2. inspire	9. surround	16. cover	23. create
3. attack	10. observe	17. twist	24. capture
4. connect	11. foster	18. trace	25. arose
5. overcome	12. keep	19. bring	26. catch
6. transfer	13. push	20. adopt	27. build
7. revise	14. wear	21. model	28. interpret

必考 句型與解析

【句型 7】被動語態。

【結構】 The town ⇨ 主詞（原受詞），was ⇨ be 動詞過去式，occupied ⇨ 被佔據，by ⇨ 被，the German Army ⇨ 原主詞。

【句子】 The town was occupied by the German army during the Second World War.

【中譯】 這個城鎮在第二次世界大戰時曾被德軍所佔據。

解　析

由句型 7 被動式【主詞 + be 動詞 + 過去分詞】此句型可得知，句首是 the town，這個城鎮，動詞為 occupy，被佔據的意思，改為過去分詞 occupied，因為發生在過去，被動語態的 be 動詞採用過去式 was，而進而推想，執行此佔據動作的真主詞是誰呢？是德軍，故用 by the German army，其中 by 有藉由、透過的意思，是被動語態常用的介系詞。完成 " 基本主詞 + be 動詞 + 過去分詞 " 的句型後，可以再加上時間副詞片語或是地方副詞片語加以修飾，在此句裡，即以 during the Second World War 在第二次世界大戰期間，來說明前段句意發生的時間。

可利用此句型，設想不同的主詞，配搭以不同的動詞，加上受詞，再轉化為被動式，從而完成 S + be 動詞 + 過去分詞的基本句型，依表格上的動詞造出各式不同變化的被動式。

必考文法概念

一般的句子都是 S + V + O，是所謂的主動式，是表達的常態，而被動式使用的時機，則運用在：

【1】　當動作行為者未知或不明的時候，句子只好以被動語態呈現。如：The painting was stolen! 這幅畫被竊走了！當發現畫作被偷時，尚不知執行動作的人是誰，因為沒有辦法以偷走畫的人當主詞故用被動式。

【2】 為了強調動作接受者的重要，把主動語態的受詞放到被動語態句子的前面，彰顯該受詞甚於動作的執行者。如：The village is surrounded by the mountains. 村莊被山所環抱，主要強調的是村莊，在敘述中，村莊是主角，而非山，所以改用被動語態。

【3】 為了比較婉轉的傳達句意。如：The article must be revised. 這個文章一定要修改。相較於主動式 You must revise the article，口吻具有 "你必做" 的 命令感，用被動式省略原主詞，只是中性的呈現此文章必須修改的事實，會讓語氣顯得更委婉。

【4】 詳細來看，被動語態是指句子的主詞是動作的承受者。
主動的句型：主詞 + 動詞 + 受詞
被動的句型：原受詞 + 時態 (be + V-pp) + by + 原主詞
兩者一般可互換，如例句的主動式為：The German army occupied the town during the Second World War.

【5】 在以下例句中，呈現的基本的現在被動式與過去被動式，發生的時間是現在或是過去，be 動詞也可依語意需要改為助動詞，如 must / can / should，代表必須、可以、應該之意，如：The problem can be solved. 這個問題可以被解決的，The issue should be addressed. 這個問題應該被討論。

就是這樣寫

2. I am inspired by your poems greatly.

   我被你的詩句所大大啟發。

3. The poor child was attacked by the stray dogs and now she is seriously wounded.

   這個可憐的孩子被流浪狗攻擊，現在她傷勢嚴重。

4. The village is connected with the highway through a bridge.

   這個村莊透過一條橋跟公路相連。

5. He was overcome by the heat.

   他熱得受不了。

6. The student was transferred to another class after a serious quarrel with his teacher.

   在與他老師嚴重的口角後，這個學生被轉移到另一個班級。

7. The article must be revised if you want it to be published.

   這篇文章一定得被修改，如果你想要它被出版的話。

8. My salary is increased, but my workload doubles.

   我的薪水增加了，但我的工作量變成兩倍。

9. The village is surrounded by snow-capped mountains.

   這個村莊被白雪覆蓋的山脈所環繞。

10. The student's abnormal behavior is observed by his teacher.

    這位學生異常的行為被他的老師注意到。

11. The idea is fostered under the support of my colleagues.

    這個想法在我同事的支持下更加強化。

12. The jewelry was safely kept in a secret place when the thief broke into the house.

當小偷闖入房子時，珠寶安全的被保存在一個秘密的地方。

13. The window was pushed open by the typhoon.

窗戶被颱風給推開了。

14. The clothes worn by the super star can be sold online at a very high price.

被超級巨星穿過的衣服在網路上可以賣很高的價錢。

15. The shoes is tailored according to the size of your feet.

這雙鞋子是根據你腳的尺寸量身訂做的。

16. The hill is covered by snow in the winter.

這座小山丘在冬天時被白雪所覆蓋。

17. My ankle was twisted from falling down the stairs.

我的腳踝因為從樓梯上跌下來被扭傷。

18. The history of Olympic Games can be traced back to the ancient Greece.

奧林匹克競賽的歷史可以被追溯到古希臘。

19. The fruits are brought to us by our relatives living in the countryside.

這些水果是由我們住在鄉下的親戚所帶來的。

20. The child was adopted by his current parents when he was only two months old.

這個孩子在他兩個月大時被他現在的父母親所收養。

21. Many scenes in the movies of Harry Potter are modeled after the colleges in Oxford.

哈利波特電影裡面的許多畫面是依據牛津大學的學院所陳設。

22. The city was developed very quickly under the mayor's leadership.

這個城市在市長的領導下發展得很迅速。

23. The story was created based on the memory of my childhood.

這個故事是根據我童年的記憶所創造。

24. He was captured by the enemy and tortured to death.

他被敵人所捕捉，被折磨致死。

25. Misunderstanding is arisen from the inadequate knowledge about the situation.

誤解是由對情況認知的不足所產生的。

26. The boy was caught stealing in a local supermarket.

這個男孩在當地的超級市場被抓到偷竊。

27. The house was built by my grandparents more than fifty years ago.

這棟房子是由我的祖父母在超過五十年前所建造。

28. The history of the castle was interpreted vividly through the guide walk.

透過徒步導覽，這座城堡的歷史被生動地闡釋著。

【句型 8 】 比較級

必考字彙表 Adj1～Adj28

1. fast	8. distinctive	15. quick	22. familiar
2. practical	9. small	16. soon	23. diligent
3. precise	10. wide	17. easy	24. close
4. popular	11. pretty	18. changeable	25. deep
5. tall	12. humble	19. optimistic	26. hard
6. common	13. impressive	20. delightful	27. powerful
7. tight	14. valuable	21. sincere	28. soulful

 句型與解析

【句型 8 】比較級。

【結構】 形容詞 / 副詞比較級。Mary ⇨ 主詞，Faster ⇨ 比較級（副詞），
Brother ⇨ 被比較的對象。

【句子】 Mary runs faster than her brother.

【中譯】 瑪麗比她的哥哥跑得更快。

解　析

由句型 8 形容詞／副詞比較級【A＋V＋比較級 than＋B.（A 比 B...。）】此句型可得知，瑪麗為 A，her brother 她的哥哥為 B，兩者來作比較，是針對跑步這個動作來相比，故用 run，由於瑪麗跑得比她哥哥快，故 fast 改為比較級 faster，嵌入句型後，為 Mary runs faster than her brother，完成句子。

可依據表格裡的不同副詞，設想不同的主詞，加上動詞，配搭以不同的副詞，加上比較的對象，則形成 A 與 B 在此動作特質上的比較。如 A 跑得比 B 快，A 唱歌唱得比 B 好聽。
　　若使用的是表格裡的形容詞，則可直接形成 A 與 B 在此形容詞特質上的比較，如 A 比 B 高，A 比 B 貴。

必考文法概念

【1】 比較級的句型為：A＋V＋比較級 than＋B.（A 比 B...。）形容詞比較級主要是比較人、事、物之間的程度差異，而副詞比較級主要是比較人、事、物執行某動作之間的特質差異。

【2】 一般比較級是在形容詞或副詞字尾直接加 er，如 tall ⇨ taller，或是去 y 加 ier，如 easy ⇨ easier，若二或三個音節以上，則加 more，如 difficult ⇨ more difficult。

【3】 A 跟 B 可以是兩個簡單的主詞，如 Mary and John, you and I，或是兩個名詞子句，如：People who exercise regularly are generally healthier than people who do not exercise. 規律運動的人通常比不運動的人較健康。其中，People who exercise regularly 整個子句就拿來跟 People who do not exercise 相比。

【4】 比較級前，可以加上副詞 much / a lot / a little 來修飾程度，如：She is a littler taller than I am. 她比我高一點點，加上 a little 來形容只高一點點。或者是 She is a lot taller than I am. 她比我高得多，加上 a lot 則拉大差異的程度。

【5】 比較級後面主詞的述語（動詞）往往省略，如：He is younger than I(am). 同時，在非正式用法中，than 後的人稱代名詞可用受格，如 I am a better singer than he is. 簡化說法可用 I am a better singer than him.

就是這樣寫

2. People with actual experiences often offer more practical advices than the ones who only dream about things.
   有實際經驗的人比起只是做夢的人，通常能提供較多實際的經驗。

3. The experiment done by the new method will have more precise results than the old ones.
   用新方法做的實驗會比舊的有更準確的結果。

4. He is more popular than his brother at school because he is more humorous.

他在學校比他的哥哥受歡迎，因為他比較幽默。

5. Maggie is taller than her brother despite she is three years younger than him.

梅姬比她的哥哥高，即便她比他小三歲。

6. This coin is more common than the others, therefore it does not worth as much for the purpose collection.

這枚硬幣比其他硬幣常見，因此在收藏目的上價值沒有那麼高。

7. My new jeans is tighter than my old ones, which makes me really uncomfortable.

我的新牛仔褲比我舊的緊，讓我真的很不舒服。

8. She has a more distinctive voice than any other actress, therefore she gets the leading role in the show.

她有比任何其他女演員更為特殊的聲音，因此她在表演裡得到主要角色。

9. The house is smaller than the one I used to live.

這棟房子比我以前住的小。

10. The streets are wider in the big cities than in the small villages.

在大城市的街道比小鄉村的寬闊。

11. Joan is prettier than all her sisters.

喬安比她所有的姊妹都漂亮。

12. Mark is more humble than anyone who is as successful as him.

馬克比任何像他一樣成功的人更謙遜。

13. Even though Allen is just a child, as a violinist his performance is more impressive than anyone older than him.

即使艾倫只是個孩子，作為一名小提琴手，他的表現較任何比他大的人都令人印象深刻。

14. The advice you gave me is more valuable than any gift.

你給我的建議較任何禮物都更珍貴。

15. David is often quicker to get my jokes than anyone else.

大衛常常比任何人都更快理解我的笑話。

16. My neighbors arrived my house sooner than the fire fighters and helped me put off the fire.

我的鄰居比消防隊員更快到達我家，幫我滅了火。

17. The exam this year is easier than the one last year.

今年的考試比去年的簡單。

18. She has a more changeable temper than her sister.

她比她的姊姊脾氣更變化不定。

19. John's tough childhood makes him become more optimistic than most people because he had learned how to overcome obstacles.

約翰艱困的童年讓他比大多數人更樂觀，因為他已學會克服困難。

20. Your new book is even more delightful than your previous one, I thoroughly enjoy reading it.

你的新書比你的前一本甚至更令人喜愛，我徹底地享受閱讀它。

21. Eddie was more sincere than all other suitors, therefore Jane decided to marry him despite he didn't have any money.

艾迪是所有追求者中最誠懇的，因此珍妮決定嫁給他，即使他沒有任何錢。

22. The surrounding looks more familiar to me than other places. This must have been the neighborhood I grew up when I was a child.

這裡周遭環境看起來比其他地方更感到熟悉，這一定是當我是孩童時長大的社區。

23. Frank is more diligent than his classmates. No wonder he always gets the best grades.

法蘭克比他的同學都認真，難怪他總是得到最好的成績。

24. Penny is closer to me than anyone else; therefore, losing her friendship is unbearable to me.

潘妮對我來說比任何人都親近，因此失去她的友情我實在無法忍受。

25. My love for you is deeper than the depth of the ocean.

我對你的愛比海的深度還深。

26. The class is harder than I thought, I might need to transfer to a new class.

這堂課比我想像中的困難，我也許需要轉到一個新的班級。

27. He is a more powerful man than the mayor because he owns a lot of businesses in the city.

他比市長是更有力量的人物，因為他擁有本市的許多生意。

28. The famous Jazz singer Billie Holiday sings more soulful songs as she grew older.

有名的爵士歌手比莉哈樂黛，隨著年紀越大唱了越來越多觸動心靈的歌曲。

【句型9】最高級

100學測　必考字彙表 Adj1～Adj28

1. popular	8. modest	15. promising	22. aggressive
2. comfortable	9. dominant	16. enjoyable	23. potential
3. frequent	10. admirable	17. affordable	24. confusing
4. hostile	11. fearful	18. costly	25. intensive
5. confident	12. delightful	19. conspicuous	26. exciting
6. radical	13. intense	20. artificial	27. embarrasing
7. competitive	14. considerate	21. reliable	28. disappointing

必考　句型與解析

【句型9】最高級

【結構】 The Great Canyon（主詞）+ is one of the most（最高級）popular tourist attractions + in the United States（在限定的範圍內）. The Great Canyon（大峽谷）⇨ 主詞，most popular tourist attraction（最受歡迎的景點）⇨ 最高級。

【句子】 The Great Canyon is one of the most popular tourist attractions in the United States.

【中譯】 大峽谷是美國最受歡迎的景點之一。

由句型 9 最高級【S. + V. + the 最高級（+ in / on / at /... + 群體）】此句型可得知，主詞為 The Great Canyon 大峽谷，加上 be 動詞 is，the most popular 為 popular 的最高級，前面加上定冠詞 the，用來形容最受歡迎的景點，故為 the most popular tourist attraction。因為只是最受歡迎景點之一，所以加上 one of....，attraction 後加 s。

在基本上鋪陳出句子後，後面加上限定範圍作修飾，in the United States，代表是在美國這個範圍內，大峽谷是最受歡迎的景點之一，完成句子。

可依照表格內的形容詞，變換為最高級，來說明主詞 S 在何種群體內最具有什麼特質，即可變化完成不同句式。

必考文法概念

【1】 形容詞的最高級，一般只要在原級後加上 est 就可以了，如 tall ⇨ tallest，hot ⇨ hottest，或去 y 加 iest，如 easy ⇨ easiest，pretty ⇨ prettiest，若為兩至三音節的形容詞，則加上 most，如 beautiful ⇨ most beautiful。

【2】 在寫最高級句型時，可加入限定範圍（＋in／on／at／…＋群體），以說明 S 是某個群體裡面相較起來最具有某特質的事物，如 He is the tallest student in my class. 他是我班上最高的學生，並不是全世界最高的學生，也不是全市最高的學生，而是在我的班上這個群體內，最高的學生。如果只是 He is the talles student. 則句意略為不明。

【3】 注意最高級形容詞前面要加定冠詞 the，如：I am the eldest children in my family. 要加上 the。

就是這樣寫

2. This is the most comfortable hotel I have ever stayed.
   這是我住過最舒適的旅館。

3. The most frequent cause of death is heart attack.
   心臟病是最常發生的死因。

4. He is the most hostile person I have ever met.
   他是我遇過最有敵意的人。

5. The boy is the most confident performer in the competition.
   在這場比賽裡這個男孩是最有自信的表演者。

6. He was known as the most radical reformer in the country.
   他被認為是這個國家裡面最激進的改革者。

7. This is the most competitive position in the company. You must work very hard to get it.
   這是這個公司裡最競爭的職位，你一定要很努力工作才能得到。

8. He lives the modest lifestyle in the village despite his wealth.
   儘管他的財富很多，他在鄉村裡過著最簡樸的生活。

9. Joe is the most dominate player in the basketball team.

喬是籃球隊裡主導性最強的球員。

10. She is the most admirable professor in the university.

她是這所大學裡最受景仰的教授。

11. It is her most fearful thought that someday she may lose her job due to her illness.

有天她也許會因病失去她的工作,這是最讓她感到害怕的想法。

12. This is the most delightful trip I have ever taken.

這是我去過最令人愉悅的旅程。

13. He experienced the most intense pain in his life when he had the car accident.

當他出車禍時他經歷了這一生最強烈的疼痛。

14. She is the most considerate person I have ever met, no wonder everyone likes to work with her.

她是我遇過最體貼的人,難怪每個人都喜歡跟她工作。

15. He is the most promising young actor in his generation.

他是他的時代裡最有前途的年輕演員。

16. This is the most enjoyable conversation I have had.

這是我經歷過最享受的談話。

17. This is the most affordable house in the city.

這是這個城市裡最平價的住宅。

18. The highway is the most costly construction the city has ever undertaken.

這條高速公路是這個城市所進行花費最高的工程。

19. Her blonde hair made her the most conspicuous person when she traveled in rural Asia.

當她在亞洲的鄉下旅行時，她的金色頭髮使她成為最顯眼的人物。

20. She has the most artificial manner I have ever seen which makes me really uncomfortable.

她有我見過最虛偽的舉止，讓我實在很不舒服。

21. He is the most reliable worker in the company.

他是公司裡最可信賴的工作者。

22. He becomes the most aggressive person I know if he receives any criticism.

一旦他受到批評，他就變成我所知最有攻擊性的人。

23. The girl has the most potential to succeed as a pianist among her classmates.

在她的同學之中，這個女孩最有潛力成功地成為一名鋼琴家。

24. This is the most confusing map I have ever seen. The scale is all messed up.

這是我見過最令人困惑的地圖，尺度都全弄錯了。

25. You will receive the most intensive training once you join the swimming team.

一旦你加入游泳隊，你會接受最密集的訓練。

26. Riding the roller coaster in Disneyland is the most exciting moment in my life.

在狄斯耐樂園坐雲霄飛車是我一生最令人興奮的時刻。

27. Falling down from the stage during the performance was the most embarrassing memory in my childhood.

在表演的時候從舞台上跌下來，是我童年最尷尬的回憶。

28. Our family trip to Europe was cancelled due to my father's busy work. This is the most disappointing thing ever happens to me!

因為我父親繁忙的工作，我們到歐洲的家庭旅遊取消了，這是發生在我身上最令人失望的事！

【句型 10】數量不定代名詞

1. solution	8. insect	15. interpretation	22. anxious
2. candidate	9. soil	16. error	23. enemy
3. landmark	10. assistance	17. laboratory	24. adventure
4. gallery	11. injury	18. popularity	25. protection
5. company	12. confusion	19. power	26. love
6. tablespoon	13. excitement	20. color	27. expressions
7. suspicion	14. disappointment	21. danger	28. instinct

必考 句型與解析

【句型 10】數量不定代名詞

【結構】　many ⇨ 很多，形容可數名詞，much ⇨ 很多，形容不可數名詞，
　　　　　solution ⇨ 可數名詞加 s，many ⇨ 形容可數名詞。

【句子】　There are many easy solutions to this problem.

【中譯】　這個問題有很多簡單的解決方法。

解　析

由句型 10【 many ＋可數名詞 / much ＋不可數名詞 】此句型可得知，There are 為 "這裡有" 的意思，solution 因為為可數名詞，故加上 many 代表有很多解決方法，solution 加 s，成為複數，而再以 easy 修飾 solution，many easy solutions 代表有很多容易的解決方法。

to 是介系詞，代表針對這個問題 problem，有很多解決的方法，完成句型。

可依表格上的名詞造出各式不同變化的句子，試想主詞跟名詞的關係，（用各種不同動詞來表示，如擁有 S ＋ have、創造 S ＋ create、購買 S ＋ buy 等等，依據動詞使用有無限可能），之後的名詞，若為可數名詞，為 many ＋可數名詞，若為不可數名詞，為 much ＋不可數名詞，變化延伸出許多不同的句子。

必考文法概念

【1】 many ＋複數可數名詞（可以明確數出的人事物），如筆 pencil、椅子 chiar、樹 tree 等等。much ＋不可數名詞（不可明確數出的人事物），像是沙子 sand、液體 water、某項抽象的物質如時間 time、資訊 information，或是一種無形的特質如 kindness 親切、grace 高貴、appreciation 感激等等。但要注意，許多名詞可作可數名詞，也可作不可數名詞，

如：Do not drink too much wine. 不要喝太多酒。

在這裡，酒為不可數名詞，用 much 修飾。

但：This is a very good wine! 這是一支很好的酒！

指特定的一種葡萄酒，則為可數名詞，單數可以加 a。或是像抽象物的名詞 troube 麻煩，如：I have had much trouble learning English. 我學英文有很多困難。

在此作不可數名詞用 much 修飾，但在其他句子裡，亦可做可數名詞用 many 修飾：I have many troubles. 我有很多麻煩。因此在使用時，一開始可先查字典以確認詞性，日久便能逐漸熟練。

【2】寫作時，若要表達有很多某項事物，可依據所用名詞之詞性選擇用 many 或 much，若不確定，也可以用 a lot of，或是 lots of 代替，a lot of 和 lots of 可以修飾可數名詞，也可以修飾不可數名詞。

He has many books ⇨ He has a lot of books. ⇨ He has lots of books.
他有很多書。

He has much money ⇨ He has a lot of money. ⇨ He has lots of money.
他有很多錢。

There is not much butter left. ⇨ There is not a lot of butter left.
沒有剩下很多奶油了。

就是這樣寫

2. There are many candidates running for the election.
   有許多候選人參與競選。

3. Paris has many landmarks such as the Eiffel Tower and the Louvre.
   巴黎有很多地標像是艾菲爾鐵塔和羅浮宮。

4. There are many art galleries in the city.
   這城市裡有許多美術館。

5. There are many companies offering the same kind of services, so the market becomes very competitive.
   有很多公司提供同樣的服務，所以市場變得非常競爭。

6. She bought many tablespoons for her daughter's new house.
   她為她女兒的新家買了許多湯匙。

7. People have many suspicions about his true intention to donate such a large amount of money to the association.
   人們對他捐一大筆錢給協會的真正動機有許多懷疑。

8. The campfire in the darkness attracted many insects.
   在黑夜中的營火吸引了很多昆蟲。

9. The typhoon has caused much soil to be eroded from the slope.
   颱風導致許多土壤從斜坡上被侵蝕。

10. He gave me much needed assistance when I first moved into the neighborhood.
    他給我很多需要的幫助，當我一搬到這個鄰里來時。

11. The passenger has many injuries from the car accident.
    這個乘客因為車禍受了很多傷。

12. There is much confusion about the actress's true age.

關於這個女演員的真實年齡有許多困惑。

13. The news generated much excitement in the room.

這個新聞在房間裡製造了很多興奮。

14. The result of John's entrance exam for college has caused much disappointment in his family.

約翰的大學入學考試結果讓他家人很失望。

15. There could be many interpretations about this poem. There is no right or wrong.

關於這首詩可以有很多不同的詮釋，沒有對或錯。

16. The letter contains many typing errors.

這封信含有很多打字錯誤。

17. I sent the samples to many laboratories, but none can tell what the material really is.

我把樣本寄給很多家實驗室，但沒有人可以告訴我這個材料真正是什麼。

18. The comedian enjoyed much popularity during the 60s.

在六零年代時這個喜劇演員享有很多知名度。

19. I do not have much power over him to tell him what to do.

我對他沒有很多影響力可以告訴他怎麼做。

20. There is not much color on her face. She looks so pale.

在她臉上沒有很多顏色，她看起來好蒼白。

21. There are many dangers ahead, please be careful.

前方有很多危險，請小心。

22. The exam has caused him much anxiety.

這個考試導致他有很多焦慮。

23. We made many enemies in the company.

   我們在這個公司裡製造了很多敵人。

24. My father had many exciting adventures when he was a sailor.

   我的父親有很多刺激的冒險，在他當水手的時候。

25. The insurance policy will provide you much protection in case there is an accident.

   如果有意外的話，保險條約會提供給你很多保障。

26. I receive so much love from my grandmother, even though I meet her only once a year.

   我從我的奶奶那得到好多的愛，即使我一年只見她一次。

27. He has many funny facial expressions.

   他有很多好笑的臉部表情。

28. Animals have many survival instincts.

   動物有很多生存的本能。

【句型 11】介詞 at / on / in

1. publish	8. awake	15. resist	22. influence
2. produce	9. solve	16. obtain	23. purchase
3. relieve	10. object	17. contain	24. inform
4. switch	11. preserve	18. approach	25. deal
5. maintain	12. frustrate	19. guide	26. lose
6. accept	13. hesitate	20. drill	27. satisfy
7. amaze	14. insist	21. shop	28. risk

必考 句型與解析

【句型 11】介詞 at / on / in

【結構】　she ⇨ 主詞，in the journal ⇨ 在期刊上。

【句子】　She just published an article in the journal.

【中譯】　她剛有一篇文章發表在期刊上。

解　析

由句型 11【介詞 at / on / in + 空間】此句型可得知，介詞主要是在描述主詞在什麼空間執行何種動作、或是發生什麼事件的詞。

本句句首 She 為主詞，她剛發表了一篇文章，在英文則用 publish 加上 ed 成為過去式 published，作為動詞，從而推想發表了什麼，加上 an article，代表一篇文章。

而發表在哪裡？透過什麼媒介呢？本句還可以給予更多細節，因此加上 in the journal 修飾，代表發表在一份期刊上，若為發表在報紙上，則可說 on the newspaper，若其後再加上時間副詞片語修飾，則可加上 last month 上禮拜、three weeks ago 三個禮拜前，讓句子的意義更豐富，如：

She just published on article in the journal last month.

可依表格上的動詞造出各式不同變化的句子，再試想主詞所執行動作、或事件發生的地方，然後依空間的詞性分別加 at / on / in...，完成地方副詞片語，變化延伸出許多不同的句子。

【1】 介詞 at / on / in 是表示地方或位置的介系詞，在句子後形成地方副詞片語，用來形容主詞執行動作或發生某狀況位於的地方。

【2】 at、on、in 分別用於不同性質的空間，往往很容易混淆，多半是固定用法，要靠記憶，但簡單說來，可作以下原則性區分：

(1) at 通常用於有明確地點或範圍較小的地方，有門牌號碼的特定地址：at 35 Hsinyi Road 在信義路 35 號，at 也會用在幾個特別的場所，如：

at home, at school, at work, at the party, at a meeting on 指在上面，位於⋯之上，在一個開放空間，如 on the ground 在地面上，on the third floor 在三樓上，在某條街上：on Park Road 在公園路，或介於邊界：on the border 在邊界上。

(2) in 通常位於較大的地方，泛指整個區域，如國家、城市，如：in Africa, in Taipei 或指在空間內部、場所內部，in the box 在箱子裡面，in the classroom 在教室內。

【3】 然而在實際書寫中，仍有許多通用，如本例句中，in the journal，有時常用用法也用 on the journal，或者是，指在某建築物時，有時可用 in，有時也可用 at，如：

I will meet you in the building. 我會跟你在建築物裡碰面。

I will meet you at the building. 我會跟你在建築物那碰面。

只是用 in 時，會更強調在建築物裡面。

就是這樣寫

2. The fruit trees on the farm produce a lot of peaches, pears and apples every year.

   這個農場上的果樹每年生產許多的桃子、李子和蘋果。

3. She relieved her boredom at home by watching a lot of movies.

   她透過看很多電影排解待在家中的無聊。

4. She never switches lanes when she drives on the highway.

   她在高速公路上開車時從來不轉換車道。

5. She always maintains a very graceful style when she is performing on stage.

   她在舞台上表演時總是保持非常優雅的風格。

6. We do not accept credit card in the store.

   在我們商店不接受信用卡。

7. It amazes me how people dress up at the party.

   人們在派對上的盛裝打扮使我很著迷。

8. I awoke at ten o'clock on my bed realizing that I have missed the flight.

   我十點在我的床上醒來，發覺我已經錯過了飛機。

9. Students worked very hard to solve the math problems in the final exam.

   在期末考時，學生們很努力的去解決數學問題。

10. At the meeting, everyone had objected his proposal.

    在會議裡，每個人都反對他的提議。

11. You can preserve the vegetables longer if you pickle them and put them in a jar.

你可把這些蔬菜保留的久一點，如果你將它們醃製，放在罐子裡。

12. He was very frustrated by the teammates' poor performance in their last game.

他因為隊友們在上一次比賽差勁的表現感到挫折。

13. If you need anything, please don't hesitate to come to my office. It is located on the third floor.

如果你需要什麼東西，不要遲疑請來我辦公室。它位於三樓。

14. Tony insisted that he was innocent when he was caught stealing on the train.

當被抓到在火車上行竊時，東尼堅持他是清白的。

15. The soldiers resisted the enemy attacks at the gate of the castle.

軍人在城堡的門口阻擋敵人的攻擊。

16. I obtain this book from an independent bookstore in the art district.

我在藝術區的一家獨立書店得到這本書。

17. The drink contains a lot of sugar in the bottom of the glass.

這杯飲料在杯底含有很多糖。

18. We could see the train approaching in the distance.

我們可以在遠方看到火車的接近。

19. He guided me to walk in the small alleys in the city.

他引導我在城市的小巷裡行走。

20. The plumber will drill a hole on the pipe so the water can flow out.

水管工會在水管上鑽個洞所以水可以流出。

21. I like to shop in the big department stores, because they often offer seasonal discounts.

我喜歡在大型百貨公司購物，因為他們常常提供季節性減價。

22. The teacher influenced my thinking in many ways.

這個老師在許多方面影響我的思想。

23. You can purchase tickets from the driver on the bus.

你可以在車上跟司機買票。

24. The sailor informed the captain that there were a group of dolphins swimming by the ship in the direction of 11 o'clock.

水手通知船長在船的十一點鐘方向有一群海豚在游泳。

25. I do not want to deal with you when you are in such a rage.

當你在這樣的盛怒之中，我不想處理你的問題。

26. He lost his car keys because there was a hole in his pocket.

他丟掉了他的車鑰匙，因為他的口袋有洞。

27. According to the resume, she satisfies all the requirements of the job on paper.

根據履歷表，她在書面上滿足這個工作所需要的所有條件。

28. He risked his life to save the boy in the car accident.

他在這場車禍中冒著生命的危險拯救這個男孩。

【句型12】It 虛主詞

1. throw	8. dress	15. recommend	22. consist
2. direct	9. organize	16. agree	23. breathe
3. frighten	10. behave	17. complain	24. force
4. waste	11. attend	18. advertise	25. finish
5. recycle	12. budget	19. replace	26. motivate
6. hunt	13. exchange	20. participate	27. coach
7. threaten	14. contact	21. trade	28. sponsor

必考 句型與解析

【句型 12】It 虛主詞。

【結構】 It is ⇨ 虛主詞，to throw the old TV away ⇨ 真正的主詞，wasteful ⇨ 是浪費的，代表此行為是浪費的。

【句子】 It is wasteful to throw the old TV away.

【中譯】 把這個舊電視丟掉很浪費。

解　析

由句型 12【It is... 虛主詞】此句型可得知，It is 為虛主詞，先以其開頭後，選擇適當的形容詞，來描述後面作為真主詞的動詞片語，故選擇用 wasteful 浪費的，來描述之後所發生的動作：throw the old TV away 把舊電視機丟掉，中間加上不定詞 to，來表示 " 作某某動作 / 行為 " 是很浪費的，整句便完成：It is wasteful to throw the old TV away.

可依表格上的動詞造出各式不同變化的句子，再試想主詞所執行動作、或事件發生的地方，然後依語意選擇形容詞，完成 It is + 形容詞…，然後再加上不定詞、關係副詞或是 that 子句，變化延伸出許多不同的句子。

必考文法概念

It is... 稱虛主詞、假主詞或虛構主詞，It is 放到句首後，原本的動詞加上 to + V（其實是真正主詞），便放到句尾。由於 It 沒有真正意思，只是指稱 "to + V" 這件事或這個動作，故稱為虛主詞，主要是在形容，" 做某某動作 " 是具有某種性質 / 意涵的，性質 / 意涵則以所選擇形容詞來表達。

【1】 基本句型是：It is + 形容詞 + to do something（ 去從事某項事情 ）

◆ It is cruel to kill the animals.
　　殺動物是很殘忍的。

◆ It is difficult to master a language.

要精通一個語言是很困難的。

◆ It is hard to strike a balance.

很難取得平衡。

◆ It is easy for us to make a decision.

對我們來說，做決定是很容易的。

◆ It is hard to find the perfect candidate.

很難找到完美的候選人。

◆ It is easy to throw a dinner party.

舉辦晚宴是很容易的。

也可用關係副詞來修飾虛主詞，如：

It is + 形容詞 + how / why / where / when...

It is strange how he talks to us.

他對我們說話的方式很奇怪。

或者用 that + 名詞子句來修飾虛主詞，如：

It is + 形容詞 + that 名詞子句…

It is sad that he does not want to see us anymore.

他不願意再看到我們很讓人難過。

【2】 "動名詞當主詞" 用的句型，跟 It is 虛主詞可以互換，如：

Drinking too much is bad for you. 其中 drink 由原形動詞改為 V + ing 動名詞，作為主詞，代表喝酒過量對你不好，這句子可以以 It is 虛主詞置換，等同於：

It is bad for you to drink too much.

就是這樣寫

2. It is annoying how he directs me to do things.
    他指揮我事情的方式很令人惱怒。

3. It is mean of you to frighten the little boy with such a horrible story.
    你很過分用這麼可怕的故事去嚇這個小男孩。

4. It is unfair while we waste so much food in the city, there are people starving in other parts of the world.
    當我們在都市裡浪費這麼多食物，世界的其他地方卻有人挨餓，這是很不公平的。

5. It is the company's new policy to recycle every piece of paper we use.
    這是公司的新政策去回收我們所使用的每張紙。

6. It is cruel to hunt down the lions using traps.
    用陷阱獵捕獅子很殘忍。

7. It is scary to be threatened by a guy pointing at your head.
    被用槍指著頭威脅是很恐怖的。

8. It is impolite to dress in jeans to go to the opera.
    穿著牛仔褲去聽歌劇是不禮貌的。

9. It is nice that you organize the bookshelf for me.
    你能為我整理書架真是好。

10. It is embarrassing to be at the party with my friend because he behaves very rudely to everyone.
    跟我的朋友一起參加派對很尷尬，因為他對每個人的行為都很粗野。

11. It is very kind of you to attend my farewell party.
    您能夠來參加我的餞別派對真令人感激。

12. It is sad that we cannot eat very well in Paris because we have such a low travel budget.

很可惜我們在巴黎不能吃得很好，因為我們的旅行預算很低。

13. It is inconvenient to exchange money in smaller cities.

在比較小的城市換錢並不方便。

14. It is unfortunate that I have not contacted him for more than ten years.

很遺憾的我已經超過十年沒有聯繫他了。

15. It is great that you recommended this wonderful restaurant to us.

你推薦這家美好的餐廳給我們真是太好了。

16. It is impossible that my father will agree with my travel plan.

我的父親是不可能同意我的旅行計劃的。

17. It is annoying that he always complains so much.

他一直抱怨很多真令人討厭。

18. It is very expensive to advertise the product on TV.

在電視上廣告這個產品非常昂貴。

19. It is better to replace the tire before you get on the highway.

在你上高速公路之前最好更換輪胎。

20. It is important to participate in the class if you want to be noticed by the teacher.

如果你想要被老師注意到的話，在課堂上參與是很重要的。

21. It is fun to trade stuff at second hand markets.

在二手市場交換東西很有趣。

22. It is not very good if your happiness only consists of watching TV all day.

如果你的快樂只由整天看電視所構成的話，那不是很好。

23. It is very healthy to breathe the fresh air by the seaside.

在海邊呼吸新鮮的空氣很健康。

24. It is useless to force him to follow your will.

勉強他順從你的願望是沒有用的。

25. It is our top priority to finish the project on time.

把這個計劃按照時間作為是我們的最高優先。

26. It is not easy to motivate my colleagues to do the work with me.

要激勵我的同事跟我一起工作並不容易。

27. It is necessary to find someone to coach you if you want to improve your pronunciation.

如果你想要改善你的發音的話，找到一個可以訓練你的人是必要的。

28. It is urgent that we find someone to sponsor the event.

我們要找到人贊助這個活動，這是很緊急的。

【句型13】Ving 動名詞

1. drink	8. spread	15. extend	22. improve
2. tell	9. lose	16. challenge	23. stress
3. rely	10. bring	17. arrange	24. impact
4. revise	11. carry	18. identify	25. locate
5. refresh	12. recycle	19. finish	26. imagine
6. memorizing	13. hold	20. replace	27. disturb
7. make	14. participate	21. emphasize	28. grow

必考 句型與解析

【句型 13】Ving 動名詞

【結構】 Ving 動名詞，Drinking ⇨ 動名詞當主詞，Too much ⇨ 修飾動名詞。

【句子】 Drinking too much is bad for you.

【中譯】 飲酒過量對你不好。

解　析

由句型 13【Ving 動名詞】此句型可得知，Drink 為飲酒，將原形動詞改為動名詞 Ving 後，就可置於句首當主詞，too much 為修飾主詞，代表飲酒過量，Drinking too much 形成動名詞片語。由於動名詞一律為單數，接續的 be 動詞採用現在時態 is，再推想此項行為具有什麼特質，用 bad 不好的作為形容詞，最後再指稱 " 此項行為對某人 / 某事 " 的意義，用介系詞 for，加上 you，代表 " 對你不好 "，完成整個句子。

可依表格上的動詞造出各式動名詞，設想此動名詞所具有之特質，依語意選擇形容詞，完成 Ving 動名詞 + is... 之基本句型，然後加上介系詞 for " 指對某人而言 "，變換出不同的句子。

必考文法概念

動名詞為原形動詞後加 ing（V-ing），如：

◆ study ⇨ studying
◆ speak ⇨ speaking
◆ take ⇨ taking
◆ see ⇨ seeing

【1】 動名詞本身當作主詞用，代表主詞是動作：
　　 Jogging is good for you. 慢跑對你很好。

【2】 動名詞當主詞的句子，也可以虛主詞加以置換。如：

Helping you is my pleasure. ⇨ It is my pleasure to help you.
幫助你是我的快樂。

【3】 在動名詞當主詞的句子裡，be 動詞是單數、第三人稱，若是現在式用 is，若該句子所發生的情境在過去，則用 was，如：

Cleaning the entire house last week was very tiring for me. 在上星期打掃整個房子對我來說很累。用 was 代表發生在過去。

或者為改變語意，可用 will、can、should 等助動詞。如：Taking the medicine will be very good for you. 這個藥將對你很好。

【4】 動名詞作為主詞的句型，也可以依語意改變為現在完成式、過去完成式等時態，用法就如一般 " 主詞 + have / has + 過去分詞 "，或 " 主詞 + had + 過去分詞 " 一樣。

如：Fishing has been my favorite hobby for the past twenty years.
釣魚在過去的二十年來是我最喜愛的嗜好。

He had hurt his parents' heart when he ran away from home three years ago.
他在三年前逃家時已經傷害了他父母的心。

【5】 以動名詞片語當主詞：如 Telling the truth is always the best policy。動名詞 "Telling" 是由動詞 "Tell" 加 -ing 演變而來，扮演著名詞的角色。它還是具有動詞的特性，後面加上 the truth，代表說實話，動名詞片語 "Telling the truth"（說實話）是整個句子的主詞。

就是這樣寫

2. **Telling** the truth is always the best policy.

   說實話永遠是最好的上策。

3. **Relying** on him is risky because he is not a very responsible person.

   依賴他是很冒險的，因為他不是非常負責任的人。

4. **Revising** the manuscript was not easy for the author because he loved every word he wrote.

   對於這位作者來說，修改手稿不是件容易的事，因為他愛他所寫的每個字。

5. **Refreshing** myself with a cold shower is my favorite thing to do in summer.

   在夏天洗冷水澡使我自己恢復精神，是我最喜歡做的事。

6. **Memorizing** Chinese characters is difficult for many western learners.

   對於西方的學習者來說，記憶中文字是困難的。

7. **Making** cookies is her hobby after work.

   做餅乾是她下班後的興趣。

8. **Spreading** gossips that are not even true is not a very ethical thing to do.

   散播不真實的八卦不是很道德的行為。

9. **Losing** one's hearing is a terrible tragedy, but Beethoven continued to compose many masterpieces without being affected.

   失去聽力是很不幸的悲劇，但貝多芬在之後還是繼續作出許多傑作，沒有受到影響。

10. Bringing food to the needed people in the neighborhood is a very generous thing that you do.

你為鄰里裡需要的人帶來食物是一件很慷慨的事。

11. Carrying the books in the luggage will be too heavy for you, why don't you mail them?

在行李箱攜帶這些書對你會太重了，為什麼你不郵寄呢？

12. Recycling scarp metal has become a very big business in China.

回收廢金屬在中國已經變成很大的一筆生意。

13. Holding on to the past will impede your capacity to embrace the opportunities at the present moment.

抓住過去會阻礙你擁抱當下機會的能力。

14. Active participating in the class is a requisite if you want to get a good score.

如果你想要好成績，在課堂上積極參與是必須的。

15. Extending you love and care to enemies is an honorable thing to do.

將你的愛和關懷延展給敵人是一件很榮耀的事。

16. Challenging your boss on the first day of work is not a good idea.

在上班的第一天就挑戰你的老闆可不是個好主意。

17. Arranging the appointment with the president of the company for you is not easy, how dare you fail to show up?

為你安排跟這個公司老闆的約會並不容易，你竟敢沒有出席？

18. Identifying the traits of each student in a class of big size is not easy for the teacher.

在大班裡要辨識出每個學生的特質對老師並不容易。

19. Finishing up the decoration of the house has cost me more than I expected.

完成這間房子的裝飾比我想像中花了更多錢。

20. Replacing the lamps with LED lights will save you money in the long run.

將這些燈換成 LED 燈，長期來講會為你省錢。

21. Emphasizing the child's past failures will cause him to lose his confidence.

強調這個孩子過去失敗的經驗會讓他失去信心。

22. Improving your English ability takes constant efforts.

要增進你的英文能力需要時常的努力。

23. Stressing your travel experiences worldwide may increase your opportunity to be hired by an international enterprise.

強調你世界各地的旅行經驗，也許會增加你為外商公司聘雇的機會。

24. Impacting people's lives in a positive way is the mission of his life.

對人們生命帶來正面的影響是他人生的使命。

25. Locating the small alleyway on the map is quite difficult.

在地圖上定位這條小巷相當困難。

26. Imaging how her wedding will look like brings a big smile to Sue's face.

想像她的婚禮會是什麼樣子，為蘇的臉上帶來微笑。

27. Disturbing my dad while he is taking a nap will make him very angry.

在我父親睡覺時吵到他會讓他很生氣。

28. Growing up is a wonderful adventure.

長大是一場很棒的冒險。

【句型14】副詞

1. bitterly	8. conveniently	15. shortly	22. informally
2. vividly	9. regularly	16. gradually	23. erratically
3. sensitively	10. brilliantly	17. differently	24. accidentally
4. necessarily	11. successfully	18. steadily	25. inappropriately
5. diligently	12. neatly	19. scientifically	26. healthily
6. automatically	13. recently	20. simply	27. easily
7. intentionally	14. originally	21. carefully	28. correctly

必考 句型與解析

【句型14】副詞

【結構】　He ⇨ 主詞，Smile ⇨ 動詞，Bitterly ⇨ 副詞。

【句子】　He smiles bitterly.

【中譯】　他苦澀的微笑。

解　析

由句型 14【副詞】此句型可得知，He 為主詞，他，從而設想他做了什麼動作，採用微笑 smile，因為第三人稱單數現在式加上 s，然後再尋找適當的副詞來修飾此動詞，選擇用 bitterly，代表苦澀的微笑，如此一來，He smiles bitterly. 就完成完整句子。

副詞的功能是修飾動詞，因此在構句時，先設想主詞從事了什麼動作，在思考如何描繪形容該動詞的副詞。　可依表格上的副詞搭配不同動詞，創造出各種多樣不同的句子。如：
She sleeps soundly. 她睡得很祥和。
She cried terribly. 她哭得很淒慘。

必考文法概念

【1】 副詞一般由形容詞加 ly 演變而來，如：a diligent student ⇨ study diligently 形容詞字尾為子音再加 y 時，則將 y 改成 i 後再加 -ly 便形成副詞。
如 easy ⇨ easily

【2】 副詞的位置：修飾動詞時，副詞一般置於動詞或受詞之後，如：He walks very fast. 他走得很快，或是 Mark looked at Mary sadly. 約翰難過地看著瑪麗。sadly 置於 S + V + O 之後。

【3】 副詞的不同用法：除了修飾動詞外，副詞在句子中可用來修飾形容詞或其他副詞的字。如：

He smiles pretty sadly. 他笑起來相當憂傷。其中 pretty 為 " 相當地 " 意思，用來修飾副詞 sadly。

She is really unhappy. 她真的很不快樂，really 用來修飾形容詞 unhappy。

【4】 因此再加以細分，以下幾種類型都為副詞：

- ◆ 情狀副詞：描述動作，如 slowly, happily, sadly 等
- ◆ 頻率副詞：always, usually, often, sometimes 等
- ◆ 程度副詞：quite, very, too, so, rather, really 等

就是這樣寫

2. John describes the story vividly.
   約翰生動地描述這個故事。

3. The political conflicts between the two parties need to be handled sensitively.
   兩黨之間的政治衝突必須被細膩敏銳的處理。

4. Although you love your parents, you don't have to follow everything they say necessarily.
   即使你愛你的父母，你不必然要遵從他們說的每件事。

5. Larry studies diligently in order to pass the exam.
   賴瑞認真地讀書以通過考試。

6. The camera adjusts the lens automatically.
   這個相機可以自動地調整鏡頭。

7. Jessie ignored Joe's presence at the party intentionally because she was still angry with him.

潔西故意在派對上忽略喬的出現，因為她還在生他的氣。

8. We can travel conveniently around the city with the Rapid Mass Transit system.

有了捷運我們可以方便地在城市四處旅行。

9. He goes to see a movie regularly every weekend.

他每週末規律的去看一場電影。

10. Although Katie was sick she still performed brilliantly at the concert.

雖然凱蒂生病了，她在音樂會上還是表演的很出色。

11. The project was finished successfully because of every teammate's hard work.

這個專案結束的很成功，因為每位成員的努力工作。

12. She packed her stuff neatly in a large suitcase, ready to go to the airport.

她將她的東西整齊地打包在一個大行李箱裡，準備前往機場。

13. I just move to the neighborhood recently and would like to know where to buy groceries.

我最近剛搬到這個鄰里，想要知道到哪裡買雜貨。

14. The space used to be our study room originally, but we turned it into a bedroom.

這個空間原本是我們的書房，但我們將它改為臥室。

15. We will arrive at the main station shortly.

我們很快地就會抵達總站。

16. She realized he was lying to her gradually.

她逐漸的理解到他在騙她。

17. She seems to do everything differently from everyone else.

她似乎每件事都跟每個人做得都不一樣。

18. The old car climbed the slope slowly and steadily. Finally it reached the top.

這輛舊車緩慢而穩定地爬坡，最後終於到達頂端。

19. I will not believe what you say unless it is proven scientifically.

我不會相信你所說的除非它經過科學證明。

20. She dresses simply but with a unique style.

她穿著的很簡單，但卻有獨特的風格。

21. Please drive carefully on those icy roads.

在結冰的路上請小心地開車。

22. The teacher is popular because he always speaks informally with the students.

這位老師受歡迎，因為他總是跟學生不拘小節地講話。

23. The machine is working erratically. Someone needs to come to fix it.

這個機器正不規則地運作，需要有人來修理。

24. I bumped into my high school teacher accidentally today whom I haven't met for twenty years.

我今天意外的遇見我二十年不見的高中老師。

25. The speaker behaved inappropriately for such a formal occasion.

對於這個正式場合來說，講者的舉止很不恰當。

26. Eating healthily is my grandmother's secret for longevity.

健康地飲食是我祖母長壽的祕訣。

27. I can easily move the furniture for you.

我可以輕易地幫你搬動傢俱。

28. He finally spells my name correctly.

他終於正確地拼對了我的名字。

【句型 15】連接詞 after

1. arrest	8. squeeze	15. recover	22. occupy
2. warn	9. invade	16. prepare	23. realize
3. notice	10. launch	17. imitate	24. package
4. delay	11. adopt	18. apply	25. choose
5. label	12. digest	19. involve	26. damage
6. scratch	13. consume	20. collect	27. travel
7. light	14. tolerate	21. touch	28. defend

必考 句型與解析

【句型 15】連接詞 after

【結構】 After（在）+ arresting the robber（逮捕搶匪之後）, the Police（主詞）+ kept him in the room for further interrogation（所進行的動作）. After ⇨ 在…之後，arrest ⇨ 逮捕。

【句子】 After arresting the robber, the police kept him in the room forfurther interrogation.

【中譯】 在逮捕搶匪之後，警察將他關在房裡做進一步的偵訊。

解　析

由句型 15【After 連接詞】此句型可得知，本句由 After 開頭，代表 " 在…什麼之後 "，arrest 為逮捕，在 After 連接詞之後的動詞要改為 Ving，因此用 arresting，逮捕了誰呢？設想是搶匪，故加上受詞 the robber，完成第一個子句回顧句型 1「分詞構句」的概念：當兩個句子「主詞相同」時，而兩個句子又有因果關係、條件關係時，為精簡句子就可使用「分詞構句」，因此在第一個子句逗點之後，第二個子句裡真正的主詞出現了，the police 警察是真主詞，keep 為關住、拘留的意思，在此改為過去式 kept，代表發生在過去，搶匪改為代名詞用受格，故加上 him，in the room 修飾地方，for further interrogation 修飾目的，After arresting the robber, the police kept him in the room for further interrogation. 此完整句子就完成了，說明 " 在逮捕搶匪後 "，警察所從事的動作。

可依表格上的動詞置入，設想出多樣不同的句子。

必考文法概念

After... 此句型在描述在某件事情發生後，主詞所進行的動作。

【1】 After 是屬於時間上的連接詞，連接兩個子句，通常一個句子中可能包含有兩個以上的「子句」，子句和子句之間，可要用連接詞相連接，當用 after 時，即表示兩個子句有時間上的前後關係。

【2】 當 After 放在句首，第一個子句之後要加逗點，如果放在中間…
after....，則不用加逗點。

如：

After the movie was over, I went to sleep.

I went to sleep after the movie was over.

在電影結束後，我去睡覺了。

【3】 在構句時，after 之後的動詞改為動名詞 Ving。原本 After 後面是接子
句，若主要子句的主詞和 after 子句的主詞相同，就可以用 V-ing 結尾
的動名詞代替 after 子句。

如：

After I saw the movie, I went to sleep. 因為前後兩個子句的主詞都是
I，故可省略 After 子句裡的主詞，改為 Ving：

After seeing the movie, I went to sleep.

在看完電影後，我去睡覺了。

✏ 就是這樣寫

2. After warning me to be careful with the slippery road, Joe fell down himself.

在警告我道路很滑後，喬自己跌倒了。

3. After noticing his son was very nervous, Charlie began to tell him a funny story to lighten up the atmosphere.

在注意到他的兒子非常緊張之後，查理開始告訴他一個有趣的故事讓氣氛變得比較輕鬆。

4. After delaying the press conference for two hours, the president of the company still hasn't shown up.

在將記者會延遲兩個小時之後，公司的總裁還是沒有出現。

5. After labeling the book with different stickers, you can set them aside into different categories.

在將書本分類貼上不同的標籤後，你可以將它們依據不同類別放在一邊。

6. After scratching his head for two minutes, he still had not come up with any solution.

在抓了他的頭兩分鐘之後，他還是沒有想出任何解答。

7. After lighting up the candle, he found out there was a very deep cave in front of him.

在點燃蠟燭後，他發現在他前方有個非常深的洞穴。

8. After squeezing the juice from lemons, you can still use its peels to make cakes.

在把檸檬汁擠出來以後，你還可以用它的皮做蛋糕。

9. After invading Austria, German caused a lot of tensions in Europe that set the beginning of the Second World War.

在侵略奧地利以後，德國在歐洲引發很多緊張，肇始了第二次世界大戰。

10. After launching the business, Mike works day and night to keep it going.

在開始了他的事業後，麥克日以繼夜的工作以維持它的運作。

11. After adopting the child, the couple became very content about their family life.

在領養了這個小孩後，這對夫妻變得對他們的家庭生活非常滿足。

12. After digesting what had just happened, Beth felt very lucky that she had escaped from the fire.

在消化過剛剛發生的事後，貝絲覺得很幸運她逃過這場火災。

13. After consuming much of the natural resources of our planet earth, many people finally begin to care for the environment.

   在消耗我們地球上的大量自然資源後，許多人終於開始關心環境。

14. After tolerating her husband's bad temper for twenty years, Sue finally got a divorce last year.

   在容忍她先生的壞脾氣超過二十年後，蘇終於在去年離婚。

15. After recovering from the cold, he immediately set out for the mountain climbing trip.

   在從感冒復原後，他立刻出發前往登山之旅。

16. After preparing lunch for her children, she went to take a nap.

   在幫她孩子準備午餐之後，她去睡個午覺。

17. After imitating the dance style of Michael Jackson, he quickly won popularity at local discos.

   在模仿麥可傑克森的跳舞風格之後，他在當地的狄斯可迅速地贏得歡迎。

18. After applying for the job, he did nothing but sat at home waiting for the response.

   在申請這份工作後，他什麼也沒有做，只是坐在家等待回音。

19. After involving myself in the quarrel between two of my best friends, I told myself not to get into such trouble anymore.

   在讓我自己介入我兩個最好朋友的爭執中後，我告訴我自己再也不要找這種麻煩了。

20. After collecting stamps for more than twenty years, Joseph suddenly grew tired of the hobby and wanted to give away all his collection.

   在收集郵票超過二十年以後，喬瑟夫突然對這項嗜好感到厭倦，想要送走他所有的收藏。

21. After touching her son's forehead, Maggie realized he must be having a fever.

在觸摸她兒子的額頭後，梅姬理解他一定是在發燒。

22. After occupying the backyard with his spare furnitures, how can Jeff bring in more luggages to block the hallway?

在用傢俱把後院都佔據後，傑夫怎麼可以再帶來更多的傢俱把走道給堵塞？

23. After realizing she has made a mistake, Vickie quickly made an apology to the customer.

在了解到她犯了一個錯誤後，薇琪很快的跟顧客道歉。

24. After packaging the peaches in the boxes, they will be mailed to the customers on the same day.

把桃子包裝在箱子後，它們會在同一天被寄送給顧客。

25. After choosing Harry as her future husband, Nancy never complained about any of his ill behavior.

在選擇哈利作為她未來的丈夫後，南西從來不曾抱怨他任何不好的作為。

26. After traveling around the world, I realize my hometown is the best place to be.

在旅行過全世界後，我理解到我的家鄉是最好的所在。

27. After defending for him, I was sad to find out that he had been lying to me too.

在捍衛他後，我很難過的發現他也騙了我。

【句型16】 連接詞 before

97學測 必考字彙表 V29～V56

29. escape	36. record	43. compose	50. instruct
30. inspire	37. claim	44. select	51. complete
31. feature	38. prevent	45. design	52. consider
32. recover	39. construct	46. accomplish	53. trick
33. scream	40. suggest	47. carve	54. check
34. recognize	41. rename	48. suffer	55. slow
35. sharpen	42. allow	49. expect	56. hide

 句型與解析

【句型 16】連接詞

【結構】 Before（在）+ escaping from the prison（逃出監獄之前），the prisoners（主詞）had made plans for more than three years（已經做了某事）. Before ⇨ 在…之前，escape from the prison ⇨ 進行某動作之前。

【句子】 Before escaping from the prison, the prisoners had made plans for more than three years.

【中譯】 在逃離監獄之前，囚犯已經計劃超過了三年。

解　析

由句型 16【Before 連接詞】此句型可得知，本句由 Before 開頭，代表 " 在…什麼之前 "，escape 為逃走，在 Before 連接詞之後的動詞要改為 Ving，因此用 escaping，逃出哪裡呢？設想是監獄，故加上 from the prison 地方副詞修飾，完成第一個子句。回顧句型 1「分詞構句」的概念當兩個句子「主詞相同」時，而兩個句子又有因果關係、條件關係時，為精簡句子就可使用「分詞構句」，因此在第一個子句逗點之後，第二個子句裡真正的主詞出現了，the prisoners 囚犯是真主詞，make plans 為製作計劃、籌劃的意思，在此改為過去完成式 had made plans，代表在過去時間已經完成，for more than three years 修飾時間，代表超過三年，the prisoners had made plans for more than three years 第二個子句也完成了，此完整句子說明 " 在逃離監獄之前 "，囚犯所從事的動作。

以下的其他例句也會因為動詞的變化可以延伸出許多不同的句子，讀者可以藉由自身經驗造句，推想並藉由表格上的動詞造出各式不同變化的句子。

必考文法概念

【1】 Before.... 此句型為在主詞從事動作之前，所發生的事，Before 為時間上的連接詞，連接兩個子句，通常一個句子中可能包含有兩個以上的「子句」，子句和子句之間，可要用連接詞相連接，當用 before 時，

即表示兩個子句有時間上的前後關係。

【2】 當 Before 放在句首，第一個子句之後要加逗點，如果放在中間…
before..，則不用加逗點。

如：

Before the traffic light turned green, Maggie suddenly walked
across the street. Maggie suddenly walked across the street before
the traffic light turned green.

在交通燈號轉綠之前，梅姬突然走過街。

【3】 在構句時，原本 Before 後面是接子句，若主要子句的主詞和 after 子
句的主詞相同，就可以用 V-ing 結尾的動名詞代替 before 子句，如：

Before I came to the party, I already ate dinner.

因為前後兩個子句的主詞都是 I，故可省略 Before 子句裡的主詞，改
為 Ving：

Before coming to the party, I already ate dinner.

【4】 表時間的連接詞

從屬連接詞（表時間）		
1	when　當…	
2	while　當…時 / as　當…時	
3	before　在…之前 / after　在…之後	
4	by the time　到了…之時 / as soon as　一…就	
5	once　一旦	
6	since　自從	

【5】 表讓步的連接詞

從屬連接詞（表讓步）	
1	although　雖然
2	though　雖然
3	even if / even though　即使
4	while　雖然
5	whether... or not　是否 / if　是否

【6】 表原因的連接詞

從屬連接詞（表原因）	
1	because　因為
2	as　因為
3	now that　既然
4	in that　因為
5	since　因為

【7】 表條件的連接詞

從屬連接詞（表條件）	
1	if　如果
2	as long as　只要
3	unless　除非
4	in case / in the event (that)　在…狀況下
5	provided / providing　假如
6	supposing / supposed　如果

30. Before I gave up, his encouraging words inspired me to hang on there.

    在我放棄之前，他鼓勵的話語激勵我堅持。

31. Before you go to see the movie, you should know the film features an actor who is your least favorite.

    在你看這部電影之前，你應該知道這部電影以你最不喜歡的男演員為主打。

32. Before you set out for the trip, you need to recover from your cold.

    在你出發前往旅行之前，你應該先從感冒中康復。

33. Before you screamed so loud, you should look at what the insect really was.

    在你尖叫的這麼大聲前，你應該看看這到底是哪一種蟲。

34. Before I saw her, Jane recognized me from the back even though we had not met for ten years.

    在我看見她之前，珍從我的背後就認出我來了，雖然我們已經十年不見。

35. Before you draw, you should sharpen your pencil.

    在你開始畫畫之前，你應該先把鉛筆削尖。

36. Before CDs were invented, singers often recorded their songs on tapes.

    在 CD 發明之前，歌手通常在卡帶上來錄製他們的歌。

37. Before claiming he has stolen the wallet from you, you should be certain that you have not put it somewhere else.

    在聲稱他偷了你的錢包之前，你最好確定你沒有把它放在其他的地方。

38. Before mailing the box, you should label it clearly to prevent it from

getting lost.

在郵寄這個箱子之前，你最好把它清楚的標示以避免遺失。

39. Before constructing the wall, the builder dug into the ground to make a foundation.

在建造這堵牆前，營造者挖進地面去建造地基。

40. Before suggesting us to come this restaurant, you should have known it is closed on Friday.

在建議我們來到這間餐廳之前，你應該要知道它星期五關門。

41. Before renaming the files, please write down the old file names on the list.

在為這些檔案重新命名之前，請把舊檔案名寫在這張單子上。

42. Before allowing her son to take the trip on the weekend, Helen insisted that he must finish his assignment during the weekdays.

在准許她的兒子去週末旅遊前，海倫堅持他一定要在週間完成他的作業。

43. Before composing the poem, the poet drank a glass of wine to relax himself.

在創作這首詩前，詩人喝了一杯酒以放鬆自己。

44. Before selecting the best artwork for the show, I would like to hear each artist explain his or her work.

在選擇展覽最好的藝術作品前，我希望聽到每個藝術家說明自己的作品。

45. Before designing the house, the architect tries to understand the needs of his client.

在設計這所房屋之前，建築師試著了解他客戶的需要。

46. Before accomplishing the task, I would like to know if there is any adjustment we need to make at this point.

在我們完成這項任務前，我想知道在這個時間點我們是否需要做任何調整。

47. Before carving the giant totem, the indigenous people at that time must have spent a long time collecting wood from the forest.

在雕刻這個巨大的圖騰前，當時的原住民一定花了很多時間從森林裡收集木材。

48. Before suffering from too much pain, he fainted and fell into deep sleep.

在受到更多痛苦折磨之前，他昏倒了並陷入深深的睡眠。

49. Before expecting me to do everything for you, you should reflect if you have ever done anything in return.

在期待我為你做所有事之前，你應該要反省你是否曾做任何事為回報。

50. Before instructing the soldiers to attack the enemy, the general wanted to know how much supply there was left.

在下令士兵攻擊敵人之前，將軍想要知道還有剩下多少補給。

51. Before completing the application form, Susan realized she did not want to apply for the job.

在完成申請表之前，蘇珊意識到她不想申請這個工作。

52. Before considering the matter, please make sure you are in a neutral position.

在考慮這個問題前，請確定你是在中立的位置上。

53. Before tricking the little girl, you should know such a naughty joke will make her very upset.

在作弄這個小女孩之前，你應該知道這樣頑皮的玩笑會讓她很難過。

54. Before going to bed, I went to my son's room to check if he fell asleep.

在去睡覺前，我去我兒子的房間看看他是否已經睡了。

55. Before slowing down your pace, you should see if there is any runner trying to bypass you.

在減緩你的速度之前，你應該看看有沒有其他跑者試著超越你。

56. Before hiding yourself behind the oversized coat, you should show everybody what a nice blouse you are wearing tonight.

在把你自己藏在這件過大的外套之前，你應該展現給大家看你今晚穿著一件多美的上衣。

【句型 17】By... 藉由

1. adapt	8. permit	15. upload	22. offer
2. request	9. neglect	16. fasten	23. admit
3. decide	10. segment	17. adjust	24. circulate
4. respond	11. diminish	18. defeat	25. extend
5. guide	12. divide	19. substitute	26. transfer
6. measure	13. compensate	20. advertise	27. stretch
7. constrain	14. negotiate	21. discourage	28. expand

必考 句型與解析

【句型 17】by ... 藉由

【結構】 The company（主 詞）+ increases（動 詞）+ its profits + by（透過）......。The company ⇨ 主詞，increase its profits ⇨ 增加利潤，（產生某結果、做某事）by ⇨ 透過、藉由，adapting a new marketing strategy ⇨ 採用一個新的行銷策略。

【句子】 The company increases its profits by adapting a new marketing strategy.

【中譯】 這家公司藉由採用新的行銷策略增加了它的利潤。

 解 析

由句型 17【...by 藉由】此句型可得知，主詞為 the company 公司，本句陳述簡單的事實故動詞 increase 採用簡單現在式，第三人稱單數加 s，成為 increases，公司增加了利潤，就是 the company increases its profits，到此 S + V + O 的基本句型已經出現。

然而是透過了什麼方法呢？這時用 by，就是 " 藉由…" 方法的意思，因而推想公司增加利潤的方法，動詞 adapt，中文有採用、使用的意思，在 by 介系詞之後改為 Ving，成為 adapting，adapting a new market strategy 採用一個新的行銷策略，是指公司為了增加利潤所藉由的方法。

由此完成整個句子，以下的其他例句也會因為動詞的變化可以延伸出許多不同的句子，讀者可以藉由自身經驗造句，推想並藉由表格上的動詞造出各式不同變化的句子。

必考文法概念

by 在此作介系詞，後面接 Ving，指主詞透過什麼樣的方法達到了前面子句的目的 / 形成此狀況。

【1】 S + V + by + Ving 等同於 By + Ving, S + V

如：She finally won the piano contest by practicing day and night.

By practicing day and night, she finally won the piano contest.

她藉由日夜練習終於贏得了鋼琴比賽。

但是 by + 動名詞 形成的片語，通常置於句尾，修飾句中的動詞。

【2】 by 也是 by means of 藉由某種方法的意思，可以使用 by means of 代替

如：

We can expand our worldview by traveling abroad.

We can expand our worldview by means of traveling abroad.

我們可以藉由到國外旅行擴大我們的世界觀。

【3】 by 之後也可以加名詞，如：

We are guided by the lights.

我們受到燈光引導。

或是 by + 交通工具，則為慣用用法，如：

He went to work by bus / by train / by car.

他藉由搭公車 / 火車 / 開車去工作。

或是 by 之後也可以加關係副詞，如：

In this restaurant, you will be charged by how much you eat.

在這家餐廳你會依照你吃多少付費。

就是這樣寫

2. The company saves thousands of dollars every month by requesting its employees to recycle the paper they use.

透過要求員工回收紙張，這家公司每個月省了好幾千塊錢。

3. He meant to upset his parents by deciding not to go home for Christmas.

他故意要藉由決定聖誕節不回家，讓他父母難過。

4. He shows his interest in the subject by responding every question with enthusiasm.

他透過對每個問題熱切地回答來顯示他對這個主題的興趣。

5. We were guided by the light on the shore and finally rowed the boat back to the beach.

我們受到岸上燈光的指引，終於划船回到海灘。

6. The success of a man's life cannot be measured by how much money he makes.

一個男人生活的成功不能用他賺多少錢來衡量。

7. The project is constrained by a very low budget.

這個計劃受到很低的預算所限。

8. The custom permitted us to go across the border by issuing us a visa.

海關透過發給我們簽證准許我們穿過邊境。

9. He hurt his wife's heart badly by neglecting her needs all the time.

他因為持續忽視她的需要，嚴重的傷害了他太太的心。

10. The insurance company segmented the market into three by issuing three types of policy.

保險公司透過發放三種保單將市場區分為三。

11. The mayor's opponent tries to diminish his popularity by attacking his recent policy.

市長的反對者試著透過攻擊他最近的政策以減少他的歡迎度。

12. He tries to be fair to his three sons by dividing the wealth he gives to them equally.

他試著藉由均等的分割他給兒子們的財產，以表示對他的三個兒子公平。

13. David compensated his absence from the family by giving his wife and son everything they want.

大衛為了彌補他在家庭的缺席，給他太太和兒子他們想要的一切東西。

14. I tried to negotiate a better deal by becoming friends with the seller.

透過與賣家成為朋友，我試著談判一個更好的交易。

15. She built a very beautiful website by uploading many photos.

透過上傳許多照片，她建立一個很美的網站。

16. He tried to reduce his nervousness during the turbulences by fastening his seat belt.

他試著透過繫緊安全帶，減少他在亂流中的緊張。

17. You should adjust your teaching methods by observing the needs of different children.

你應該透過觀察不同兒童的需要，調整你的教學方式。

18. The team defeated their opponent by employing a very smart tactic.

這個團隊藉由運用聰明的技巧打敗了對手。

19. The criminal tricked the police by substituting his ID.

這個罪犯透過替換證件騙過了警察。

20. The sandwich shop becomes very popular by advertising on the local newspaper.

藉由在地方報紙上廣告，這個三明治小店變得很受歡迎。

21. You will not discourage me by laughing at what I do.

你無法透過嘲笑我做的事來讓我喪氣。

22. The shopper tried to sell the old carpet to us by offering us a discount.

藉由提供給我們折扣，這個商家希望把這張舊地毯賣給我們。

23. Bob started a huge conflict with his wife by admitting that he loves someone else.

鮑伯承認了他愛著別人，開始與他太太有著巨烈的衝突。

24. We will give the teacher a Thank You card with everyone's signature by circulating the card in the class.

我們會透過在班上傳閱卡片，給老師一張有每個人簽名的感謝卡。

25. She extends her welcome to new neighbors by inviting them over for dinner.

她透過邀請新鄰居來吃晚餐，來表示她對他們的歡迎。

26. I finally got to the small village by transferring three times.

我轉三次車終於來到了這個小村子。

27. She eased the soreness of her body by stretching on the floor.

她透過在地板上伸展減輕她身體的痠痛。

28. We will expand our retail operation by opening a new shop in the city.

我們會藉由在城市裡開一間新店，擴大我們的零售業務。

【句型18】使役動詞

96 學測 必考字彙表 V29～V56

29. sing	36. quit	43. show	50. shrink
30. remove	37. confirm	44. include	51. decrease
31. retreat	38. deserve	45. relate	52. enter
32. revive	39. pamper	46. devote	53. sparkle
33. resign	40. relax	47. determine	54. climb
34. amaze	41. exercise	48. delight	55. wander
35. convince	42. supply	49. direct	56. express

必考 句型與解析

【句型 18】使役動詞。

【結構】 The teacher（主詞）＋made（使）＋Jack（受詞）＋stand up（原形動詞，站起）...。The teacher ⇨ 某事物或某人，made Jack ⇨ make ＋ O, 使傑克，make 之後接原型動詞，stand up in front of the class ⇨ 站在全班前面。

【句子】 The teacher made Jack stand up in front of the class to apologize for his mistakes.

學測篇

【96學測】V29～V56

【中譯】 這位老師要傑克站在全班的前面為他的過錯道歉。

 解　析

由句型 18【make + O + V】此句型可得知，主詞為 The teacher，make 在此是「使役動詞」，就是叫人家去做事情，受詞為 Jack，因此 The teacher made Jack 就是"老師使傑克從事某某動作的"的意思，因為為過去式，make 改為 made。

在使役動詞後，受詞 Jack 的行為不論時態，要用原形動詞，故用 stand up，代表老師要 Jack 站起來，加上地方副詞 in front of the class，代表是站在全班的前面，再加上 to apologize for his mistakes 修飾目的，站在全班面前的行為有"為他的錯誤道歉"的目的，由此完成整句。

由此句的句意可以理解，傑克原本大概不會自己站在全班面前為錯誤道歉，而 The teacher made Jack.... 的句型，是指老師要「使役」傑克、叫傑克這樣做，傑克才會去做。

故在以下造句時，可以推想是否有什麼行為是要別人「役使」才會做的，通常要帶有一點非自願或是勉強的意思，再藉由表格上的動詞造出各式不同變化的句子。

【1】 make 是個特殊的單字，除了一般的動詞意義外，還可以作為使役動詞，有 " 叫某人做某事 " 的意思，作為使役動詞時，最須注意事項是之後的第二個動詞是用「原形動詞」，不可再加 to，"make + V"，如：

My mother made me clean the room.

我媽媽叫我打掃房間。

make 之後不可再加 to，如 My mother made me to clean the room. (X) 是錯誤的。

【2】 注意與一般動詞的分別：My mother asked me to clean the room. (O) 如果是一般動詞，之後加 to。

英文中的「使役動詞」，有 make, have (使 ...), let 三個。

【3】 make 除了當使役動詞使用外，還有其它的意思，make 最常見者為「製造、製作」的意思，如：

She makes cookies at home.

她在家裡做餅乾。

並沒有「役使」、「叫某人做某事」的意思。

make 也有「使得」的意思，最常見的句型為 S + make + O + OC 受詞補語，如：

The movie makes me sad.

這部電影使得我難過。

就是這樣寫

30. The inspector made the old man remove all the rubbish from the backyard.

   檢查者使這個老人清除後院的所有垃圾。

31. The storm made him retreat from the trip.

   這場暴風雨讓他從這次旅程退卻。

32. The food makes my body revive.

   食物使我的身體重新振作起來。

33. Henry's boss made him resign last month.

   亨利的老闆讓他上個月辭職了。

34. He made the children become amazed by his magic.

   他用魔術讓這些孩子都著迷了。

35. Jeff made the jury become convinced of his innocence.

   傑夫讓陪審團相信他的清白。

36. The doctor made him quit drinking.

   醫生使他放棄飲酒。

37. You need to make the client confirm their willingness to buy the house before next week.

   下週之前你必須讓客戶確認他們要買這棟房子的意願。

38. His criticism makes me feel I do not deserve the award.

   他的批評讓我覺得我不值得這個獎項。

39. Joyce makes her boyfriend pamper her with luxurious jewelry and oversea trips.

   喬依絲使她的男友以昂貴的珠寶和海外旅遊嬌慣她。

40. The sound of the birds in the forest makes me relax thoroughly.

樹林裡的鳥叫聲讓我完全放鬆。

41. My coach makes me exercise two hours a day.

我的教練使我每天運動兩小時。

42. We need to make the food manufactures supply us only the highest quality of food.

我們需要讓食物製造商只提供我們最高品質的食物。

43. Bill made me show my paintings to him, but he laughed at me afterwards.

比爾要我給他看我畫的畫，但他之後卻笑我。

44. The manager made me include Joe's idea in the proposal.

經理要我在提案中加入喬的想法。

45. The politician made the audience relate to him by telling a personal story to make.

這位政治家透過說了一個個人故事，讓選民跟他產生連結。

46. The job has made me devote all my personal time.

這個工作讓我奉獻了所有的私人時間。

47. The TV drama "Tokyo Love Story" made her determine to go to Japan.

東京愛情故事這部電視劇讓她下定決心去日本。

48. The gift made Lisa become delighted.

這禮物讓麗莎變得非常開心。

49. The producer made the director direct the movie under a very tight budget.

製作人讓導演在非常緊縮的預算下執導這部電影。

50. The hot water made the sweater shrink.

熱水讓這件毛衣縮水。

51. The recession made many donors decrease their support to the nonprofit organizations.

經濟不景氣讓許多捐款者減少對於非營利組織的支持。

52. He made me enter the building through the back door, which was not very polite.

他讓我從後門進來這棟建築，這不是很有禮貌的。

53. The sunshine makes the diamond sparkle even further.

陽光使得這顆鑽石更加閃耀。

54. Oliver made me climb the ladder to get the book for him.

奧利佛讓我爬梯子去拿書給他。

55. His lateness made us wander around purposelessly for two hours.

他的遲到讓我們毫無目的的閒晃了兩個小時。

56. The worsening situation finally made her express her dissatisfaction.

惡化的情況終於讓她表達她的不滿。

【句型 19】 祈使句

1. pay	8. provide	15. rearrange	22. exhibit
2. move	9. hold	16. explain	23. accept
3. expose	10. depart	17. throw	24. support
4. allow	11. devote	18. deliver	25. advertise
5. conclude	12. join	19. promise	26. share
6. wear	13. loosen	20. communicate	27. reject
7. admit	14. acquire	21. destroy	28. protect

句型與解析

【句型 19】祈使句。

【結構】 pay ⇨ 原形動詞，the bill ⇨ 受詞。

【句子】 Pay the bill for me, please.

【中譯】 請幫我付帳單。

解 析

由句型 19【祈使句】此句型可得知，祈使句是對對方命令或是告知，主詞 you 通常不寫出來，所以本句子的開頭 you 省略，直接由動作開始，pay 有付錢的意思，pay the bill 為一個片語，就是付帳單，再加上介系詞 for，代表 "為某人…" 的意思，for me 是為我。所以到這裡已經完成了祈使句的句型。

在本句裡，為了使口氣較為和緩，在 pay the bill for me 之後，又加上逗點與 please，就是請幫我做的意思。

實際造句時，可按照不同語意前後句串聯，加以變化句型，但祈使句始終不脫「指示或告知對方做某事」的意思，並可因為動詞的變化可以延伸出許多不同的句子，讀者可以藉由自身經驗造句，推想並藉由表格上的動詞造出各式不同變化的句子。

必考文法概念

在學校常聽到的喊口令如 Stand up! 起立！ Sit down! 坐下，這些叫人做動作的口令，我們稱「命令句」，又稱為「祈使句」。祈使句的句子常用來對對方發出命令或指示，提出要求、建議、勸告等。

【1】 祈使句常以動詞原形開頭。第二人稱主語 you 通常不表示出來，但在要提醒對方注意時可以加入。如：

You take care of yourself.

你照顧好自己。

或者可以直接加入對方的人名，以「指定說話對象」，放在句首或句尾，如：

Kathy, look up!

凱西，看上面！

或是 Look up, Kathy!

【2】 如果表示禁止、否定不要做該行為的祈使句，則在原形動詞前加 Do not / Don't，如：

Do not open the window.

不要打開窗戶。

Don't walk so fast.

不要走這麼快。

【3】 表示勸告的祈使句，通常用 Be 動詞＋形容詞，來表示對方應該要有如此特質，如：

Be careful.

小心哦！

Be open-minded when you make friends.

當你交朋友時應心胸開放。

就是這樣寫

2. **Move** the box over, will you?

   你可以把箱子搬過來嗎？

3. **Expose** the wet tower under the sun, or it will dry up quickly.

   把濕毛巾曝露在陽光下，否則它會很快乾。

4. **Allow** yourself to have some free time.

   容許讓你自己有些空閒時間。

5. **Conclude** your speech in one minute. Your time is running out.

   把你的演講在一分鐘內結束，你的時間已經用完了。

6. **Wear** a jacket, it's getting chilly.

   穿件夾克，天氣變冷了。

7. **Admit** that you have made a mistake.

   承認你犯了錯誤。

8. **Provide** us some food, please! We will return your favor someday.

   請提供給我們一些食物吧！我們有天會回報你的恩惠。

9. **Hold** on to the rope tightly!

   緊緊的抓住那繩索！

10. **Depart** immediately, or you will miss the train.

    立刻出發不然你會錯過火車。

11. **Devote** yourself into the project, do not seek more excuses.

    全心投入這計劃，不要再找更多藉口。

12. **Join** our side, or you will be our enemy.

    加入我們這一邊，不然你就是我們的敵人。

13. **Loosen** the rope!

    把繩索鬆開！

14. Acquire the estate as soon as it is on sale.

只要這個地產一拍賣就盡快買下。

15. Rearrange my meeting with Mr. Huang, please.

請幫我重新安排與黃先生的會議。

16. Explain to me why you are late for two hours.

解釋給我聽為什麼你晚到了兩個小時。

17. Throw the ball to me, boy!

男孩，把球丟給我！

18. Deliver the parcel to my house as soon as possible.

盡快將這個包裹遞送到我家。

19. Promise me you will come back to see me.

跟我保證你會回來看我。

20. Communicate with your subordinates instead of commanding them!

跟你的下屬溝通，而不是命令他們。

21. Destroy everything in the village!

把這村莊裡的一切毀滅！

22. Exhibit these great paintings in the hallway!

在走廊裡展示這些很棒的圖畫！

23. Accept the fate, don't fight with it.

接受命運，不要與之爭戰。

24. Support your brother, do not make fun of him all the time.

支持你的哥哥，不要總是嘲笑他。

25. Advertise the product on major shopping websites!

在主要的購物網站上廣告這個產品！

26. Share your resources with others, don't be selfish.

與其他人分享你的資源，不要自私。

27. **Reject** all the unqualified applicants!

把不合格的申請者都拒絕掉！

28. **Protect** the castle from being attacked!

保護這座城堡不受攻擊！

【句型20】 have difficulty + Ving

29. recognize	36. dwell	43. forget	50. drive
30. realize	37. imagine	44. invite	51. believe
31. acquaint	38. lose	45. notice	52. neglect
32. command	39. estimate	46. count	53. prove
33. kick	40. see	47. attract	54. stay
34. wear	41. forgive	48. understand	55. instruct
35. make	42. maintaining	49. challenge	56. describe

必考 句型與解析

【句型 20】 have difficulty + Ving（做⋯）很困難。

【結構】 have difficulty + Ving（做⋯）很困難。I（主詞）+ have difficulty（有困難）+ recognizing（Ving）+ Jane's face.

【句子】 I have difficulty recognizing Jane's face.

【中譯】 我有困難認出珍的臉。

解　析

由句型 20【have difficulty + Ving（做⋯）很困難】此句型可得知，主詞是 I，因為為現在是第一人稱，故動詞用原形 have，have difficulty 乃是片語，difficulty 這裡也是不可數名詞，是困難、障礙的意思，所以不加 s，在這裡，主詞 I 表示有困難做某事，是什麼事呢？可利用不同的動詞變換加以組織句子，如本句中，採用 recognize 辨認的意思，have difficulty 之後因為省略了 in，動詞須改為 Ving，故用 recognizing，最後再加上有困難辨識的目標：Jane's face 珍的臉，因而完成本句子。

在本範例中，並沒有說明我有困難辨識珍的臉的原因，可依語意自行變化句型，加上 "because.... 因為 " 等等，可在之後的例句詳見。並可因為動詞的變化可以延伸出許多不同的句子，讀者可以藉由自身經驗造句，推想並藉由表格上的動詞造出各式不同變化的句子。

必考文法概念

【1】 have difficulty + Ving（做⋯）很困難，為一片語，代表要做某事很困難，不易做到某事，have 在此是一般動詞 " 有 " 的意思，故可隨人稱與時態變化為 has / had，如：

She has difficulty studying English.

她有困難學英文。

I had difficulty starting the car yesterday.

我昨天有困難發動車。

【2】 原本的句型為 have difficulty(in) + Ving，省略了 in，之後動詞要改為動名詞 Ving，注意 difficulty 在此皆用單數。

若要修飾有困難的程度，可以用 a little, much, a lot of, no 來修飾，如：

Maggie has a lot of difficulty finishing the project.

梅姬有很大的困難完成這個專案。

My son had no difficulty learning swimming when he was a little boy.

我的兒子在他是小男孩的時候，學游泳完全沒有困難。

也 可 變 化 為 S + has / have + trouble / difficulty / a hard time / problems + V-ing.. 如：

Joy has a hard time memorizing all the exam materials.

喬伊有段艱難的時間背誦所有的考試材料。

I had problems fixing the car.

我有困難修理這台車。

就是這樣寫

30. She has difficulty realizing what has just happened to her.

要她了解到她身上剛發生了什麼事很困難。

31. Mary has difficulty getting acquainted with people because she is always so cold.

瑪麗跟人們熟識很困難，因為她總是很冰冷。

32. The captain has difficulty commanding his crew because his lack of experience.

這個船長很難指揮他的船員，因為他缺乏經驗。

33. Jack has difficulty kicking the ball. Maybe he is not suited to play soccer.

傑克很不會踢球，也許他不適合玩足球。

34. Allen has difficulty wearing a tie because he does not like to dress formally.

艾倫很難戴著領帶，因為他不喜歡正式穿著。

35. I have difficulty making the decision to tear down the old houses because I concern about the people who are living there.

我沒有辦法下決定去拆除掉這些老房子，因為我關心居住在裡面的人們。

36. I have difficulty imagining if anyone can dwell in such a horrible condition.

我沒有辦法想像有任何人可以在這麼可怕的條件下定居。

37. He has difficulty attending the meeting because there is a time conflict.

他沒有辦法參加這場會議，因為時間衝突。

38. She has difficulty losing weight because she always indulges herself with a pint of ice cream after work.

她沒有辦法減輕體重，因為她總是放縱自己在工作後吃一品脫的冰淇淋。

39. The analyst has difficulty estimating the losses of the company.

分析師沒有辦法預測公司的損失。

40. I have difficulty seeing what is in front of me because the sun shines on me.

我沒有辦法看到我前面有什麼東西，因為陽光照著我。

41. I have difficulty forgiving his behavior because he annoys me again and again.

我沒有辦法原諒他的行為，因為他一次又一次的激怒我。

42. She has difficulty maintaining her independence because her parents always interfere with her life.

她沒有辦法保持獨立，因為她的父母總是干涉她的生活。

43. He has difficulty forgetting about the girl because she has amazed him so much.

他沒有辦法忘掉那女孩，因為她讓他感到如此驚奇。

44. My mom has difficulty inviting Mark to come to the party because he was so rude to her last time.

我媽媽沒有辦法邀請馬克來到這派對，因為上次他對她很粗魯。

45. The teacher has difficulty noticing the little boy because he barely speaks.

老師沒有辦法注意到這個小男孩，因為他幾乎都不說話。

46. I have difficulty counting more than ten.

我沒有辦法數超過十。

47. Paul has difficult attracting girls.

保羅很難吸引女孩子。

48. I have difficulty understanding why parents mistreat their children.

我沒有辦法了解為什麼家長會虐待他們的孩子。

49. Frank has difficulty challenging authorities.

法蘭克沒有辦法挑戰權威。

50. I have difficulty driving in the snow. I try to avoid driving when it snows.

我沒有辦法在雪中開車，下雪的時候我試圖避免駕駛。

51. He has difficulty believing that the once unspoiled coastline has been ruined by this huge modern hotel.

他沒有辦法相信一度純淨的海岸線被這間大型現代旅館給毀了。

52. I have difficulty neglecting the scars on his face.

我沒有辦法忽視他臉上的疤。

53. Joe has difficulty proving that he is innocent to the judge.

喬沒有辦法向法官證明他是清白的。

54. She has difficulty staying awake without refreshing herself with a cold shower.

如果沒有辦法洗個冷水澡恢復精神的話，她沒有辦法保持清醒。

55. I have difficulty instructing you how to make spaghetti because I rarely cook.

我沒有辦法教導你怎麼做義大利麵因為我很少煮飯。

56. He had difficulty describing how the scenery was like because he was sleeping during the bus ride.

他沒有辦法描述風景是什麼樣子，因為他在公車途中睡著了。

指考篇

【句型21】 未來式

1. face	8. predict	15. require	22. challenge
2. plan	9. escape	16. waste	23. fulfill
3. achieve	10. identify	17. increase	24. measure
4. examine	11. advise	18. enhance	25. lead
5. deny	12. attract	19. occur	26. reduce
6. cover	13. serve	20. appear	27. inhabit
7. approve	14. associate	21. regret	28. establish

必考 句型與解析

【句型21】未來式。

【結構】　未來式 "S + will + V"，The basketball team ⇨ 籃球隊，Will ⇨ 即
　　　　　將（未來式），Face ⇨ 面對，Strong opponent ⇨ 強勁的對手，in
　　　　　tomorrow's game ⇨ 在明天的比賽。

【句子】　The basketball team will face a strong opponent in tomorrow's
　　　　　game.

【中譯】　籃球隊明天的比賽會面對很強的對手。

解　析

由句型 21【未來式 "S + will + V"】此句型可得知，主詞是 The basketball team 籃球隊，will 是表示即將、將來的意思，不分主詞單複數都用 will，動詞 face 是面對的意思，面對什麼呢？受詞採用 strong opponent 代表強勁的對手，然後進而推想在什麼樣的場合會面對強勁的對手，並且是一個未來的時態，故寫上 in tomorrow's game：在明天的比賽的意思，完成此句子：The basketball team will face a strong opponent in tomorrow's game. 籃球隊明天的比賽會面對很強的對手。

在後續的造句中，可由不同的主詞，搭配動詞的變化可以延伸出許多不同的句子，在句子中，也可說明 "未來會發生此狀況 / 動作" 的時間 / 地點 / 場合 / 條件等等，以讓語意更完整。讀者可以藉由自身經驗造句，推想並藉由表格上的動詞造出各式不同變化的句子。

必考文法概念

【1】 未來式指將來會發生的動作及會存在的狀態，will + "原形動詞"：是一個最簡單的表達法，不管主詞是什麼人稱、單數複數，都用 will，而 will 的中文意思相當於「將要、將會」。

They will go to the movies tonight.
他們今晚會去看電影。
She will cook dinner for me.

她會為我煮晚餐。

It will be a wonderful party.

這將是場很棒的派對。

可以見到以上不論主詞人稱，都是用 will。

【2】 S + will V 也可以用 S + V + going to 代替，但就需注意主詞的人稱單複
數，加以變化：

I am going to sing a song.

我即將唱一首歌。

He is going to the United States.

他即將去美國。

They are going to move to a new house.

他們即將搬去一個新家。

【3】 will 跟 can 一樣，都是助動詞，因此在否定時，可以用 will not，或是
縮寫為 won't，代表即將不做此項動作。

I will not go to the office on Friday.

我星期五不會去辦公室。

She won't eat the cake.

她將不會吃那蛋糕。

就是這樣寫

2. I will plan for a family trip to Europe once I finish this project at work.

   只要我一完成這份專案,我將計劃一趟家庭歐洲旅遊。

3. You will achieve success if you work this hard all the time.

   如果你一直這麼努力,你將會成功。

4. The doctor will examine the patient once the check up room becomes available.

   一旦診間空下來,醫生將會檢視病患。

5. He will deny the facts like he always does.

   如同他一向所做的,他將否認事實。

6. I will cover the bicycle with a piece of cloth if it rains.

   如果下雨的話,我將在腳踏車上蓋一塊布。

7. The boss will approve your idea once it gets refined.

   如果再經過修改的話,老闆將會贊成你的意見。

8. The fortuneteller will predict your future if she knows your birthday.

   只要知道你的生日,這個算命者將能預測你的未來。

9. Nothing will escape the teacher's eyes because the teacher watches his students closely.

   沒有什麼能逃得過老師的眼睛,因為這位老師很仔細的看著他的學生。

10. The manager will identify the priorities tomorrow morning.

    經理明天早上將會確認優先要做的事。

11. The doctor will advise you not to smoke.

    醫生將會勸告你不要抽煙。

12. Tracy will attract more suitors if she dresses up more.

    如果多打扮一點,崔西將會吸引更多的追求者。

13. The flight attendant will serve us drink shortly after the plane takes off.

飛機起飛不久後，空服員將會很快提供我們飲料。

14. People will associate you with the criminal because you have got the same name.

人們將會把你聯想成罪犯，因為你們有同樣的名字。

15. I will require you to hand in the form tomorrow.

我將會要求你明天交回這張表格。

16. We will waste a lot of money if we cannot go to the concert. The tickets cannot be refunded.

如果我們不能去這場音樂會，我們將會浪費很多錢。票是不能退錢的。

17. The revenue of the company will increase next year.

明年公司的收入將會增加。

18. The new purple paint on the wall will enhance of the atmosphere of the room

牆上新的紫色油漆將會增強這個房間的氣氛。

19. An accident will occur if you continue to drive so carelessly.

如果你繼續開車這麼不小心的話，會發生意外。

20. The movie star will appear at the theater at 10 pm.

電影明星將會在晚上十點的時候出現在戲院。

21. You will regret what you do in the future.

你將來會後悔你所做的事的。

22. The boy will challenge any authority without fear when he grows up.

這個男孩長大後將會無懼於挑戰任何權威。

23. I will fulfill your dream, no matter what it is.

我將會滿足你的夢想，不管那是什麼。

24. The tailor will measure your height in order to make the suit.

為了製作西裝，裁縫將會測量你的身高。

25. He will lead us out of the darkness with his visionary thinking.

他將會以他充滿遠見的思考領導我們走出黑暗。

26. I will reduce your wage because we are having very little business lately.

因為我們最近生意清淡，所以我將會減少你的薪水。

27. The birds will inhabit in the wetland once the polluted river gets cleaned up.

一旦受污染的河川受到整治，這些鳥將會棲息這片溼地。

28. He will establish his own business when he graduates.

他畢業後將會建立自己的生意。

【句型22】現在進行式

29. cross	36. confirm	43. create	50. celebrate
30. gain	37. carve	44. connect	51. form
31. imagine	38. address	45. repeat	52. decide
32. discuss	39. copy	46. impress	53. train
33. capture	40. organize	47. receive	54. demonstrate
34. allow	41. process	48. craft	55. add
35. conduct	42. improve	49. place	56. spread

必考 句型與解析

【句型 22】現在進行式。

【結構】 現在進行式 "S + be 動詞 + Ving"，The cars ⇨ 車子（主詞），Are
⇨ be 動詞，crossing ⇨ 通過（Ving），Bridge ⇨ 橋樑。

【句子】 The cars are crossing through the bridge.

【中譯】 車子正在通過橋樑。

由句型 22【現在進行式 "S + be 動詞 + Ving"】此句型可得知，主詞是 The cars 這些車子，因為是複數，動詞用 are，動詞 cross 是通過的意思，因為是現在進行式，改為 Ving 用 crossing，在通過什麼地方呢？本範例中用介系詞 through，來表示通過這座橋樑。

The cars are crossing through the bridge. 車子正在通過橋樑，可以用在報導、或是觀察上，代表此項事實正在發生，就用現在進行式。

在後續的造句中，可由不同的主詞，搭配動詞的變化延伸出許多不同的句子，在句子中，也可補充 " 正在發生此狀況 / 動作 " 的地點 / 情況 / 條件等等，以讓語意更完整。讀者可以藉由自身經驗造句，推想並藉由表格上的動詞造出各式不同變化的句子。

【1】 現在進行式指將來會發生的動作及會存在的狀態，現在進行式的句型
構成是 S + be 動詞 + Ving，其中，Ving 是所謂的現在分詞，動詞後加
ing，如：cry ⇨ crying，walk ⇨ walking，work ⇨ working。

【2】 而 be 動詞則依主詞的人稱而改變，如：
I am working. 我正在工作。
He is studying. 他正在唸書。
They are playing. 他們正在玩。

【3】 簡單現在式通常用來表示現在的事實、狀態、習慣性動作或敘述不變
的真理。如：He is my father. 他是我的爸爸。
I live in Canada. 我住在加拿大。
而現在進行式則是現在發生的動作，或是某動作的進行、持續或發展。
She is crying in the room. 她正在房裡哭。
I am thinking about going to study in Europe.
我正在想考慮去歐洲唸書。

【4】 現在進行式的用法除了表示說話時正在進行或發生的動作外，在口語
中表示主語計劃將要作的動作，如：
I am hosting a party next week, please do come.
我計劃在下禮拜主辦一個派對，請務必要來。

【5】 有的動詞用於現在進行式表示「逐漸」的含義，如：

The situation is becoming more and more interesting.

情況越來越有趣了。

【6】 或是，當現在進行式與 always 等副詞連用時帶有 " 總是 "、" 老是 "
的意味，如：

She is always complaining about her husband.

她老是抱怨她的丈夫。

My mother is always worrying about me.

我的媽媽老是擔心我。

就是這樣寫

30. I am gaining a lot of knowledge from talking with you.
    我正從與你談話中得到很多知識。

31. He is imaging he will be rich and successful someday.
    他正在想像有一天他會變得有錢又成功。

32. She is discussing with her classmates on the other side of the room.
    她正在跟她同學在房間的另一端討論。

33. The police is capturing the thief in the subway station.
    警察正在地下鐵車站裡捕捉小偷。

34. You are allowing everybody to take advantage of you.
    你正在容許每個人占你便宜。

35. He is conducting an experiment that needs careful attention. I cannot let any visitor come into the lab now.

他正在進行一項需要小心注意的實驗，我現在不能讓任何訪客進入實驗室。

36. The report is confirming my worst fear.

這個報告正印證我最深的恐懼。

37. The sculptor is carving the wood in his studio.

雕刻家正在他的工作室裡雕刻木頭。

38. The teacher is addressing to you now, please listen to him.

老師正在跟你說話，請注意聽他所說。

39. My brother is copying what I do again, which really annoys me.

我弟弟現在又在模仿我做的事了，這真讓我生氣。

40. She is organizing the files in her computer.

她正在整理她電腦裡的檔案。

41. I am processing what you are saying, please give me a minute.

我正在理解你說的話，請給我一分鐘。

42. I am really happy that my grandmother's health is improving.

我真高興我祖母的健康正在改善。

43. She is creating the most beautiful art piece that I have ever seen.

她正在創作我所看過最美麗的藝術作品。

44. I am connecting you with my best friend Aaron who will know how to answer your questions.

我會將你跟我最好的朋友艾倫連結，他將知道如何回答你的問題。

45. The comedian is repeating the same joke again.

這個喜劇演員又正在重複同樣的笑話了。

46. The boy is impressing his mother with the new tricks he just learned.

這個男孩正在以他剛學的戲法向他母親炫耀。

47. I feel I am receiving lots of insults from you.

我覺得我正接受來自於你許多的侮辱。

48. I am crafting a beautiful speech for tomorrow's event.

我正為明天的場合打造一段美麗的講辭。

49. The waiter is placing wine glasses on each table.

侍者正在每個餐桌上放置酒杯。

50. The famous actress is celebrating her birthday with many guests in her mansion.

這位知名女演員正在她的豪宅裡與許多賓客慶祝她的生日。

51. I am forming a different opinion about him after I knew what he has done.

自從我知道他做了什麼以後，我正對他形成不同的看法。

52. She is deciding whether she should go to this trip.

她正在決定是否參加這次旅行。

53. Oliver is training his dog to understand instructions.

奧利佛正訓練他的狗聽懂指令。

54. I am demonstrating to you the best method I have discovered to cook spaghetti.

我正在示範給你看我所發現最好的煮義大利麵方法。

55. She is adding too much salt into the pot which is going to spoil the dish.

她正在把太多鹽加到鍋子裡，這將會毀了這道菜。

56. The news is spreading really quickly, you had better respond to the public.

消息正迅速的傳播開來，你最好對大眾有所回應。

【句型 23】現在完成式

1. dine	8. withstand	15. humiliate	22. crumble
2. realize	9. warn	16.accommodate	23. establish
3. design	10. irritate	17. brush	24. radiate
4. show	11. liberate	18. replace	25. hide
5. undertake	12. kidnap	19. harbor	26. explore
6. conceive	13. evacuate	20. maintain	27. transfer
7. execute	14. suffocate	21. accumulate	28. observe

必考　句型與解析

【句型 23】現在完成式

【結構】 She ⇨ 主詞，Has dined ⇨ 曾經用餐。

【句子】 She has just dined in the restaurant two weeks ago.

【中譯】 她在兩個禮拜前才剛在這家餐廳用過餐。

解　析

由句型 23【現在完成式 "S + have / has + 過去分詞"】此句型可得知，主詞是 She 她，因為是單數第三人稱，用 has，just 是時間副詞，表示剛剛的意思，用來表示主詞執行的動作才剛剛發生，動詞 dine 是用餐的意思，因為是現在完成式，改為過去分詞 pp 用 dined，在什麼地方呢？本範例中用 in the restaurant，來表示在這家餐廳，最後，再加上時間 two weeks ago，代表是兩個星期前的事。

She has just dined in the restaurant two weeks ago. 她兩個禮拜前才剛剛在這家餐廳用餐，是描述過去的某個動作，不久前才剛剛發生或完成。

在後續的造句中，可由不同的主詞，搭配動詞的變化可以延伸出許多不同的句子，在句子中，也可補充 "正在發生此狀況 / 動作" 的地點 / 情況 / 條件等等，以讓語意更完整。讀者可以藉由自身經驗造句，推想並藉由表格上的動詞造出各式不同變化的句子。

【1】 現在完成式是用來描述現在已經完成或仍在進行中的行為、動作跟事件，有 " 已經 "、" 曾經 " 的意思。

【2】 結構是：主語（單數）+ has + 動詞過去分詞

主語（複數）+ have + 動詞過去分詞，如：

He has seen the movie. 他已經看過電影。

They have seen the movie. 他們已經看過電影。

【3】 完成式的否定，因為 have / has 為助動詞，所以用 have not, has not，簡寫為 haven't, hasn't.

She has not seen the movie. 她還沒有看過這電影。

They haven't seen the movie. 他們還沒有看過這電影。

【4】 一般現在完成式的使用時機為：

◆ 過去的某個動作，到現在已經完成，或是已經造成某種結果：

I have finished the project.

我已經把這個專案做完。

You have hurt your mother's heart.

你已經傷害你母親的心。

◆ 過去的某個動作，不久前才剛剛完成：

I have just seen the movie.

我剛剛才看過這個電影。

◆ 從過去到現在累積的經驗，或是某個動作持續進行一段時間直到現在：

I have lived in Taiwan for more than twenty years.

我已經住在台灣超過二十年了。

◆ 在句型裡，常用 since 或 for 表時間的介系詞，for 表示一段時間，
  since 表示從過去的某一時間點，一直到現在：

We have known each other for ten years.

我們已經彼此認識十年了。

She has been my best friend since we were high school students.

從我們是高中生時，她就是我最好的朋友。

就是這樣寫

2. She has difficulty realizing what has just happened to her.

   要她了解到她身上剛發生了什麼事很困難。

3. I have designed the dress especially for you.

   我已為你特別設計了這件洋裝。

4. He has shown us what a great politician he is.

   他已展現給我們看他是一個多偉大的政治家。

5. He has undertaken this task under great pressure.

   他是在極大壓力下才承接這項任務的。

6. I have conceived this idea since three years ago.

   我自從三年前就有了這個構想。

7. You have executed the project perfectly.

   你已將這個計劃執行得很完美。

8. The house has withstood the test of the most sever typhoon ever in
   the history.

   這棟房子已經通過了史上最強烈颱風的考驗。

9. I have warned him over and over but he would not listen to me.

我已經警告他一次又一次，但是他不聽我的。

10. The boy sitting next to me has irritated me from the beginning of the concert by making a lot of noises.

這位坐在我旁邊的男孩從音樂會的一開始就製造很多噪音，已經惹惱我了。

11. Your kind forgiveness has liberated me from self-blaming.

你慷慨的原諒使我從自我責備中解脫出來。

12. The notorious gangsters have kidnapped several people over the years.

惡名昭彰的幫派份子在過去幾年已綁架了數人。

13. The fire fighters have evacuated people from the nearly burned down building.

消防隊員已經將人撤出這棟幾乎快燒光的建築。

14. The smoke in the subway has suffocated several people.

地下鐵裡的煙使好幾個人窒息。

15. Your behavior has humiliated your parents.

你的行為羞辱了你的父母。

16. The family has accommodated an exchange student from Germany over the past three months.

這個家庭讓一個德國來的交換學生在過去的三個月寄宿。

17. I have brushed the muddy floor several times this morning, but it still looks dirty.

我早上已經刷了這個泥濘的地板好幾次，但它看起來還是很髒。

18. I have replaced the batteries in the remote control.

我已經把遙控器裡的電池換掉了。

19. New York City has harbored many artists to realize their dreams.

紐約市孕育了許多藝術家去實現他們的夢。

20. He has maintained his calm despite all the difficulties.

他一直保持冷靜，即使困難重重。

21. Joseph has accumulated a fortune through years of hard working.

喬瑟夫透過歷年來的辛勤工作已經累積了一筆財務。

22. The cob wall has crumbled and needs to be repaired.

這個泥牆已經碎裂，需要被修復。

23. Owen has established one of the best private schools in the city.

歐文在城裡建立了最好之一的一所私立學校。

24. You have radiated love and kindness like the sunshine in my life.

你放射出愛與慷慨，就像我生命中的陽光。

25. He has hidden the bad news from his family and keeps the sorrow to himself.

他將這個壞消息藏匿不讓他家人知道，獨自承受悲傷。

26. Tony has explored all the hiking trails in this region.

東尼已經探索了這個區域裡所有的健行步道。

27. I have transferred you to another class due to your misconduct to your teacher.

因為你對老師不恭敬的行為，我已將你轉到另外一個班級。

28. I have observed the river for several days, but I can't see any salmon return upstreams.

我已經觀察這條河流好幾天了，但我看不到任何鮭魚上溯回流。

【句型24】 未來進行式

29. conduct	36. boost	43. discriminate	50. refund
30. propose	37. emigrate	44. puzzle	51. convert
31. order	38. block	45. investigate	52. modify
32. digest	39. detect	46. isolate	53. wipe
33. purchase	40. indicate	47. thrive	54. engineer
34. possess	41. incorporate	48. decentralize	55. transmit
35. confirm	42. participate	49. reverse	56. infect

必考 句型與解析

【句型 24】未來進行式。

【結構】 He ⇨ 主詞，will be conducting ⇨ 未來進行式，在未來將持續發生，在某一時刻正在發生，將執行計劃，for the next three month ⇨ 在未來三個月的時段內。

【句子】 He will be conducting the market survey for the next three months.

【中譯】 他將在未來的三個月持續進行這個市場調查。

由句型 24【未來進行式 "S + will + be + Ving"】此句型可得知，主詞是 He 他，助動詞 will 不分人稱單複數，之後接原形動詞 be，conduct 有執行、進行的意思，因為是未來進行式，改為 Ving 成為 conducting，will be conducting 就是即將持續進行的意思。繼而再推想 conducting 的受詞，從事什麼事情呢？就是進行一項市場調查：the market survey。最後加上介系詞 for，指明時間是未來的三個月以後：for the next three months，完成本句。

He will be conducting the market survey for the next three months. 他將在未來的三個月持續進行這個市場調查，是描述主詞在未來即將進行，而且將持續一段時間的動作，在後續的造句中，可由不同的主詞，搭配動詞的變化可以延伸出許多不同的句子，在句子中，也可補充 " 正在發生此狀況／動作 " 的地點／情況／條件等等，以讓語意更完整。讀者可以藉由自身經驗造句，推想並藉由表格上的動詞造出各式不同變化的句子。

153

【1】 未來進行式是指在未來某個時間「將正在」做的事，或是要強調未來將發生的動作，它的基本句型為：主詞 + will be + Ving。

【2】 使用的時間主要在：

◆ 表示在某個時間點時，預測或希望某事會發生

I will be going home at 7 o'clock.

我將在七點回家。

My mother will be making dinner when we arrive home.

當我們到家時，我的母親會在做晚餐。

◆ 表示確信某事肯定會發生，或是主詞在未來將執行的動作。

He will be trying again and again until he succeeds.

他將會一次又一次的嘗試直到他成功。

I will be moving in a month.

我在一個月內就將要搬家了。

【3】 雖然 will + V 的未來簡單式可以用 am / are / is going to V 代替，但一般未來進行式造句中，會避免用 am / are / is going to be Ving 這種句型，以免過度繁冗。

如：

We will be cleaning the classroom at nine tomorrow morning.

我們將在明天早上九點打掃教室。

替換成 We are going to be cleaning the classroom at nine tomorrow morning. 並非嚴重錯誤，但應避免。

就是這樣寫

30. He will be proposing this ideas again and again until it gets accepted.
他將會提議這個點子一次又一次直到它獲得接受。

31. She will be ordering meals for us in the restaurant when we get there.
當我們到餐廳時，她將正在為我們點餐。

32. I have just eaten. I will be digesting my dinner while you eat.
我剛吃過了，你吃東西的時候，我正好將消化我的晚餐。

33. Jack will be purchasing all the needed supplies for the mountain climbing trip in the next month.
傑克將在接下來的一個月購買登山之旅所需要的一切裝備。

34. The painting will be possessing amazing color qualities once it gets done.
這幅畫將具有迷人的顏色特質，當它被完成的時候。

35. I will be confirming your travel itinerary with you in a week.
我會在一個星期內跟你確認你的旅遊行程。

36. The advertisement on TV will be boosting our sales for the next season.
在電視上的廣告將會在下季大大增長我們的銷售。

37. Many people will be emigrating to New Zealand due to the new policy.
這個新政策會讓許多人移民到紐西蘭。

38. The building will be blocking our window view once it gets completed.
等到這棟建築完成它將會擋住我們窗外的景觀。

39. You will be sending to prison once the public detects your crime.

一旦大眾偵知你的犯罪，你會被送到監獄。

40. We will be knowing what to do next when the client indicates her preference.

當客戶表明她的偏好後，我們將會知道接下來該怎麼做。

41. We will be incorporating your ideas in the future edition of the book.

在未來這本書的編輯中我們會容納你的想法。

42. He will be participating in the marathon next weekend.

他下週末將會參與馬拉松比賽。

43. I will be filing a complaint if you continue to discriminate my ability.

如果你繼續歧視我的能力，我將提出申訴。

44. Susan will be searching for an answer because the situation really puzzles her.

蘇珊會去尋找答案，因為這個情況真的使她迷惑。

45. Nancy will be investigating the situation on behalf of me.

南西將會代表我調查這個情況。

46. I will be feeling very isolated in the village during the winter.

在冬天我在這個村莊會覺得很孤立。

47. The plants will be thriving in summer if the soil is fertile.

如果土壤是肥沃的，植物在夏天會繁盛。

48. The company will be decentralizing its system of decision making in response to its growing business worldwide.

這公司會將它的決策系統分散化，以因應它在世界各地成長中的生意。

49. People will be reversing their attitude toward the poor boy when they know that he is actually a prince.

當人們發現這男孩其實是王子時，人們對這可憐男孩的態度會完全翻轉。

50. I will be refunding you the money if you bring your receipt.

如果你帶你的收據來的話，我會退還你錢。

51. I will be having enough money tomorrow after I convert my traveler's check.

當我兌換我的旅行支票後，明天我會有足夠的錢。

52. We will be publishing the book once you modify the conclusion.

一旦你修正結尾，我們就會出版這本書。

53. I will be wiping the floor all day tomorrow. You are welcome to help me!

我明天整天都會在擦地板，歡迎你來幫我！

54. We will be having a better chance to get the business if we can engineer a further meeting with her.

如果我們可以籌劃跟她更進一步的會面的話，我們會有更好的機會得到這筆生意。

55. You will be transmitting your own fears to your son if you do not control your emotions.

如果你不控制情緒的話，你會把你自己的恐懼傳導給你的兒子。

56. The patient will be running a fever if he is infected with the virus.

如果病人被病毒感染的話，他將會發燒。

【句型25】過去進行式

1. dust	8. select	15. struggle	22. contribute
2. record	9. invite	16. access	23. reach
3. fantasize	10. prevent	17. reduce	24. market
4. inspire	11. check	18. experience	25. release
5. suggest	12. construct	19. burn	26. labor
6. undergo	13. produce	20. rise	27. replicate
7. decide	14. threaten	21. spread	28. manipulate

必考 句型與解析

【句型25】過去進行式

【結構】 過去進行式 "S + was / were + Ving"，Maggie（主詞）was dusting the table（A 行為）when her son came back from school（B 時間）。Maggie ⇨ 梅姬（主詞），was ⇨ be 動詞過去式，dusting ⇨ 撣灰塵（Ving），the table ⇨ 桌子。

【句子】 Maggie was dusting the table when her son came back from school.

【中譯】 當她兒子從學校回來時，梅姬正在為桌子撢灰塵。

 解 析

由句型 25【過去進行式 "S + was / were + Ving"】此句型可得知，主詞是 Maggie 梅姬，因為是第三人稱單數過去式，故動詞用 was，之後接原形動詞 dust，有打掃、撢灰塵的意思，因為是過去進行式，Ving 成為 dusting，was dusting 就是在過去的時段裡，持續、或正在進行撢灰塵的意思。繼而再推想 dusting 的受詞，以 table 代表打掃的對象為一張桌子。

當前面的子句完成後，後面的關係子句以 when 作為連接，when... 代表 "在什麼時間發生之前動作" 的時間，when her son came back from the school. 意指前面子句的動作：梅姬正在撢桌子的灰塵，發生的時間點為當她的兒子從學校回來的時候，完成本句。

過去進行式是描述在過去某個時間點 / 某件事發生時，主詞正在進行的動作，在後續的造句中，可由不同的主詞，搭配動詞的變化可以延伸出許多不同的句子，在句子中，也可補充 在過去 "正在發生此狀況 / 動作" 的地點 / 情況 / 條件等等，以讓語意更完整。讀者可以藉由自身經驗造句，推想並藉由表格上的動詞造出各式不同變化的句子。

【1】 過去進行式的基本句型為：主詞 + was / were + Ving。過去進行式指過去某一時刻或某段時間正在發生的動作，跟簡單過去式比起來，特別強調該行動進行與發生的狀態。

【2】 在構句時，可以先描述主詞過去正在進行的行為（A 行為），再說明是在 B 時間點發生的，而 B 是一個過去的時間。如：

The students were all playing when the teacher came into the classroom.

當老師進到教室時，學生們都在玩。

【3】 The students were all playing. 代表的是主詞學生們正在進行的 A 行為，而 the teacher came into the classroom 是發生的時間點，兩者間用 when 來連接，代表 A 行為剛好在 B 的時間點發生。當此句被陳述出來時，顯然該件事已發生過了，故屬「過去時間」，用過去進行式。

【4】 簡單歸納，過去進行式可用於：

◆ 過去的某個時間點，某動作正在進行、或持續進行，如：

He was eating ice cream all afternoon last Saturday.

上周六整個下午他都在吃冰淇淋。

◆ 由過去某時持續到另一時間的過去動作：

I was traveling in Europe from August to October last year.

去年的八到十月，我在歐洲旅行。

◆ 在過去的時間裡，當某一情境發生時，某動作正在進行，經常用

when 來引導描述時間的子句，如：

◆ When the thief came in through the back door, Mary was soundly sleeping in her room.

◆ 當小偷從後面進來時，瑪麗正在她的房間裡熟睡。

✐ 就是這樣寫

2. He was recording the music on radio all afternoon.
   他整個下午都在錄收音機的音樂。

3. He was fantasizing his lover when the teacher called his name.
   他正在幻想他的愛人，當他老師叫他的名字的時候。

4. The book "On the Road" was inspiring to many young people at that time.
   「在路上」這本書當時激勵了許多的年輕人。

5. He was suggesting a different way of doing things, that's all.
   他不過只是在建議一種做事情不同的方法罷了。

6. The road to the village was undergoing a major repair when we took our excursion.
   當我們出遊時，這條通往村莊的道路正在經歷重大的維修。

7. He was doing the work all by himself when I decided to join him.
   當我決定加入他時，他正自己一個人在做所有的工作。

8. Joe was considering of giving up playing basketball when the coach selected him to join the school team.
   當教練選他在參加校隊時，喬正在考慮放棄打籃球。

9. I was going to spend the night alone when you invited me to the party.
   當你邀請我來參加派對時，我正想要自己一個人度過今夜。

10. The city was enforcing strict rules to prevent youth crime.

這城市在執行嚴格的法規以防範青少年犯罪。

11. My daughter was crying when I went to check her.

當我去看視我女兒時，她正在哭。

12. The city was constructing the largest aquarium in the world when we visited it last time.

上次我們拜訪這座城市時，它正在建造世界最大的水族館。

13. The composer was producing his greatest work when the accident suddenly struck.

當意外突然降臨時，作曲家正在創造他最好的作品。

14. I was not feeling scared when he threatened me with his knife.

當他用刀威脅我時，我沒有覺得害怕。

15. The deer was struggling to get out of the trap when we came to rescue her.

當我們去解救牠時，這頭鹿正掙扎要從陷阱裡脫逃。

16. The hacker was trying to access the database when the police detected his action.

當警察偵測到他的行動時，這位駭客正試著要進入資料庫裡。

17. Fanny was spending a lot of money buying luxuries when her husband told her to reduce her expenses.

當她的先生告訴她必須減少花費時，芬妮正在花很多錢買奢侈品。

18. I was hoping you would like this village when you experienced how beautiful it was.

我正希望你會喜歡這個村莊，當你體驗它有多漂亮時。

19. The man was attempting to burn down the house when the police got there.

當警察趕到時，這男人正在意圖把房子燒了。

20. The sun was rising when we got home yesterday morning.
昨天早上當我們回到家時，太陽正在升起。

21. The news was spreading quickly and there was nothing we could do about it.
消息正在快速地散播，而我們什麼也不能做。

22. We were not knowing what to do when he contributed the idea to us.
當他把這個點子貢獻給我們時，我們正不知道該怎麼辦。

23. I was reaching the finishing line when someone suddenly hit me.
當有人突然撞到我時，我正快抵達終點線。

24. He was trying everything he could to market the product, but the sales would not go up.
他試盡他一切所能行銷這產品，但銷售就是不上昇。

25. The public was running out of patience when the company finally released the news.
當大眾正耗盡耐心時，公司終於釋出消息。

26. I was laboring day and night to build the house all by myself when my neighbor came to visit me.
當我鄰居來探訪我時，我正日夜自己一個人為蓋這間房子而努力。

27. She was painting the postcards one by one while it would be much easier to replicate the cards with computer.
她一張一張畫明信片，即便用電腦複製這些卡片會容易多了。

28. The police was suspecting the accuracy of the data because the company might have manipulated the figures.
警方在懷疑資料的正確性，因為這公司有可能篡改數據。

【句型 26】過去完成式

29. strike	36. remain	43. bear	50. invest
30. resonate	37. appear	44. notice	51. complete
31. associate	38. freeze	45. slip	52. create
32. announce	39. block	46. realize	53. express
33. deliver	40. flow	47. wake	54. post
34. save	41. count	48. record	55. trap
35. increase	42. insist	49. arrange	56. destroy

必考　句型與解析

【句型 26】過去完成式

【結構】 the thunder ⇨ 主詞，雷電，had struck ⇨ 過去完成式，在過去某一時間或某一動作之前已經完成的動作或經驗，已經被雷電擊中，more than ten years ago ⇨ 發生在過去十年前的事。

【句子】 The thunder had struck the trees more than ten years ago.

【中譯】 十年前雷電就擊中了這些樹。

解　析

由句型 26【過去完成式 "S + had + 過去分詞 "】此句型可得知，主詞是 The thunder 雷電，因為是過去完成式，不分人稱與單複數都用 had，之後再加上過去分詞，strike 有雷擊打的意思，過去分詞 pp 為 struck，受詞為 the trees，代表這些樹，The thunder had struck the trees，代表雷電在過去已經打中了這些樹，而發生在什麼時候呢？用 more than ten years ago 來修飾，代表此事發生在超過十年以前，而完成了本句。

The thunder had struck the trees more than ten years ago. 十年前雷電就擊中了這些樹，過去完成式代表在過去某個時間點，某件事已然發生或完成，在後續的造句中，可由不同的主詞，搭配動詞的變化可以延伸出許多不同的句子，在句子中，也可詳細敘述 在過去發生此狀況 / 動作的地點 / 情況 / 條件等等，更加豐富語意。讀者可以藉由自身經驗造句，推想並藉由表格上的動詞造出各式不同變化的句子。

【1】 過去完成式的基本句型為：主詞 + had + 過去分詞，動作開始在過去的過去，並在過去結束，主詞後都接 had，表示過去某一時刻之前已經完成的動作，在構句時，可加上過去的時間點、情境，常與由 by，before 引導的時間狀態語連用。

【2】 過去完成式的使用時機是：

◆ 表示過去某一動作之前已經完成的動作或經驗，常與由 when，before 等連接詞引導的時間副詞子句連用。如：

When he woke up the phone had stopped ringing.

當他醒來的時候電話已經停止不響了。

She had made a lot of efforts before she won the competition.

在她贏得比賽前，她已做了很多努力。

◆ 使用的情境，常常是在敘述在過去的時態中，已經發生或完成的事，故常常用在說故事、回憶的情境中。

◆ 某些動詞的過去完成式表示一個在過去預計要做的事（但通常未發生），如：

We had planned to publish the book last year, but we were short of funding.

我們原本預計在去年出版這本書，但我們的資金不足。

He had hoped to receive a scholarship to study abroad, but unfortunately it didn't happen.

他原本希望能得到到國外唸書的獎學金，但很不幸地結果並沒有發生。

就是這樣寫

30. The story had resonated with me the moment I heard it.

這個故事在我一聽到時，我就有所共鳴。

31. The boy had associated a group of gangsters when his parents started to notice something went wrong.

當他的父母開始注意到有些事不對勁的時候，這個男孩已經跟一群幫派份子有所糾葛。

32. The manager had announced the plan to the company.

經理已經將這個計劃向全公司宣布了。

33. The postman had delivered the package more than two weeks ago.

郵差已經在超過兩個月前就送出了包裹。

34. I had saved more than two million dollars during working for the company.

我在為這公司工作的期間，已經存了超過兩百萬元。

35. My boss had increased my wage twice during the past four years.

我的老闆在過去的四年間已經加了我兩次薪。

36. He had remained an important figure in the company until he retired in his 70s.

一直到他七十歲退休，他在公司裡都持續是個重要人物。

37. The actor had appeared on TV frequently in the 90s, but he stopped performing afterwards.

這位演員在九零年代時還常常出現在電視上，但他之後就停止表演。

38. My father had frozen the meat in the freezer, therefore throughout the winter we had enough food supply.

我父親已把肉冷凍在冷凍庫裡，因此整個冬天我們有足夠的食物供給。

39. Jane realized she could not get out of her house because the cars had blocked the road.

珍察覺到她無法離開她的房子，因為車子已經堵住路了。

40. The river had always flown in this area until they built a dam upstream.

一直到他們在上游蓋水壩之前，這條河一直在這區域流動。

41. He had counted the number of books in stock three times

他已經算了庫存書的數量三次了。

42. She had insisted on giving the best education to her children despite she was very poor.

即使她很貧窮，她也堅持給她的孩子最好的教育。

43. Nancy had born the weight of keeping the secret until she couldn't stand it any more.

南西一直承受保守秘密的重擔，直到她再也忍耐不住。

44. I had noticed the boy's talent the first day when he came to the school.

這男孩來學校的第一天我就注意到他的天份。

45. Before I told him not to touch the letter he had slit open the envelope.

在我告訴他不要碰那封信之前，他已經把信封拆開來了。

46. I had scolded the innocent boy badly before I realized it was not his fault.

在我理解到這不是他的錯之前，我已經把這個無辜的男孩狠狠的罵了一頓。

47. The phone had stopped ringing before Martha woke up.

在瑪莎醒來之前，電話已經停止響了。

48. He had recorded many folk songs sung by the local elderly before they passed away.

在老人還未凋零前，他已經錄下了當地耆老唱的許多傳統民謠。

49. She had arranged many interviews for me before I even asked her.

在我要求她之前，她已經為我安排了很多面試。

50. Before you had invested so much money, you should have known about the firm's reputation.

在你投資這麼多錢前，你早該知道這個公司的評價。

51. He had completed the novel more than three years ago.

他在三年之前就完成了這部小說。

52. Josh had created the sculpture when he was an art student.

當他是藝術學生時，賈許製作了這個雕像。

53. I had expressed my gratitude to you in the past, and I am going to express it again.

我以前就跟你表達過我的感謝了，我要再表達一次。

54. He had posted the letter before realizing that the address was wrong.

他在意識到住址是錯的之前就寄出了那封信。

55. The hunter had trapped the lion after weeks of tracing.

經過好幾個星期的追蹤，獵人終於以陷阱捕獲了獅子。

56. The bomb had destroyed the town in the Second World War.

炸彈在第二次世界大戰時就摧毀了這個城鎮。

【句型 27】 There is / There are

1. gallery	8. passenger	15. developer	22. message
2. resort	9. consumer	16. character	23. founder
3. activity	10. campaign	17. plaza	24. installation
4. exhibition	11. politician	18. essay	25. celebration
5. puppet	12. comedian	19. skyscraper	26. reflection
6. performer	13. pill	20. basement	27. discussion
7. festival	14. pilot	21. aircraft	28. citizen

必考 句型與解析

【句型 27】There is / There are

【結構】 There is ＋單數名詞 / There are + 複數名詞，There is（這裡有）
a（一個）very famous art gallery（有名的藝廊）in the city（在這
個城市）. There is ⇨ 這裡有，a famous art gallery ⇨ 一個有名的
美術館，in the city ⇨ 在這個城市

【句子】 There is a very famous art gallery in the city.

【中譯】 這城市裡有一個很有名的美術館。

解 析

由句型 27【There is ＋單數名詞 / There are ＋ 複數名詞】此句型可得知，There 是副詞，和 be 動詞 is 或 are 連用，用於表示某物或某人的存在，代表 "這裡有…" 的意思，從 There 引導的句子，因為之後要敘述的真主詞 art gallery 美術館是單數名詞，故用 There is，名詞前再加上 very famous 來形容美術館很有名，而美術館在哪裡呢？設想在這個城市裡，故用 in the city，在這個城市裡的地方副詞片語來修飾，完成本句子。

在後續的造句中，可由不同的名詞，依據其單數、複數，搭配 There is 或 There are，來描述在什麼樣的狀態 / 情況 / 地點 / 時間，有什麼樣的人、事、物（名詞），讀者可以藉由自身經驗造句，推想並藉由表格上的動詞造出各式不同變化的句子。

必考文法概念

There 是副詞，there 和 be 動詞用以代替主語，是虛主詞，而不是真正的主詞，真正的主詞是後面的名詞。所以後面的名詞是單數名詞時，there 就接 be 動詞 is，如果是複數名詞，be 動詞就接 are。

【1】 There is / are 代表有什麼東西、事物，可以在「句尾」的部分，加上了「在…地方」in / on / at /… ＋ 地方。如：
There is a book in my bag.
在我的袋子裡有一本書。

There is a plate on the table.

在桌上有一個盤子。

【2】 也可改變時態 There was / were...，描述過去存在的事物，如：

There was a big banyan tree in the school long time ago.

這學校很久以前曾有一棵很大的榕樹。

【3】 There is / There are 的疑問句為將 be 動詞提到句首，如：

Is there a book on the table?

在桌上有一本書嗎？

Are there two girls in the classroom?

在教室裡有兩個女孩嗎？

【4】 表示「在某處有某人正在做某動作」的句型，用 "There is / are + a / one / two + 名詞 + Ving + 地方副詞片語" 表示，如：

There are three girls playing on the beach.

有三個女孩在沙灘上玩。

【5】 There is / There are 後也可以加以 who / which / that 引導的子句，如：

There is a book that I would like you to read.

有一本書我想讓你看。

There is someone whom I would like you to meet.

有一個人我想讓你見見。

就是這樣寫

2. There is a beautiful resort near the beach.
   在海邊有一個美麗的度假村。

3. There are many extra curriculum activities you can do in this high school.
   這所高中裡有很多你可以做的課外活動。

4. There is a computer exhibition this weekend in the World Trade Center.
   這個週末在世貿中心有電腦展。

5. There is an old puppet in the drawer that used to be my favorite toy.
   這個抽屜裡有個舊偶人，曾是我最喜歡的玩具。

6. There is an excellent ballet performer who is going to join this show tomorrow.
   有個很傑出的芭蕾舞表演者將加入明天的這場演出。

7. There is a great festival coming up celebrating the autumn harvest.
   有一場很棒的節慶即將到來，慶祝秋季的豐收。

8. There is a passenger who has not boarded the plane.
   有一名乘客還沒有登上飛機。

9. There are many consumers expressing dissatisfaction toward this product.
   有許多消費者對這項產品表達不滿。

10. There is a campaign for animal rights tomorrow if you would like to join.
    明天有一場有關動物權的宣傳活動，如果你要參加的話。

11. There are few politicians who can fulfill their promises after the election.

有很少的政治家可以在競選後達成承諾的。

12. There is a famous comedian in town. Let's go see his show!

有個很有名的喜劇演員來到城裡了，我們去看他的演出！

13. There are many pills you need to take if you want to stay out of the hospital.

你必須吞很多藥丸，如果你不想進醫院的話。

14. There are many pilots in the Smith family.

史密斯家庭有許多飛行員。

15. There is a developer who wishes to transform the rolling hills into a golf course.

有一個開發商想要將這片起伏的山坡轉變成高爾夫球場。

16. There are many characters in Harry Potter's movies that are very well liked by the young audience.

哈利波特電影裡有許多人物廣受年輕觀眾的喜愛。

17. There are many lively plazas in Italian cities.

義大利的城市裡有許多活躍的廣場。

18. There is an essay about this place written by a famous writer.

有一篇關於這個地方的散文，是由一個著名的作家寫成。

19. There are many skyscrapers in New York.

紐約有許多摩天大樓。

20. There is a basement in the house that can be used as a storage.

這個房子有個地下室，可以當儲藏空間使用。

21. There is an exhibition on the aircrafts in the Second World War in the avian museum.

航空博物館裡有一場關於第二次世界大戰飛機的展覽。

22. There is a message for you, Mr. Brighton.

有給你的一則留言，布萊頓先生。

23. There was a strong founder behind each successful organization.

在每個成功組織的背後都有一個堅強的創辦人。

24. There is an art installation on the wall. Please do not damage it.

在牆上有一個藝術裝置，請不要損傷它。

25. There is a celebration for my mother's birthday this afternoon.

下午會有為我母親生日舉行的慶祝。

26. There are many reflections I have about my life in the army.

關於我在軍中的生活我有許多反思。

27. There is a discussion about alternative energy this evening.

今晚有一場關於替代能源的討論。

28. There are many citizens protesting against the use of nuclear power throughout the country.

在全國各地都有很多公民反對核能的使用。

【句型28】 連接詞 In addition to

1. convince	8. persist	15. tighten	22. arrest
2. assume	9. prevent	16. direct	23. investigate
3. evaluate	10. addict	17. appear	24. attempt
4. cause	11. contribute	18. offer	25. attract
5. tackle	12. inspire	19. criticize	26. destroy
6. stroll	13. entertain	20. phone	27. create
7. motivate	14. crush	21. collect	28. return

必考　句型與解析

【句型28】連接詞 In addition to。

【結構】　In addition to 除了…之外，還有 In addition to his speech（A 事物），Jack prepared（準備）a video showing the actual research process（B 事物）for the conference in order to（為了以下目的）convince his audience. In addition ⇨ 除了，his speech ⇨ 演講，he ⇨ 主詞，prepared a video showing the actual research process ⇨ 還準備了的其他東西。

【句子】 In addition to his speech, Jack prepared a video showing the actual research process for the conference in order to convince his audience.

【中譯】 除了他的演講外，傑克為了這會議準備了一個錄影帶顯示實際的研究過程以使他的聽眾信服。

解　析

由句型 28【In addition to...】此句型可得知，in addition to 表示除…以外（還有），是介系詞片語，後接名詞或動名詞，故用 In addition to 開頭後，接名詞 his speech，指他（主詞）的演講，便開始設想主詞除了演講以外，還做了什麼事，在 In addition to his speech 後，用逗號區格，開始進入主詞的主要動作，主詞 Jack 傑克還準備了一段影片，英义用 prepare a video，過去式改為 prepared a video，這段影片並不只是隨便一段影片，加上 showing the actual research process 修飾後，我們知道它是能夠展現實際研究過程的影片。而為了什麼場合呢？加上介系詞 for，for the conferece 代表是為了會議的場合，接著再設想是為了什麼目的，則加上 in order to convince his audience，指目的是為了說服他的聽眾，而完成整個句子。

"In addition to" 放在句首，有除了某事物以外，主詞還做了某事物的意思，在後續的造句中，可由不同的動詞，來描述主詞所做的不同行動，讀者可以藉由自身經驗造句，推想並藉由表格上的動詞造出各式不同變化的句子。

In addition to 意指 "除了…之外，還有…"，代表 A 與 B 兩者同時都有，是介系詞片語，使用的時機，是用來轉承句子結構，讓句子的語意更加順暢。在結構上，"In addition to + N / Ving"，因為為介系詞，之後接名詞，若接動詞的話，注意要改成動名詞。

【1】 在構思句子時，In addition to 前後的名詞或動名詞在許多情況中，有對等、類比、或是相互補充的關係，如：

In addition to hamburgers, I had french fries for lunch.

除了漢堡之外，我在午餐還吃了薯條。

"漢堡" 與 "薯條" 有類比性質，兩者是相對的東西。

In addition to giving me the old TV, my parents bought me a sofa for my new apartment.

除了給我一台舊電視以外，我的父母為我的新公寓買了一個沙發。

【2】 In addition to 也可以放在句中，由主詞先開頭引導，再加入 in addition to，中間不加逗點分隔，如：

Sophie made a pie in addition to the pizza.

蘇菲除了披薩以外又做了一個派。

【3】 in addition 與 in addition to 的分別：in addition 表示 "此外"，是副詞片語，用來附加說明，可用逗點和句子的其他部分分開，如：

Jenny is a very well known professor. In addition, she is a very popular writer.

珍妮是很知名的教授，除此之外，她還是很受歡迎的作家。

就是這樣寫

2. In addition to watermelons, I assume there are mangos produced on the island.
   除了西瓜外，我假設這個島上也生產芒果。

3. In addition to the taste, the appearance of the food is also evaluated in the cooking competition.
   除了味道之外，食物的外表也在烹飪比賽中加以評鑑。

4. In addition to smoking, air pollution is another factor that causes the patients to have lung cancer.
   除了抽煙以外，空氣污染是導致病人罹患肺癌的另一個原因。

5. In addition to R& D department, we need to include marketing department to tackle this problem.
   除了研發部外，我們必須請行銷部也來一起解決這個問題。

6. In addition to an ice cream, she ate a hot dog while she was strolling down the road this afternoon.
   除了冰淇淋以外，今天下午當她在路上散步時她也吃了一支熱狗。

7. In addition to the physical training, the coach motivated us by developing our mental strength.
   除了體能訓練外，教練培養我們心理力量以激勵我們。

8. In addition to running, she persists to strengthen her body by lifting weight.
   除了跑步外，她持續的透過舉重來強化她的身體。

9. In addition to setting up the fence, the school installed video camera to prevent theft.
   除了架起柵欄之外，學校裝設了攝影機以防範偷竊

10. In addition to chocolate, it is unfortunate I am addicted to ice cream now.

除了巧克力之外，不幸的我現在也對冰淇淋上癮了。

11. In addition to science, Dr. Li also contributes to the art field greatly.

除了科學以外，林博士對藝術界也貢獻良多。

12. In addition to literature, my teacher inspires me to pursue my interest in music.

除了文學外，我的老師也啟發我追求我對音樂的興趣。

13. In addition to kids, the movie entertains adults alike.

除了孩子外，這部電影對人也一樣有娛樂性。

14. In addition to two bicycles, the car crushed into a tree.

除了兩輛腳踏車以外，這輛車撞上了一棵樹。

15. In addition to the thighs, you should tighten your arms in this yoga posture.

除了繃緊大腿外，在這個瑜伽動作裡你也應該繃緊你的手臂。

16. In addition to Crouching Tiger, Hidden Dragon, An Lee directed The Life of Pi, which was also won him an Oscar.

除了臥虎藏龍外，李安導演了少年 Pi 的漂流日記，也讓他得到奧斯卡。

17. In addition to TV shows, the actress appeared in several movies.

除了電視秀以外，這個女星在好幾部電影出現。

18. In addition to tea, the host offered us delicious cakes.

除了茶以外，主人提供給我們好吃的蛋糕。

19. In addition to her look, she was criticized for her voice.

除了她的長相外，她因為她的聲音而受批評。

20. In addition to the police station, I think we should phone the hospital in case someone is hurt in the robbery.

除了警察局以外，我想我們還應該打電話給醫院，以免有人在這次搶劫中受傷。

21. In addition to jade, he collects diamond.

除了玉以外，他收集鑽石。

22. In addition to the president, the police arrested the manager of the company because both of them seemed to violate the law.

除了總裁外，警察逮捕了公司的經理，因為他們兩人似乎都違反了法律。

23. In addition to rivers, the researchers also research the lakes to investigate how the number of fish has changed due to the construction of reservoir.

除了河川外，研究者也研究湖泊，去調查水庫的興建對魚的數量有何種改變。

24. In addition to swimming, I attempt to try throwing the discus in the sports competition.

除了游泳，我想要在今年的運動會嘗試丟鐵餅。

25. In addition to cockroaches, the rotten garbage attracts a lot of mice.

除了蟑螂，這發霉的垃圾吸引了許多老鼠。

26. In addition to the train station, the bomb destroyed our city hall.

除了火車站，炸彈摧毀了我們的市政府。

27. In addition to a sculpture, she created several paintings during the workshop.

除了一個雕像外，她在這個工作坊創作了好幾幅畫。

28. In addition to books, Caroline returned the CDs that she had borrowed from me.

除了書以外，卡洛琳把她跟我借的 CD 也還我。

【句型 29】 連接詞 Although

1. recall	8. circle	15. detect	22. identify
2. clarify	9. cool	16. relieve	23. admit
3. transform	10. contradict	17. disclose	24. train
4. polish	11. mediate	18. condense	25. harvest
5. perform	12. generate	19. provoke	26. collect
6. manage	13. notice	20. retain	27. reform
7. overcome	14. recruit	21. deny	28. omit

必考　句型與解析

【句型 29】連接詞 Although。

【結構】　Although ⇨ 雖然，I cannot recall his name ⇨（某種情況），I remember his face vividly. ⇨（在這種情況下）我還是清楚地記得他的臉。

【句子】　Although（雖然）I cannot recall his name（某種情況），I remember his face vividly.

【中譯】　雖然我無法記得他的名字，我還是清楚地記得他的臉。

解　析

由句型 29【連接詞 Although 】此句型可得知，Although 代表 "雖然"，置於句首開頭，之後接主詞 I，此時推想，雖然主詞不能達成某種狀況，I cannot recall his name 我不能記得他的名字，但卻達成另外一種結果，因此設想，I remember his face vividly 我生動地記得他的臉，兩個子句中用逗點隔開，便完成整個句子。

使用 Although 的造句，主要是兩個子句的確要具有主詞 "雖然如何"，"但是卻如何" 的連接關係，這是形成句子的關鍵，唯有當設想出具有此關係的情境，造出的句子才有意義，可以不同主詞，參照表格上的動詞，試著造出各種不同變化的句意。

必考文法概念

【1】　連接詞 Although.... 引導的句子，為副詞子句，最貼切的中譯為 "雖然…但是"，修飾主要子句。

Although Jane is very hungry, she decides not to eat dinner so that she can lose weight.

本句的主要子句位在逗點之後，是珍妮為了減重決定不要吃晚餐，前面 Although 引導的副詞子句，是在修飾主要子句，說明珍妮其實很饑餓的狀態，使用 Although 開頭串連兩個子句，讓兩個子句間有連接關係，句意也更豐富有層次，否則若變成 Jane is very hungry. 以及 Jane decides not to eat dinner so that she can lose weight. 兩個獨立句子，便無法顯示出這兩個情況的相連關係。

【2】 注意有 although 的句子中不可再用 but，否則會造成有兩個連接詞的錯誤，如：

Although the book is very popular, but I do not like it. (X)

雖然這本書很受歡迎，但是我不喜歡。在中文翻譯上雖然通順，但在英文上，一個句子同時有 although 又有 but 卻是錯誤，應該只能使用一個連接詞。

【3】 although 也可以 tough 代替，特別在口語中更為常見，though 為副詞，表達 " 但是 "、" 不過 "，通常置於句尾，如：

I have had a huge dinner, I am still hungry though.

我已經吃了豐盛的晚餐，但我還是很餓。

等同於 I have had a huge dinner, although I am still hungry.

就是這樣寫

2. Although he tries to clarify his position, people are skeptical about where he really stands.

雖然他試著澄清他的立場，人們還是對他真正的立場感到質疑。

3. Although the actor has been on stage for more than twenty years, he transforms himself and surprises his audiences all the time.

雖然這名演員已經在舞台上超過二十年，他不停的自我轉型，一直讓他的觀眾感到驚訝。

4. Although this is a pair of old shoes, my father cherishes it and polishes it all the time.

雖然這是一雙舊鞋子，我父親很愛惜他，時時將它擦亮。

5. Although Helen performs at local theater regularly, she still feels very nervous about her first performance at the National Theater.

   雖然海倫經常在地方戲院表演，她對於她在國家劇院的第一場演出還是覺得很緊張。

6. Although he is very busy lately, he manages to read a book every day.

   雖然他最近很忙碌，他設法每天讀一本書。

7. Although she dislikes public speaking, eventually she overcomes her shyness and gave a speech in the graduation ceremony.

   雖然她不喜歡公眾演說，最終她克服了她的害羞在畢業典禮上演講。

8. Although the thief tried to get way, the police circled the ground of houses with guard dogs which made the escape impossible.

   雖然小偷設法逃跑，警衛將房子地面以警犬包圍，讓他插翅難飛。

9. Although the situation is very annoying, Ted always cools my temper with his good humor.

   雖然這個情形很令人惱怒，泰德總是以他絕佳的幽默感冷靜我的脾氣。

10. Although Joan seems to be a very obedient child in school, she always contradicts with her parents at home.

    雖然瓊安在學校看起來像是個聽話的小孩，在家她總是反駁她的父母。

11. Although the negotiators try to mediate the dispute, the conflict still escalated.

    雖然談判者試圖調停這個爭端，衝突還是持續上升。

12. Although the factory will cause some pollution, it will generate 120 new jobs.

    雖然這個工廠會製造些污染，它會帶來 120 個新的工作。

13. Although I tried to get the teacher's attention, he could not notice

me because there was a such a distance between us.

雖然我試圖引起老師的注意，他無法注意到我因為我們兩個距離很遠。

14. Although he does not have related experience, he is still recruited by the company.

雖然他沒有相關經驗，他還是受到這家公司所招聘。

15. Although the recession has lasted for a long time, financial experts have detected signs that the economy is beginning to improve.

雖然不景氣持續了好長一段時間，財金專家已觀察到經濟即將好轉的跡象。

16. Although she was not allowed to go out to play, she relieved her boredom at home by reading a lot of books when she was a child.

雖然她不被准許出去玩，當她是小孩時，她透過閱讀許多書減輕她待在家的無聊。

17. Although the company has disclosed a profit of over two million, its stock price still goes down.

雖然這家公司公開有超過兩百萬的盈餘，它的股價還是下跌。

18. Although he tries to condense his speech, it still goes for more than three hours.

雖然他試圖壓縮他的演說，還是超過了三個小時長。

19. Although the mayor has been careful in his wording, what he said still provoked a lot of controversy in the public

雖然市長的用字很小心，他所說的話在大眾間還是引發了很大的爭議。

20. Although Joe's father passed away when he was just a little boy, he still retains a very vivid memory of his father.

雖然喬的父親在他是小男孩時就過世了，他還是保留對他父親鮮明的記憶。

21. Although Jeff has been denying his love toward Mary, everybody can see that he really adores her.

雖然傑夫一直否認他對瑪麗的愛，每個人都看得出來他真的很喜歡她。

22. Although I have been to his house several times, I still have a hard time identifying the street he lives.

雖然我曾經去過他的房子好幾次，我還是很難辨識出他住的那條街。

23. Although she admitted she had made a mistake, she refused to make an apology publicly.

雖然她承認她犯了一個錯誤，她拒絕公開的道歉。

24. Although Joyce is the youngest one among her colleagues, she trains herself to be more assertive at work and soon wins much respect.

雖然喬伊絲是她同事裡最年輕的，她訓練自己變得更堅持自我，也迅速的贏得許多尊敬。

25. Although there is a severe drought in the region, the farmer harvests more rice than the previous year.

雖然這區域有很嚴重的乾旱，這個農夫比去年收獲了更多的稻米。

26. Although she did not have a lot of money, she started to collect antiques from the flea market.

雖然她沒有很多錢，她開始在跳蚤市場收集古董。

27. Although the politician has promised to reform the government, so far we cannot see any result.

雖然這名政治人物承諾要改革政府，到目前為止我們沒有看到任何成果。

28. Although I have worked a lot for the project, I was disappointed to find my name was omitted from the list of contributors in the report.

雖然我為這個計劃工作良多，我很失望的發現我的名字在報告上被遺漏在貢獻者的名單以外。

【句型 30】 頻率副詞

100指考 必考字彙表 V29～V56

1. handle	8. appreciate	15. surpass	22. measure
2. request	9. minimize	16. decline	23. conduct
3. approve	10. distress	17. explore	24. enforce
4. adjust	11. mask	18. fade	25. ensure
5. refuse	12. upset	19. dare	26. reveal
6. disappoint	13. anguish	20. attract	27. shrink
7. solve	14. control	21. inform	28. postphone

必考 句型與解析

【句型 30】頻率副詞 always / often / sometimes / never

【結構】 查理（主詞）+ always（頻率副詞，總是）+ handles +（動詞）+ accidents with great clam. Charlie ⇨ 主詞，always ⇨ 頻率副詞，指永遠、總是，handle accidents with great calm ⇨ 以很大的冷靜面對意外，發生某事的時候。

【句子】 Charlie always handles accidents with great calm.

【中譯】 查理總是以很大的冷靜面對意外。

解　析

由句型 30【頻率副詞 always / often / sometimes / never】此句型可得知，Charlie 為主詞，加上頻率副詞 always，意指總是、永遠是，既然是總是，就是個一直發生的狀態，採用簡單現在式，故動詞 handle 加上 s，成為 handles，意指處理、面對，之後的受詞，採用 accidents，先完成 S + V + O 的基本句型，然而句子到此仍未臻完整，再設想查理永遠以何種態度處理意外狀況？因此想到 with great calm，以很大的冷靜來處理意外狀況，而完成整個句子。

使用頻率副詞造句，主要是修飾句子裡主詞執行某動作 / 做某事情的頻率狀況，是經常、常常、或是從來不，可使用不同主詞，參照表格上的動詞，加上不同的頻率副詞，試著造出各種不同變化的句意。

【1】 always（總是）/ often（常常）/ sometimes（有時候）/ never（從不）
這些頻率副詞是用來形容主詞從事某動作發生的頻率或次數，其中
always 代表 100%，幾乎總是發生，常常，也許可說是 50%，發生的
頻率或次數很普遍，sometimes 為 25%，在有的時候發生，而 never
就屬於 0%，從來不會發生。

【2】 在構句時，可先完成主詞＋動詞＋受詞的基本句型，再思考什麼樣的
頻率副詞適合該情境，常常 (often)、有時候 (sometimes)、或是總是
(always)、從不 (never)，再補充進句子中，用來修飾句意。

【3】 在放置的位置上，通常頻率副詞位於 be 動詞之後，如：
He is never late.
他從來不會遲到。
助動詞之後：
You should always tell the truth.
你應該永遠說實話。
一般動詞之前：
She sometimes goes swimming after work.
她有時在下班後去游泳。
但有時也依文氣放於一般動詞之後，如：
I see him often.
我常跟他碰面。
I love you always.
我永遠愛你。

✍ 就是這樣寫

2. He always requests me to do impossible things for him.

   他總要求我為他做不可能的事情。

3. My boss never approves any proposal that I make.

   我老闆從來不同意我做的任何提案。

4. The manager adjusts the plan often to suit the reality.

   經理常常修正計劃以符合現實。

5. He never refuses to do anything his daughter asks.

   他從來不會拒絕他女兒要求的任何事。

6. I am sometimes disappointed in his lack of efficiency.

   我常常因他的缺乏效率而失望。

7. Jack always solves problems in a way out of our expectation.

   傑克總是用超乎我們預期的方式解決問題。

8. My sister never appreciates anything I do for her.

   我姊姊從來不感激我為她做的事。

9. The manager always minimizes the contribution of his team.

   這經理總是貶低他團隊的貢獻。

10. His parents' health conditions always distress him.

    他父母的健康情況總使他煩惱。

11. He sometimes masks himself behind a happy face although he is actually sad.

    他有時候會把自己藏在快樂面孔的面具後，雖然他其實很悲傷。

12. Linda is often upset by her son's naughty behavior.

    琳達有時候會為她兒子的頑皮行為而生氣。

13. Whatever you do it will never anguish me.

不管你做什麼都不會惹我生氣。

14. Carrie always controls her temper perfectly.

凱莉永遠完美的控制她的脾氣。

15. It is always his dream to surpass the standard set by his father.

他一直以來的夢想是去超越他父親設下的標準。

16. The number of visitors to the amusement park rises up and never declines.

到遊樂園的訪客持續上升從來沒有降低。

17. Ken always wants to explore the world by himself.

肯總是想要自己探索這個世界。

18. The memory of him will never fade away.

有關他的回憶永遠不會褪去。

19. He never dares to try bungee jumping in his life.

他一輩子永遠不敢試高空彈跳。

20. The outdoor performances on the square always attract a lot of audiences.

在這廣場上的戶外表演總是吸引許多觀眾。

21. My secretary never fails to inform me what's going on in the company even when I am away.

我的秘書從來沒有錯過告知我公司的情況，即使我不在。

22. You need to always measure the size of the room before you go out to buy any furniture.

你在出去買任何傢俱前，永遠要先測量房間的尺寸。

23. The scholar often conducts research with several assistants.

這位學者通常與好幾位助理進行研究。

24. We need to always wear a seatbelt because the police enforces the law pretty strictly.

我們需要一直繫著安全帶，因為警察執行法律相當嚴格。

25. The insurance policy you have signed up will always ensure you to get the best protection.

你加入的這張保單會一直保證你得到最好的保障。

26. He never reveals his heart to anyone.

他從來不會向任何人揭露他的心。

27. The kind of cloth will sometimes shrink in hot water.

這種布料有時候會在熱水中縮水。

28. The child always postpones his study until last minute.

這孩子總是拖延唸書直到最後一分鐘。

【句型 31】 Too...to

1. superficial	8. harmful	15. popular	22. scary
2. exceptional	9. changeable	16. active	23. complex
3. indifferent	10. common	17. detail	24. abstract
4. unconvincing	11. lazy	18. expensive	25. sensual
5. direct	12. proper	19. surprising	26. conflicting
6. diligent	13. essential	20. ripe	27. cruel
7. powerful	14. sloppy	21. earthy	28. loyal

必考　句型與解析

【句型 31】 too...to（太…以至於不能）

【結構】　Ruby's idea（主詞）is too（太）superficial（膚淺）to（以至於不能從事某件事…），Ruby's idea ⇨ 主詞，superficial ⇨ 形容詞，膚淺。

【句子】　Ruby's idea is too superficial to be taken seriously.

【中譯】　露比的想法太膚淺以至不能被認真看待。

解 析

由句型 31【too.. to..】此句型可得知，Ruby's idea 為主詞，因為是第三人稱現在式，be 動詞用 is，之後便加上 too..to 的句型結構，形容詞 superficial，意思是膚淺的，露比的想法太膚淺，以至於不能做什麼呢？在本句裡，to 之後加上 be 動詞，指被動式，take 改為過去分詞 p.p. 成為 taken，再加上副詞 seriously 修飾，代表不能被認真的對待，因此本句的句意就是：露比的想法太膚淺，以致不能被認真看待。

本句型中並沒有出現否定字 not，但 "too.. to" 太⋯以至於不能卻有否定的意思，導致整句的意思其實是 Ruby's idea cannot be taken seriously. 這是因為 Ruby's idea is too superficial 的原因。

在 too..to 的造句裡，最主要是要掌握句子的內在連繫，因此在構思句型時，可試想因為什麼特質（形容詞），以至於主詞不能從事某項行為、達成某項目的，或是被用於從事某目的。可由不同的主詞，推想並藉由表格上的動詞造出各式不同變化的句子。

"too...to" 的結構其實是："too ＋形容詞／副詞＋不定詞 to ＋ 原形動詞 "，
中文的意思，通常可解釋為 " 太…以致不能…"、" 太…無法…"。

【1】 "too ＋ adj / adv ＋ to V" 是 too...to 的最基本的常用句型。too 之後
可加形容詞或副詞，如：

The girl is too young to travel by herself.

這個女孩年紀太小，不能自己旅行。

She walks too slowly to arrive on time.

她走得太慢不能準時到達。

【2】 "too...to ＋ to be V-pp " 這是不定詞後接被動式的用法，代表主詞是
不定詞後動作的承受者，如在範例句中的：

Ruby's idea is too superficial to be taken seriously.

露比的想法太膚淺以至不能被認真看待。

The girl's voice is too beautiful to be ignored.

這個女孩的聲音美到無法被忽略。

【3】 "too ＋ adj / adv ＋ for S ＋ to V"，在結構中加上一個 for 某人或某
物，主要是強調這對某人或某物才具有句中所說的影響，對其他人或
物則不一定如此，可使句子的意義更為清楚、精確，如：

The problem is too complicated for me to understand.

這個問題對我來說太複雜以至於難以明白。

（對其他人不一定是這樣）

The weather is too hot for David to go out.

對大衛來說，這樣的天氣太熱而無法出去。

就是這樣寫

2. John is too exceptional to be treated as an ordinary student.

約翰太傑出，以致於不能被當一個一般學生對待。

3. Martha is too indifferent to notice if there is any change in the house.

瑪莎太漠不關心以致於不會去注意這個房子有什麼改變。

4. The story is too unconvincing to be believed as true.

這個故事太沒有說服力，以致於難以被當真。

5. Her communication style is too direct to be accepted by everyone.

她溝通的風格太直接了，以致於難以被每個人所接受。

6. The student is too diligent to be failed from the class based on one test result.

這位學生太認真了，以致於不能只憑一次考試結果就把他當掉。

7. The rich man is too powerful to be ignored by the crowd.

這位有錢人太有力量，以致於難以被群眾忽視。

8. The pollutants are too harmful to not be treated seriously.

污染物對人太有害，以致於不能个被嚴肅處埋。

9. The weather is too changeable for us to be planning a hiking trip now.

這天氣太變幻莫測了，不適宜我們現在計劃一個健行之旅。

10. The style of the clothes is too common to attract the buyers' attention.

這衣服的樣式太平凡，以至於不能引起買者的注意力。

11. She is too lazy to walk to work.

她太懶了，不想走路去工作。

12. Her manner is too proper to be considered as a comedian.

她的態度太正經了，很難被當成是一個喜劇演員。

13. The work is too essential to be done by a novice.

這份工作太必要了，以至於不能讓一個新手來做。

14. His hand writing is too sloppy to be understood.

他的手寫筆跡太潦草以致於不能被辨認。

15. The movie is too popular to be missed. You must see it.

這電影太受歡迎以致於不能錯過，你一定要看。

16. The boy is too active to be confined in the small room.

這個男孩太活躍以致於不能被限制在這個小房間裡。

17. The story is too detailed to be covered in full length on the newspaper.

這個故事有太多細節，無法在報紙上以全文呈現。

18. The big house is too expensive for the family to maintain.

這幢大宅的維護費對這家人來說太昂貴了。

19. The news is too surprising for me to believe.

這個消息太令人吃驚了，以致於我不能相信。

20. The peaches are too ripe to be left unpicked on the trees.

這些桃子已經太成熟，以致於不能被留在樹上未採收。

21. She has a too earthy sense of humor to be appreciated by everyone.

她有太粗俗的幽默感，以至於不能被每個人所欣賞。

22. The movie is too scary to be watched by a child.

這個電影太嚇人，以致於不能讓小孩看。

23. The math problem is too complex to be solved by junior high school students.

這個數學問題太複雜，以至於不能被國中學生所解決。

24. The theory is too abstract to be comprehended by the freshmen.

這個理論太抽象了，以至於不能被新鮮人所理解。

25. Her dress is too sensual to be accepted by the older generation.

她的衣著太性感了，以致於不能被老一輩所接受。

26. His report is too conflicting to be considered to be well written.

他的報告太互相矛盾，以致於不能被認為是份好報告。

27. The king was too cruel to be well liked by his people.

這個國王太殘忍，以至於不能被他的人民所愛戴。

28. The solider is too loyal to his country to consider running away from the battlefield.

這個士兵對他的國家太忠誠，以致於不可能考慮從戰場上逃走。

【句型 32】Not only...but also

1. serve	8. exhibit	15. recommend	22. schedule
2. offer	9. monitor	16. absorb	23. abbreviate
3. appeal	10. interpret	17. release	24. remove
4. convey	11. convert	18. continue	25. criticize
5. inform	12. assume	19. target	26. ignore
6. demand	13. promote	20. symbolize	27. issue
7. approve	14. understand	21. grasp	28. devote

句型與解析

【句型 32】Not only... but also 不只… 而且

【結構】　Not only... but also 不只… 而且，The kind hostess ⇨ 主詞，親切的女主人，not only.. but also ⇨ 對等連接詞，不只 ……而且還…。

【句子】　The kind hostess not only served us drinks, but also provided us with many fresh fruits.

【中譯】　這位親切的女主人不只提供給我們飲料，而且還給予我們許新鮮水果。

解　析

由句型 32【not only... but also 不只…而且】此句型可得知，主詞是 the kind hostess，親切的女主人，not only 有不但的意思，serve us drink，指不只執行提供給我們飲涼的動作，but also 指而且…，provide us with many fresh fruits 提供給我們許多新鮮水果，而 serve 和 provide 兩個動詞，都因為發生於過去而加 ed，改為過去式，因而完成整個句子。

在 not only.. but also... 的造句裡，最主要是要掌握句子的內在關係，因此在構思句型時，可試想主詞不只做了什麼事，還又做了什麼事，可由不同的主詞，推想並藉由表格上的動詞造出各式不同變化的句子。

必考文法概念

not only...but also 為對等連連接詞，雖然有 not，但意思卻是「肯定的」，not only A but also B ”，意思是「不只是 A 而且連 B 都 …」，即 前後 A 和 B 兩者都…。

【1】 "not only A but also B" 所連接的兩個單字，詞性需一樣，如 A 為名詞，則 B 也是名詞，A 是動詞，B 也應是動詞。
He gave us not only food but also a place to stay.
他不只給我們食物，也給我們一個可以停留的地方。（名詞）
She is not only smart but also beautiful.

她不只聰明，也很漂亮。（形容詞）

The basketball player not only runs fast, but jumps very high.

這個籃球員不只跑得很快，也跳得很高。（動詞）

【2】 注意在 not only...but also 前後的動詞時態須對稱一致，如：

He not only cleaned the windows but also swept the floor of the classroom yesterday.

他昨天不只清潔了窗戶，也打掃了教室的地板。（都用過去式）

就是這樣寫

2. The man not only offered me a job, but also gave me an opportunity to change my life.

這個男人不只提供給我一份工作，還給我一個改變我生命的機會。

3. The charity not only appealed for clothes to be sent to the devastated region, but also requested volunteers to join the relief work.

這個慈善機構不只呼籲人們把衣服寄到災區，還要求志願者加入救災工作。

4. The poem conveys not only the writer's emotion to his lover, but also his determination to marry her.

這首詩不只傳達詩人對於他愛人的感情，也傳達他想要與她結婚的決心。

5. Mike not only informed the police about the stealing, but also led the police to find the thief.

麥克不只告訴警察這樁竊案，他還帶領警察去找到了小偷。

6. The authority not only demanded the farmers to pay a huge amount of tax, but also required the farmers to donate part of the harvest to the local office.

當權者不只要求農夫付很高的稅金，還要求農夫們將部分的收成捐給當地辦公室。

7. My mother not only approves of my decision to quit my job, but also supports my dream to travel around the world.

我的母親不只贊成我辭職的決定，還贊成我環遊世界的夢想。

8. The museum not only exhibits Picasso's work, but also holds an annual seminar on the art theory of Picasso.

這所博物館不只展示畢卡索的作品，也舉辦有關於畢卡索藝術理論的年度研討會。

9. The machine monitors not only the temperature of the room, but also the moist level in the air.

這個機器不只監測房間裡的溫度，也監測空氣裡的濕度。

10. The teacher not only reads the essays word by word, but also he tries to interpret the meaning of the essay to his students.

這位老師不只是逐字念這篇文章，他還試著將這篇文章的意義傳達給他的學生。

11. The architect not only converted the small bedroom into a wondering living room, but also added a nice penthouse for us in the house.

這位建築師不只將這個小的臥室改造成一個很棒的起居室，他還在這個屋子裡幫我們加了一個很不錯的閣樓。

12. I assume you are not only careless but also very self-centered so you can make such a mistake!

我假設你不只要很粗心，還要很自我中心才能犯下這種錯誤！

13. You should promote not only the product but also the philosophy of thecompany when you do your sales pitch.

當你做銷售演說時，你不止要推銷產品，還要推銷公司的哲學。

14. She understands not only Spanish but also Catalan because she used to live in eastern Spain.

她不只了解西班牙語，也了解加泰羅尼亞語，因為她曾經在西班牙東部住過。

15. She recommended not only the steak but also the seafood in the restaurant.

除了牛排外，她還推薦這間餐廳的海鮮。

16. The soil absorbs not only water but also pollutants from the air.

土壤不只吸收水分，也吸收來自空氣的污染物質。

17. Trees not only releases oxygen but also phytoncide into the air.

樹木不只釋放氧氣也釋放芬多精到空氣中。

18. Despite the warning from the doctors, Joe not only continues drinking, but also maintains his unhealthy lifestyle.

儘管醫生給予警告，喬不只繼續喝酒，也維持他原本不健康的生活方式。

19. The campaign targeted not only college students, but also young people above twenty-five years old.

這個宣傳不只針對大專學生，也針對二十五歲以上的年輕人。

20. The ring symbolizes not only my love for you, but also my desire to spend my life with you.

這個戒指不只象徵我對你的愛，也象徵我想要跟你共度一生的願望。

21. She not only had a hard time grasping the meaning of the text, but also had great trouble understanding the technical terms in each paragraph.

    她不只難以抓住文章的意思，也難以理解每個段落裡的專有名詞。

22. My secretary scheduled a meeting for me not only in the early morning but also during the lunch time.

    我的秘書不只在一大早，也為我在午餐時間安排會議。

23. His name was not only abbreviated, but also misspelled on the certificate.

    他的名字不只被縮寫，還在證書上被拼錯。

24. My gardener not only removed the tree branches from the garden, but also cleared off the weeds for me.

    我的園丁不只從花園裡把樹木的枝幹移除，也幫我清除了雜草。

25. My teacher not only criticized our performance, but also forbid us to rehearse the show.

    我的老師不只批評我們的表演，還禁止我們排練這場演出。

26. The government not only ignores the wishes of the majority, but also disregards the basic principle of democracy.

    政府不只忽視了多數人的願望，也罔顧了民主最基本的原則。

27. The school not only issued a statement but also exhibited a blueprint of its expansion plans to the press.

    學校不只發出聲明，也對新聞界公開展示了它擴張計劃的藍圖。

28. Mary devotes not only her energy but also her lifelong experience in creating this artwork.

    瑪麗不只投入她的精力，也付出她一輩子的經驗來創作這件藝術作品。

【句型33】 Have to / has to

1. store	8. circulate	15. promote	22. lower
2. purchase	9. operate	16. convince	23. come
3. guide	10. investigate	17. abolish	24. voice
4. receive	11. include	18. modify	25. provide
5. promise	12. estimate	19. document	26. reserve
6. scatter	13. reform	20. prevent	27. collect
7. release	14. surpass	21. associate	28. expose

必考 句型與解析

【句型33】Have to / has to。

【結構】 have to... 必須去做，You（主詞）+ have to（必須去做）+ store（V，儲存）+ the food（受詞）...。You ⇨ 主詞，have to ⇨ 必須，store ⇨ 儲存，otherwise it will turn rotten ⇨ 為什麼必須如此做的原因或條件。

【句子】 You have to store the food in the refrigerator otherwise it will turn rotten.

【中譯】 你必須將食物儲存在冰箱不然它會腐敗。

解　析

由句型 33【 have to / has to 】此句型可得知，土詞是 You，因為是第二人稱，採用 have，帶有命令、指揮的意思，have to，to 為不定詞，因此之後的動詞必須接原形動詞，設想主詞必須要做什麼事，store 為儲存，受詞為 food 食物，You have to store the food，就是 " 你必須將食物儲存 " 的意思，儲存在什麼地方呢？加上地方副詞來修飾，in the refrigerator 代表在冰箱裡，這時候句子已初步完成了，但為了求句意更完整，還可以加上為了什麼目的、因為什麼原因、否則會發生什麼情況，來解釋為什麼叫你做此事的原因，在本句裡，採用 otherwise it will turn rotten，otherwise 為否則，it 是代名詞，代表食物，will turn rottern，意思是否則食物會腐壞的意思。

在 "have / has to" 的造句裡，可試想主詞需要、必須做什麼事，並設想須做這件事的原因、背景，並藉由表格上的動詞造出各式不同變化的句子。

【1】 "have / has to" 之後加原形動詞，有強烈表達某人必須做某事之意，

用在第二人稱，有命令、要求對方的意思，如：

You have to return the book to me.

你必須把書還給我。

用於第一人稱，則有「必須」的意思，如：

I have to study for the exam, so I cannot go to the party with you.

我必須為考試唸書，所以我不能跟你去派對。

【2】 否定式為 "S + doesn't / don't / didn't have to"，指某人不需要做某

事，如：

You don't have to lend your money to me.

你不用把錢借我。

John does have to work so hard.

約翰不用這麼努力工作。

就是這樣寫

2. You have to purchase the tickets two weeks in advance; otherwise, they will be sold out.

   你必須在二個星期前事先買票，不然它們會被賣光。

3. John has to guide the little girl because she doesn't know her way.

   約翰必須引導這個小女孩因為她不知道路。

4. He has to receive the money sent by his mother, so he can pay the rent.

   他必須收到他母親寄來的錢，他才可以付房租。

5. You have to promise me you will come back.

   你必須承諾我你會回來。

6. The hay has to be scattered to cover the filed.

   稻草必須被散布以覆蓋田野。

7. You have to release the prisoners immediately.

   你必須立刻釋放囚犯。

8. You have to circulate the pamphlets among the group.

   你必須在團體裡傳閱這個手冊。

9. She has to operate the machine all by herself.

   她必須自己一個人操作機器。

10. You have to investigate the case in detail.

    你必須在細節上深入調查這個案子。

11. You have to include the new students to play with the group.

    你必須讓新學生加入跟團體一起玩。

12. He has to estimate how much money the trip will cost him.

    他必須估計這趟旅行將會花他多少錢。

13. I have to reform the company during my term as CEO.

在我當執行長的期間我必須改革這公司。

14. You have to surpass your previous performance in order to win.

你必須超越你以往的表現才能勝利。

15. The ambassador has to promote a mutual understanding of the two countries.

這名外交官必須去增進兩國間的彼此了解。

16. You have to convince me that the spending is necessary.

你必須使我信服這項花費是必要的。

17. We have to abolish the cruel custom of bullfighting.

我們必須廢除鬥牛這項殘忍的習俗。

18. You have to modify your proposal to incorporate the boss's feedback.

你必須修改你的計劃以涵蓋老闆的意見。

19. Lisa has to document the story because it is of great personal importance to her.

麗莎必須要記錄這個故事，因為這對她有很大的個人重要性。

20. You have to prevent the situation from deteriorating.

你必須防範情況惡化。

21. He has to associate with people of a higher class to satisfy his vanity.

他必須和更高階級的人來往以滿足他的虛榮心。

22. You have to lower your standard if the kid cannot meet your expectation.

你必須降低你的標準，如果這個孩子不能滿足你的期待。

23. The manager has to come up with creative solutions if the company's financial situation worsens.

如果公司的財務情況惡化的話，經理必須要提出創意的解決方法。

24. You have to voice your concern, do not suffer in silence.

    你必須說出你的顧慮，不要在沈默中受苦。

25. The host family has to provide enough food to the students.

    接待家庭必須為學生提供充分的食物。

26. You have to reserve a ticket for me.

    你必須為我保留一張票。

27. The people in the village have to collect wood to make fire everyday.

    村子裡的人必須要每天收集木材以生火。

28. You have to be careful and do not expose yourself in danger.

    你必須小心，不要將你自己暴露在危險中。

【句型34】That + 名詞子句

29. underrepresent	36. hide	43. survey	50. lock
30. aim	37. represent	44. develop	51. expand
31. encourage	38. attract	45. eliminate	52. exclude
32. explore	39. serve	46. volunteer	53. qualify
33. provide	40. raise	47. dye	54. practice
34. appear	41. gain	48. defeat	55. achieve
35. symbolize	42. download	49. rob	56. report

必考　句型與解析

【句型34】that + 子句 S1 + V1 + that + S2 + V2

【結構】 The Asian people want to change the fact（第一個子句），that they are underrepresented in the U.S. politics（第二個子句）. The Asian people want to change the fact. ⇨ 第一個子句 S1 + V1，They are underrepresented in the U.S. politics. ⇨ 第二個子句 S2 + V2 that ⇨ 中間加 that 加以串連。

【句子】 The Asian people want to change the fact that they are

underrepresented in the U.S. politics.

【中譯】 亞洲人想要改變他們在美國的政治中代表性不足的現象。

 解 析

由句型 34【that + 子句　　S1 + V1 + that + S2 + V2】此句型可得知，主詞是 The Asian people，want 是想要，The Asian people want to change the fact 亞洲人想要改變這個事實，這是第一個子句，然後加上 that，代表想要改變的事實，想要改變的事實是什麼呢？這就是 that 之後的第二個子句，they are underrepresented in the U.S. politics 他們在美國的政治中代表性不足，完成整個句子。

在 第 一 個 子 句 中，The Asian people 為 主 詞 (S1)，其 動詞 為 want (V1)，在 第 二 個 子 句 中，主 詞 為 they (S2)，動 詞 為 are (V2)，under；但 整 個 (that) 之 後 的 they are underrepresented in the U.S. politics 為修飾第一個子句。

在構思 "that 子句" 的句型時，主要也是先找到合理的句意，如 that 之後的子句跟主要子句的關係如何建立，可依照表格上的動詞造句，變化推演出不同的句子。

● 必考文法概念

"that" 在此句型中，是連接詞，使用的時機有以下幾種：

【1】 作為動詞的受詞，像是 tell, think, feel, see, find, guess, hope, notice, believe 等動詞，之後常常接 that 引導的子句，如：

He thinks that Paula is a great singer.

他覺得波拉是個很棒的歌手。其中，that 引導後的整個子句 that Paula is a great singer 都是前面 He（第一個主詞）thinks（第二個動詞）後的 " 受詞 "，因此不要因為句子裡有 think、is 兩個動詞，而感到奇怪，其實這是某人認為某人 / 事 / 物具有某種特質的意思，句子裡有第一個主詞所做的動作，和第二個主詞所做的動詞，用 that 串聯在一起。

有時候，"that" 也會被省略，如：

I believe (that) he will be successful.

我相信他會成功的。

【2】 放在 " 主詞 + V + 形容詞 / 副詞 " 之後的 that 子句，表示主詞對 that 子句所陳述事件的一種感受，這些形容詞 / 副詞，包括 excited, bored, glad, confused, angry, happy, surprised 等等，如：

I am very happy that you are coming to my birthday party.

我很高興你將來參加我的生日派對。

She feels excited that she is going to perform in front of the school.

她覺得興奮她將在全校前表演。

【3】 在句意上，"that" 子句也可以補充說明主要子句，如：

The worst thing is that he forgets about my birthday.

最糟的事是他忘記我的生日。

He forgets about my birthday 是主要子句 "The worst thing" 的補充說明。

就是這樣寫

30. He is aiming to achieve his goal that someday he will become the president of the company.

    他正計劃達成有一天成為這間公司總裁的目標。

31. Maggie feel encouraged that John speaks so highly of her achievement.

    約翰對她的成就盛讚，梅姬覺得受到鼓勵。

32. Joy is anxious that she is going to explore the cave all by herself.

    喬依很焦慮她將自己一個人探索洞穴。

33. Jack is proud that he can provide a livelihood to a family of six.

    傑克以他能為六口之家提供生計為傲。

34. She was shocked that a stranger appeared behind her all of a sudden.

    有一個陌生人突然出現在她後面，讓她很受驚嚇。

35. Doreen was happy to show that Eddie has given her a golden ring to symbolize his love to her.

    朵琳很高興展現艾迪給她的一個金戒指，象徵他對她的愛。

36. My grandmother was quick to hide her disappointment that the family had forgotten about her birthday.

    對於家人忘記她的生日，我的奶奶很快的隱藏她的失望。

37. It is certainly a great achievement that women are now well represented in the politics of Taiwan.

    女性在台灣的政治有充份的代表性，這絕對是一項重大的成就。

38. He was surprised that his idea has attracted a lot of attention.

    他很驚訝他的想法吸引了這麼多的注意。

39. I am delighted that I can serve a kind gentleman like you.

我很高興我可以服務像你這樣一位紳士。

40. We are all worried that the church cannot raise so much money in such a short time.

我們都很擔心教會不能在短時間籌出這麼多錢。

41. After learning for two years I can finally say that I have gained confidence in playing guitar.

在學了兩年之後我終於可以說我在彈吉他方面已獲得自信。

42. She is excited that she can download all the free movies from the internet.

她對可以從網路上下載所有的電影感到興奮。

43. He does not believe that he can survey all the animal spices in this national park within a year.

他並不相信他可以在一年內調查完這個國家公園內所有的動物物種。

44. Jack looks forward that he will have the opportunity to develop his skills in programing in his new position.

傑克期待在他的新職位上，他將會有機會培養他寫軟體的技能。

45. He was very disappointed that he was eliminated in the cooking competition.

他很失望他在烹飪比賽中被淘汰了。

46. The locals are very touched that so many people came to volunteer after the earthquake.

當地人很感動在地震之後有這麼多人前來義務協助。

47. Wayne is angry that his daughter has dyed her hair purple.

韋恩很生氣他的女兒把她的頭髮染成紫色。

48. The basketball team players were very disappointed when they got defeated by the opponent.

籃球隊球員對於他們被對手打敗感到非常失望。

49. She still cannot believe that she was robbed in the middle of the day.

她還是不能相信她在光天化日下被搶劫。

50. She was angry that she has locked herself out of her car again.

她很生氣她又把自己鎖在車外了。

51. It is a risky move that the company decides to expand its business during recession.

公司決定在不景氣時擴張是個很冒險的行動。

52. The feminists come to protest the fact that women are still excluded from this club.

女權主義者來此抗議女性仍被排除於這個俱樂部之外的事實。

53. He is relived that he passes the exam that qualifies him to teach in any secondary school in the country.

他鬆了一口氣他通過一項考試，讓他有資格在全國各地中學任教。

54. The company denies that it has practiced any discrimination against its employees.

這個公司否認它有從事任何針對員工的歧視措施。

55. She becomes very obsessed that she must achieve her ambition to visit South America.

她變成非常的執著她一定要完成造訪南美洲的野心。

56. The journalist was determined that he would report nothing but the truth.

這名記者下定決心他只會報告事實。

【句型35】Need to + V

1. resign	8. suspend	15. attract	22. destroy
2. hire	9. dismiss	16. function	23. maintain
3. refresh	10. exceed	17. protect	24. compete
4. remedy	11. retrieve	18. affect	25. improve
5. apologize	12. diversify	19. color	26. obey
6. notify	13. interact	20. memorize	27. return
7. fascinate	14. monitor	21. paint	28. starve

必考 句型與解析

【句型35】Need to + V。

【結構】 need to 需要，The prime minister（主詞）may need to（需要）resign（辭職）for his unpopular policy. The prime minister ⇨ 首相，主詞，need to ⇨ 需要。

【句子】 The prime minister may need to resign for his unpopular policy.

【中譯】 首相為了他不受歡迎的政策也許需要辭職。

解 析

由句型 35【need to 需要】此句型可得知，need 為動詞，need to 表示主詞 "需要" 做某事或執行某動作，口氣相較於 have to 沒有那麼強烈。在本句裡，主詞 The prime minister 是首相，加上助動詞 may，表示也許、應該的意思，在助動詞 may 之後的 need 採原形動詞，The prime minister may need to，代表首相也需應該做某件事。

做什麼事呢？這裡使用 resign，代表辭職的意思，因為接在 need to 的不定詞後面，採原形動詞，首相必須辭職的原因，則用介系詞 for 來表示 "為了…原因" 的意思，設想的原因為為了不受歡迎的政策 for his unpopular policy.

因此本句陳述了主詞 "首相也許需要辭職" 以及需要這麼做的原因，可以替換主詞，依照表格上的動詞造句，代表主詞需要做的事情，變化推演出不同的句子。

【1】 "need to" 的句型裡，need 為一般動詞，有必須、需要的意思，可依據人稱、時態作變化，後面加 s 或是 ed，to 為不定詞，之後接原形動詞，代表主詞所需要做的動作。"S need to + 原形 V" 如：

He needs to clean his room. 他必須打掃他的房間。

Joe needed to take a rest at that time. 喬那時候需要休息。

【2】 need 的其他句型：

"S need + N"，代表主詞需要某樣事物，如：

You need a heavy coat for the winter.

你需要一件厚外套過冬天。

【3】 "S need + N + to 原形 V"，代表主詞需要某人做某件事，如：

I need you to help me.

我需要你幫助我。

My sister needs me to move the boxes for her.

我的妹妹需要我為她搬這些箱子。

就是這樣寫

2. After you put in the time, effort, and investment to hire the best employees, you need to retain that talent.

   在你花了時間、精力、投資去聘雇最好的員工，你需要留住這些有天份的人。

3. It was such a hot night that I need to refresh myself by taking a cold shower.

   這晚好熱，我必須沖個冷水澡讓我自己振作起來。

4. We need to remedy the disparity in academic achievement of students in the city and in the rural area.

   我們必須彌補在城市與鄉村學生之間學術表現的差異。

5. You need to apologize for your behavior.

   你必須為你的行為道歉。

6. If you're moving there's a range of people and organizations that you need to notify.

   如果你要搬家，你必須通知一大堆人和單位。

7. The advertisement needs to fascinate customers to create an exciting connection.

   廣告必須要使顧客著迷以創造令人興奮的連結。

8. If during your studies personal circumstances arise in which you need to suspend your studies then you must contact your Education centre.

   如果在你學習中，有個人因素發生讓你必須中斷學業，你一定要聯繫你的教育中心。

9. If you need to dismiss an employee, it must be for valid reasons.
   如果你要解聘員工，一定要有有根據的理由。

10. Many organizations say that they need to exceed customer expectations.
    許多組織都說他們需要超越顧客期待。

11. I need to retrieve photos from my phone but my screen is completely damaged.
    我需要從我的手機取出照片但我的螢幕完全毀損了。

12. You need to diversify your investment accounts to make sure when one sector is down another might make up for it.
    你需要多樣化你的投資帳戶，確保當一個部門下跌時，另一個部門可以平衡它。

13. Musicians need to interact with their fans to develop a sustainable career.
    音樂家需要跟樂迷互動以發展永續的表演事業。

14. We need to monitor the pollutants in the river.
    我們需要監測河流裡的污染物。

15. I believe we need to attract a new generation of the best and brightest to public service .
    我相信我們必須吸引最優秀與聰明的新一代投入公共領域。

16. The machine needs some maintenance in order to function properly.
    這機器需要些維修以運作恰當。

17. School rules need to protect kids better.
    學校的規定需要更好的保護孩童。

18. The painting we are looking for needs to affect the atmosphere of the room.

我們在找的話要能改變房間裡的氣氛。

19. We need to color these parts black.

我們需要把這些部分塗黑。

20. When you need to memorize something, it is often helpful to associate it with an image.

當你需要記憶某事時，把它跟一個圖像連結通常有用。

21. I am moving and need to paint back my old apartment white.

我要搬家，必須把我的舊公寓漆回白色。

22. You need to destroy your files before recycling your computer.

你在回收你的電腦前必須刪毀你的檔案。

23. How many calories do you need a day to maintain your current weight?

每天你會需要多少的卡洛里以維持現在的體重？

24. They do not have the skills they need to compete effectively.

他們沒有為了效競爭所需具備的能力。

25. The students need to improve reading skills to get the most from their books.

學生們需要增進他們的閱讀技巧以從書裡獲得最大收獲。

26. Do children always need to obey their parents?

孩子們永遠需要服從他們的父母嗎？

27. I need to return the books to the city library,

我需要把書還給市立圖書館。

28. If you're obviously skinny then you don't need to starve yourself to reduce weight.

如果你已經明顯的那麼瘦削了，你不用再把自己受餓以減輕體重。

【句型 36】 So...that

29. remarkable	36. cooperative	43. superficial	50. mysterious
30. intimate	37. complicated	44. diligent	51. emotional
31. efficient	38. fascinating	45. obvious	52. valuable
32. poor	39. premature	46. annoying	53. independent
33. fundemantal	40. spontaneous	47. rare	54. memorable
34.extraordinary	41. remote	48. amusing	55. accidental
35. objective	42. scarce	49. popular	56. shining

必考 句型與解析

【句型 36】So...that。

【結構】 so... that 如此 … 以至於 The scientist's achievement（主詞）is
so（如此）remarkable（卓著）that（以致於）＋產生的結果…。
The scientist's achievement ⇨ 主詞 remarkable ⇨ 形容詞，卓
著、特殊 everyone remembers him in the science field ⇨ 產生的
結果。

【句子】 The scientist's achievement is so remarkable that everyone remembers him in the science field.

【中譯】 這個科學家的成就如此卓著,以至於科學界的每個人都記得他。

解　析

由句型 36【so...that..】此句型可得知,so...that 代表主詞因具有某種性質,以至於導致某結果。在本句裡,主詞是 The scientist's achievement 代表科學家的成就,動詞採第三人稱單數 is,so...that 之間要加形容詞,形容科學家的成就,因此用 remarkable,卓越、卓著的來代表,而科學家的成就如此卓越,產生了何種結果呢?導致於每個在科學界的人都記得他,就用 that 之後的子句來代表,that everyone remembers him in the science field.

在構思 "so...that" 句型時,主要先要設想兩個子句間的因果關係,然後再用 so...that 的結構來串連,可以不同的主詞造句,搭配表格上的動詞,變化推演出不同的句子。

【1】 "so...that" 是表示結果的副詞子句，so 是副詞，用以修飾形容詞或副詞，that 是連接詞引出副詞子句表結果。

【2】 在構思句型時，可設想主詞具有什麼樣的特質，給予一個形容詞，然後設想導致了什麼樣的結果。或是主詞的動作具有什麼樣的特質，以副詞來修飾，然後再設想導致什麼樣的結果。

【3】 "so + adj + that"：He is so fat that he cannot run very fast.
他很胖以至於他不能跑非常快。

"so + adv + that"：She speaks so fast that nobody can understand her.
她說話說得很快，以至於沒有人能了解她。

就是這樣寫

30. The couple is so intimate together that other people on the tour find it hard to interact to them.

這對情侶在一起如此親密，其他在旅行團的人覺得很難跟他們產生互動。

31. His work style is so efficient that there is hardly any time wasted.

他的工作風格如此有效率，幾乎沒有任何時間被浪費掉。

32. The old man is so poor that he cannot afford to buy a meal.

這個老人如此貧窮，他付不起買一餐飯。

33. Your question is so fundamental that I must spend an hour to answer it.

你的問題是如此的根本，我一定得花一個小時來回答。

34. Yo Yo Ma's musical talent was so extraordinary that he was recognized as the greatest cellists of our time.

馬友友的音樂天份如此卓越，以至於他被認為是我們這個時代最偉大的大提琴家。

35. His point of view is so objective that you can trust his decision.

他的觀點很客觀，你可以相信他的決定。

36. The naughty boy was so cooperative in class today that I began to wonder if he was plotting something behind me.

這個頑皮的男孩今天在課堂上這麼合作，讓我不禁懷疑他是不是在我背後計劃著什麼。

37. She is so complicated that I have stopped to figure her out.

她是如此的複雜我已經停止去了解她了。

38. The movie is so fascinating that it attracts all the audience's attention.

這部電影吸引人以至於它吸引了所有觀眾的注意力。

39. Your plan is so premature that it is doomed to fail.

你的計劃如此的未成熟，它註定會失敗的。

40. Mary's communication style is so spontaneous that nobody knows what she will say in the next minute.

瑪麗的溝通方式非常的隨性，以至於沒有人知道她下一分鐘會說什麼。

41. The village is so remote that it is hardly reached by any traveler.

這個村莊如此偏遠，以至於它幾乎從沒有任何旅行者抵達過。

42. Water is so scarce in the desert that we must use it for irrigation efficiently.

水在沙漠如此稀少，以至於我們用它來灌溉時必須有效率的使用

43. Her remarks are so superficial that I do not even want to respond to it.

她的評論如此膚淺，以至於我甚至不想回應。

44. The student is so diligent that he deserves the first prize in the class.

這名學生如此勤奮，以至於他值得獲得班上的第一名。

45. The spelling mistake on the sign was so obvious that everyone saw it right away.

在招牌上的拼字錯誤如此明顯，以至於每個人馬上就看到它。

46. The boy is so annoying that I refuse to sit with him anymore.

這個男孩如此的令人討厭，以至於我拒絕再跟他坐在一起。

47. The precious stone is so rare that it will worth a lot of money on the market.

這塊寶石很稀有，在市場上它會值一大筆錢。

48. I find your behavior so amusing that I cannot stop laughing.
    我覺得你的行為很有趣，我不能停止笑。

49. Jackie Chen is so popular that even people in India know about him.
    成龍很受歡迎，即使是印度人也知道他。

50. The man is so mysterious that even his neighbor does not know where he is from.
    這個男人很神秘，即使是他的鄰居也不知道他是從哪來。

51. Her reaction is so emotional that I decided not to tell her the truth.
    她的反應很情緒化，以致於我決定不要告訴她真相。

52. Your opinion is so valuable that I will take it seriously.
    您的意見很寶貴，我會將它慎重以待。

53. The girl was so independent that at the age of six she took airplanes all by herself.
    這個女孩從小就非常獨立，她在六歲的時候就自己搭飛機。

54. My honeymoon trip was so memorable that I still think about it everyday.
    我的蜜月旅行很難忘，以至於我每天都還想起。

55. Our bumping into each other in the city is so accidental that it may not happen again.
    我們兩個在城市撞見彼此是如此的巧合，它可能不會再發生了。

56. The floor is so shining that it looks like a mirror.
    地板如此光亮以至於看起來像鏡子一樣。

【句型 37】 間接問句

【96 指考】V1 ～ V28 +【句型 37】間接問句

29. diagnose	36. overlook	43. commit	50. understand
30. exploit	37. update	44. behave	51. count
31. percieve	38. occur	45. attack	52. voice
32. concern	39. advance	46. innovate	53. affect
33. appreciate	40. respond	47. imagine	54. isolate
34. operate	41. contribute	48. overtake	55. influence
35. confirm	42. excite	49. complain	56. happen

必考　句型與解析

【句型 37】間接問句

【結構】　The doctor tried to diagnose（主要子句）+ where（疑問詞）+ the tumor（主詞）+ is（助動詞 / 動詞）。

【句子】　The doctor tried to diagnose where the tumor is.

【中譯】　醫生試著診斷腫瘤在哪裡。

由句型 37【間接問句】此句型可得知，疑問詞之後接名詞子句時，稱為間接問句，就是兩個子句以疑問詞 where / who / how / when 相連。在本句中，主詞為 The doctor 這名醫生，嘗試用 try，因為為過去式改為 tried，繼而推想醫生試著做什麼，不定詞 to 後採用 diagnose，表示診斷的意思，到此，The doctor tried to diagnose 完成了第一個子句。

至於醫生在診斷什麼呢？這裡用代表疑問 " 在哪裡 " 的 where 作連接詞，引出第二個子句，the tumor 是腫瘤的意思，where the tumor is，代表醫生試圖診斷腫瘤在哪裡，完成了整個句子。

在構思 " 間接問句 " 句型時，可以設想主詞試圖取得答案的是什麼類型的資訊，是什麼地方、是誰、如何、或是何時，然後選擇用 where / who / how / when 來引導接下來的子句，可搭配表格上的動詞，變化推演出不同的句子。

【1】 間接問句就是包含在句子裡的提問，在句中發問。當把一個問句併入另一個句子中，結構是：

"主要子句＋疑問詞＋主詞＋動詞）"

前一句為主要子句，後一句為從屬子句

S＋V（主要子句）＋疑問句（從屬連接詞）＋S＋V（從屬子句，作為前項主要子句動詞的受詞），如：

I wonder where he is going to eat tonight.

我好奇他今晚會在哪裡吃東西。

其中，I wonder 就是主要子句，where 為從屬連接詞，連接 he is going to eat 的從屬。

【2】 如原本有兩個句子：

He tries to understand something.

Why does his son like to play video games so much?

可以透過 why 連接詞連結成一句：He tries to understand why his son likes to play video games so much. 把問句放入主要子句裡面發問，但因 He tries to understand 已是直述句，把第二個子句的問句改為直述句（去掉 does, like 加 s），然後句尾打句號。

【3】 也可使用其他疑問詞 who / why / where / how / when

如：We do not know who the man is.

我們不知道這個男人是誰。

He does not know when the train will come.

他不知道什麼時候火車會來。

就是這樣寫

29. We do not know how the first aboriginals learned to exploit metal.
我們不知道最早的原住民如何學會利用金屬。

30. You don't know how you are perceived by the public.
你不知道大眾是如何認知你的。

31. He tries to find out what people are concerning about.
他試著找到人們擔心的是什麼。

32. He can't understand why the students do not appreciate his devotion.
他不了解為什麼學生不感激他的付出。

33. Jack does not know how he can operate the machine.
傑克不知道他可以如何操作這台機器。

34. Jane forgets to confirm where she will meet with us.
珍妮忘記確認她會在哪裡跟我們見面。

35. Owen tries to find where he can overlook the river.
歐文試著找可以眺望河的地方。

36. I do not know when our company will update the contact list.
我不知道我們的公司什麼時候會更新通訊錄。

37. She does not know when the violence will occur again.
她不知道什麼時候暴力又會發生。

38. David does not know who can advance his career.
大衛不知道誰可以幫助他事業前進。

39. I do not know who can respond to my jokes.
我不知道誰可以回應我的笑話。

40. She is eager to know how she can contribute to the club.

她很急迫想知道她可以如何對這個社團貢獻。

41. I am excited to find out where you will bring me tomorrow.

我很興奮地想知道你明天會帶我到哪去。

42. I do not understand why he committed the crime.

我不了解為什麼他會犯這項罪。

43. She does not know how her son behaves this way.

她不知道為什麼她的兒子有如此行為。

44. I was shocked how the man attacked me out of the blue.

我很驚訝這個男人沒有預兆的攻擊我的行為。

45. The researchers are studying how the society is innovated by the use of computer.

研究者在研究電腦的使用如何創新了社會。

46. I was trying to imagine where you would put your glasses.

我正在想像你會把你的眼鏡放在哪裡。

47. I do not know how I can overtake the other car on such a small road.

我不知道在這麼小的路上我要怎麼超另外那台車。

48. Our neighbor downstairs just came to complain about the noise. The children do not understand why they are not allowed to bounce up and down anymore.

我們樓下的鄰居才剛上來抱怨噪音，孩子們不了解為什麼他們不准再跳上跳下了。

49. The president did not understand why the policy had resulted such a riot.

總統不了解為什麼這個政策引發這麼大的動亂。

50. The children do not know how to count yet.

孩子們還不知道如何數數字。

51. Young people do not know why they are not allowed to voice out their concern about the society.

年輕人不知道為什麼他們不被允許提出他們對社會的看法。

52. She is worried how her son is affected by the violent online games.

她擔心暴力線上遊戲對她兒子的影響。

53. Nobody knows how isolated I felt when I was in the army.

沒有人知道當我在軍隊裡，我覺得有多孤立。

54. You probably do not know how you have influenced me.

你也許不知道你如何的影響了我。

55. He describes how the accident happened again and again.

他一次又一次的描述這意外是如何發生的。

【句型38】承轉詞 therefore

29. figure	36. satisfy	43. descriminate	50. sponsor
30. survive	37. shrink	44. burden	51. establish
31. conform	38. retire	45. message	52. earn
32. research	39. rehire	46. destroy	53. beat
33. negotiate	40. estimate	47. devote	54. refine
34. increase	41. hesitate	48. introduce	55. export
35. influence	42. punish	49. degrade	56. rebel

句型與解析

【句型38】承轉詞 therefore。

【結構】　I am still figuring my taxes（句子 1）; therefore（承轉詞，因此），結果…。I am still figuring my taxes ⇨ 我還在算我的稅金（因為此一狀況）therefore ⇨ 因此，I can't pay my taxes yet. 我還不能付我的稅（導致後一結果）。

【句子】　I am still figuring my taxes; therefore, I can't pay my taxes yet.

【中譯】　我還在算我的稅金，所以我還不能付稅。

解　析

由句型 38【承轉詞 therefore】此句型可得知，轉承詞是連接兩個子句的連接副詞，代表兩者之間的因果關係，有 " 所以、結果 " 的意思。本句的主詞為 I，動詞用 figure，有計算、搞清楚的意思，進行式用 I am still figuring out my taxes，代表主詞還在計算、整理自己的稅務，而這樣的情況產生什麼結果呢？用 therefore 語氣上的轉承詞來連接其後的結果：I can't pay my taxes yet. 所以我還不能付我的稅。

基本上，可以將兩個有因果關係的句子，用承轉詞 therefore 來連接，就會使句子更平順、婉轉，可採用不同的主詞，以表格上的動詞設想不同的行為，推導出不同的結果，變化演繹出不同的句子。

必考文法概念

【1】 therefore 為呈接兩個因果關係子句的副詞，稱為承轉詞，又稱為連接副詞，用來連接兩個獨立而對等的子句，一般在第一個子句後，以分號區隔後加 therefore，連接第二個子句。或是也可以在第一個子句後句號，再用 Therefore 大寫開頭，之後加逗點，引出第二個句子。第三種用法，可以用逗點與前一句子區隔，然後加上 and therefore，再連接第二個句子。如：

她覺得不舒服，所以她今晚會待在家。

◆ She is not feeling well; therefore, she will stay at home tonight.

◆ She is not feeling well. Therefore, she will stay at home tonight.

◆ She is not feeling well, and therefore she will not stay at home tonight.

【2】 therefore 也可用 thus、consequently、accordingly 代替，都有所以、結果、因此的意思：

雨停了，所以，野餐將如計劃中舉行。

◆ The rain stops; therefore, the picnic will be taking place as planned.

◆ The rain stops; thus the picnic will be taking place as planned.

◆ The rain stops. Consequently, the picnic will be taking place as planned.

◆ The run stops. Accordingly, the picnic will be taking place as planned.

就是這樣寫

30. Sue hid herself in the cave; therefore she was the only one that survived the snow storm.

蘇躲在洞窟裡，因此她是這暴風雪中唯一生還的人。

31. The students are required to conform to the standard; therefore there is no place for originality.

學生被要求遵從標準，因此，容不得原創性。

32. She has been researching for the topic for thirty years; therefore everyone knows about her in the field.

她已經研究這個題目三十年了，因此每個在這領域的人都知道她。

33. She is good at negotiating; therefore she always gets the best deal.

    她很擅長談判，因此她永遠得到最好的價格。

34. Mark is trying everything he can to save the business; therefore the profit slowly increases.

    馬克正試盡一切所能拯救這生意，所以，利潤慢慢增加。

35. My father is a doctor. Therefore, I was influenced to choose a career in medicine at a very young age.

    我的父親是一位醫生，因此，我在很年輕的年紀就受到影響，選擇以醫學為職志。

36. We are all intrigued by the mysterious man; therefore we request him to tell us his story to satisfy our curiosity.

    我們都被這位神秘的男子所吸引，因此，我們請求他告訴我們他的故事，滿足我們的好奇心。

37. My skirt has shrunk after wash; therefore I have to buy a new one.

    我的裙子洗過後縮水了，因此我必須去買一件新的。

38. My dad retired at a very young age; therefore he had a lot of time topursue his hobby.

    我父親在很年輕的年紀就退休了，因此他有很多時間追求他的嗜好。

39. Lisa is the most talented designer I have ever seen; therefore we must rehire her.

    麗莎是我見過最有天份的設計師，因此我們一定要重新聘用她。

40. Bob made a mistake in estimating the cost of opening the cafe; therefore he almost went bankrupt.

    鮑勃在估計開咖啡店上算錯了要花多少錢，因此他幾乎破產。

41. She is a very shy person; therefore, she hesitates to tell Mark how much she likes him.

她是個很害羞的人，因此她遲疑告訴馬克她有多麼喜歡他。

42. Drunken driving can be punished with a prison sentence in this country; therefore, everyone is careful not to do it.

酒醉駕駛在這個國家可能會被關進監獄，因此每個人都小心避免去做。

43. I feel I was discriminated in the company; therefore, I quit my job.

我覺得我在公司裡被歧視，所以我辭職了。

44. He always burdens people with his problems; therefore, everyone tries to avoid contacts with him.

他總把他的問題給人們造成負擔，因此每個人都試著避免跟他接觸。

45. Charlie has messaged me several times therefore, I had better get back to him.

查理已經發訊息給我好幾次了，所以我最好回他。

46. Most of the old part of the city was destroyed; therefore, people had to rebuild the city after the war.

城市裡的老城區大半被摧毀了，因此人們必須在戰後重建城市。

47. She has devoted her life to teaching; therefore, when she retired hundreds of students came to thank her.

她將她的一生奉獻給教學，因此當她退休的時候，好幾百位學生來跟她道謝。

48. Frank was worried that I will feel lonely after moving to the new city; therefore, he introduced many friends to me.

法蘭克擔心我搬到新城市後會覺得孤單，所以他介紹了許多朋友給我。

49. The local environment degraded quickly; therefore people decided to form an environmental group to do something about it.
當地環境惡化的很快,因此人們決定成立一個環保團體去做點什麼。

50. The school will sponsor the travel expenses; therefore we can finally conduct the field trip.
學校會贊助旅費,因此我們終於可以進行這次田野之旅。

51. The brewery was established in 1822; therefore many pieces of the equipment are priceless antiques.
酒廠建於 1822 年,因此許多設備是無價的古董。

52. As an artist he cannot earn a living from selling his painting; therefore, he has to wait in the restaurants.
身為一個藝術家他無法靠賣他的畫作維生,因此他必須在餐館裡侍應。

53. His father beats him all the time; therefore, he does not like to stay at home.
他的父親總是打他,因此他不喜歡待在家。

54. My boss is a very picky person; therefore, I have to refine the proposal if I want an approval from her.
我的老闆是個很挑剔的人,所以我必須改進這個提案,如果我想要從她那得到批准的話。

55. Our domestic market is not large enough; therefore, we must export the goods abroad.
我們的國內市場不夠大,因此我們必須出口產品到國外。

56. She has had a very strict upbringing; therefore, she rebelled against her parents very badly when she grew up.
她過去有非常嚴格的成長過程,因此當她長大時,她反叛父母得很嚴重。

【句型 39】 No matter how

1. access	8. demonstrate	15. regulate	22. prepare
2. convey	9. acquire	16. highlight	23. overwhelm
3. deprive	10. interprete	17. formulate	24. determine
4. equip	11. condense	18. command	25. unfold
5. pass	12. desert	19. range	26. offer
6. stablize	13. exclude	20. boil	27. accept
7. vary	14. remove	21. experiment	28. award

必考 句型與解析

【句型 39】No matter how（無論如何）。

【結構】 No matter how（無論如何）+ hard I try 主詞（從事某項動作）+ 產生的結果…，no matter how ⇨ 不管，no matter how hard I try ⇨ 不管我試得再辛苦，I ⇨ 主詞，I cannot access the computer system of my university ⇨ 達成的結果。

【句子】 No matter how hard I try, I cannot access the computer system of my university.

【中譯】 不管我多嘗試得多努力，我無法進入我大學的電腦系統。

解析

由句型 39【No matter how】此句型可得知，no matter how 有不管、無論如何的意思，放在句首，之後接 hard，有辛苦、努力的意思，主要是修飾之後主詞所執行的動作 I try，代表嘗試得非常努力的意思，而 no matter how hard I try 便指 " 無論我試得多努力 "，逗點之後，再說明達成的結果，在這用 access 代表進入、取得管道的意思，"I cannot access the computer system of my university"，代表我無法進入我大學的電腦系統。

"no matter how" 的句子通常有無論怎麼做，都無法達成某目的的否定意思，因此在構思句意時，可以設想不論主詞如何執行某動作，都無法達成某個目的，將兩個句子以 no matter how 為首整併為一句，便可以產生 " 無論如何 " 的語氣，較平鋪直述兩個句子更有表達力，寫作上，可採用不同的主詞，以表格上的動詞設想不同的行為，構思不同的結果，變化演繹出不同的句子。

必考文法概念

【1】 "No matter how" 為一連接詞，可放在句首或句中，代表無論主詞如何做某項動作，都不能達成想要的結果。

【2】 句型結構上為 "No matter how S + V"，動詞因應主詞人稱與單複數而改變，也依過去或現在，而有不同時態，如：

◆ No matter how poor he becomes, he always remains content.

無論他變得多們貧窮，他一直保持滿足。（第三人稱）

◆ No matter how hard you work, you need to spend time with your family.

無論你多麼努力工作，你必須花時間陪伴家人。（第二人稱）

◆ No matter how the English fought against the German army, they lost several battles in the Second World War.

無論英國人如何與德軍對戰，他們在第二次世界大戰輸了多場戰役。（過去式）

◆ 但是當在敘述 " 未來式 "，緊跟著 no matter how 的句子須改為現在式。

【3】 "No matter how S + V" 的句型，可改為 "No matter how adv. S + V"，以副詞來修飾主詞所執行的動詞，如：

◆ No matter how hard he studies... 不論他多麼努力唸書…

◆ No matter how seriously she cries... 不論她哭得多麼厲害…

◆ No matter how stupid the movie is... 不論這部電影有多愚蠢…

就是這樣寫

2. No matter how Jeff conveys his love to Susan, she would not marry him.

無論傑夫再怎麼傳達他對蘇珊的愛，她不願嫁給他。

3. No matter how you insult me, you cannot deprive my dignity.

無論你如何污辱我，你不能剝奪我的尊嚴。

4. No matter how Harry equipped himself with the best mountain climbing gears, he failed to reach the peak.

無論哈瑞如何以最好的登山裝備裝備他自己，他攻頂失敗了。

5. No matter how hard I study, I cannot pass the exam.

無論我讀得多努力，我無法通過考試。

6. No matter how Kevin pursues Lisa, she does not want to be stabilized with him.
無論凱文如何追求麗莎，她不想跟他定下來。

7. No matter how our appearances vary, we are all the same at heart.
無論我們長相多麼不同，我們心裡都是一樣的。

8. No matter how we begged him, he did not want to demonstrate his special techniques in making cookies in front of us.
無論我們如何求他，他不願意在我們面前展示他做餅乾的特殊技術。

9. No matter how the job acquires you to travel, you should always come home for Christmas.
無論這個工作有多麼需要你旅行，你在聖誕節永遠該回家。

10. No matter how complicated the data is, he always interprets the statistics accurately.
無論資料有多複雜，他永遠正確的詮釋這些統計數字。

11. No matter how I condense the article, it still exceeds ten pages.
無論我如何壓縮這篇文章，它還是超過十頁長。

12. No matter how difficult the situation becomes, we will never desert each other.
無論情況變得多麼困難，我們永遠不會拋棄彼此。

13. No matter how time has changed, women are still excluded from the club.
無論時代如何改變，女人還是被排除在這個社團之外。

14. No matter how I asked my neighbor to remove the rubbish in his backyard, he would not listen to me.
無論我如何請我的鄰居把他在後院的垃圾移除，他就是不聽我的。

15. No matter how the police regulates the traffic, speeding problems become worse and worse in the city.

無論警察怎麼規範交通，超速問題在這城市越來越嚴重。

16. No matter how the report highlights the need for immediate actions, nobody does anything.

無論這份報告如何強調立刻行動的需要，沒有人做任何事。

17. No matter how you are attached to your own idea, we need to formulate a new plan.

無論你如何執著你自己的想法，我們必須形成新的計劃。

18. No matter how hard he tries, he cannot command the soldiers.

無論他怎麼嘗試，他都不能命令這些士兵。

19. No matter how the teacher reminded us to get focused, our topics ranged over many current issues.

無論老師如何提醒我們聚焦，我們的題材涵蓋了許多當今議題。

20. No matter how hard we try, the water does not get boiled.

無論我們如何努力嘗試，水就是無法滾。

21. No matter how I encourage my son, he does not want to experiment new ways of doing things.

無論我如何鼓勵我的兒子，他不想實驗新的做事方式。

22. No matter how much time I spent on preparing for the exam, it seems I will never improve my score.

無論我在這個考試花多少時間準備，看起來我永遠也不會成績進步。

23. No matter how I feel overwhelmed by the stress, I always feel much better after exercise.

無論我覺得壓力如何的讓我難以應付，我在運動過後總覺得好得多。

24. No matter how determined he is, he finds achieving the goal is really

difficult.

無論他如何的有決心，他發現要達到目標非常困難。

25. No matter how old you are, in the Harry Potter movies, as the story unfolds you will still be fascinated by the plot.

    無論你多大，在哈利波特電影裡，隨著故事的展開你仍然會對劇情著迷。

26. No matter how cold my neighbor was to me last time, I will still offer her tea when she comes to my house.

    無論我鄰居上次對我有多冷淡，當她到我家時我還是會請她喝茶。

27. No matter how much money the company offers him, he does not want to accept the position.

    無論這公司提供給他多少錢，他不願意接受這職位。

28. No matter how poorly Judy performs in the movie, she will still be awarded the Best Actress because audiences just love her.

    無論朱蒂在電影裡表現得有多差勁，她還是會被頒獎為最佳女影員因為觀眾就是喜愛她。

【句型 40】承轉詞 as a result

29. fight	36. exterminate	43. respect	50. end
30. deliver	37. consider	44. reveal	51. report
31. wrap	38. adore	45. react	52. swallow
32. shock	39. threaten	46. spread	53. perform
33. attain	40. advocate	47. smuggle	54. refine
34. display	41. mislead	48. disappear	55. fix
35. persuade	42. direct	49. imagine	56. accomplish

必考 句型與解析

【句型 40】承轉詞 as a result

【結構】 The two brothers were always fighting when they were little（原因）. As a result（表因此）, they do not get along when they grow up（導致的後果）. The two brothers were always fighting when they were little ⇨ 兩兄弟小的時候永遠在爭吵，A 項事實 as a result ⇨ 結果。They do not get along when they grow up ⇨ 當他們長大後感情也不好，導致 B 項結果。

【句子】 The two brothers were always fighting when they were little. As a result, they do not get along when they grow up.

【中譯】 這兩兄弟小的時候永遠在爭吵，結果，當他們長大後感情也不好。

解　析

由句型 40【as a result】此句型可得知，as a result 有結果、導致的意思是副詞，放在句首是用來修飾句子裡的結果是由前一項原因所導致。如在本句中，第一句為 "The two brothers were always fighting when they were little"，這兩個兄弟小時候總是在吵架，用過去進行式代表常常、一直，這是在過去一直發生的狀態，這樣的原因產生了什麼樣的結果呢？ As a result，逗點，產生的結果是 "They do not get along when they grow up." 他們長大後也無法好好相處。

基本上，要書寫 As a result 的句子，只要構思兩個有因果的句子，中間以 as a result 串連，主要是強調語氣，A 事實導致 B 結果，會使文意較為連結，相較於兩個獨立的句子，會讓文章漸漸由單一的句子有承接的連續感。

寫作上，可用可採用不同的主詞，以表格上的動詞設想不同的行為，構思不同的結果，變化演繹出不同的句子。

【1】 "as a result" 一般用於句中，以逗點與句子分開，表示前面句子是後面句子的原因。因此注意書寫時，前後要有因果關係。

He got up very late today. As a result, he missed the class at 8 o'clock.

他今天起得非常晚，結果，他錯過了八點的課。

【2】 "as a result" 有導致某結果的意思，"as a result of" 有因為某原因的意思，通常，as a result of 後接名詞或名詞片語，如：

⇨ He reacted to everything negatively. As a result, he doesn't have many friends.

【3】 他因為對事情的反應都很負面，結果他並沒有很多朋友。

⇨ He reacted to the everything negatively as a result of his poor health.

他因為健康不佳，對所有事情的反應都很負面。

Jack pulled his muscle as a result of moving the piano all by himself.

傑克因為一個人搬鋼琴，拉傷了肌肉。

（去掉主詞 he，動詞 move 改為 moving）

就是這樣寫

30. The postman delivered the mail to the wrong address. As a result, I never received his letter.

這個郵差把信件送錯地址了，以致於我從來沒有收到他的信。

31. She wrapped herself in an oversized coat. As a result, nobody could tell if she is a man or a woman.

她把自己包在一件過大的外套裡，以致於沒有人可以分辨她是男人還是女人。

32. I was in shock for about two weeks after the accident. As a result, I did poorly for the exam.

我在那意外發生後的兩個禮拜都在驚嚇狀態，以至於我考試考得很差。

33. He has attained the highest grade in his music exams. As a result, he won the scholarship to study in Paris.

他在音樂考試裡獲得最高分，使他能獲得到巴黎唸書的獎學金。

34. She displays a photo of a crystal waterfall on her wall. As a result, the room feels cooler on a hot summer day.

她展示了一張晶瑩瀑布的照片在她的牆上，以致於這個房間在炎熱的夏日感覺起來比較清涼。

35. He persuaded the customer to buy the product by giving false information. As a result, he received a complaint from the customer afterwards.

他透過給予不實資訊來說服顧客購買產品，結果，之後他就收到顧客投訴。

36. Our newly invented pesticide is very effective. As a result, all the cockroaches are exterminated at once.

我們最新發明的殺蟲劑非常有效，結果，所有的蟑螂一下都被根除了。

37. She made the decision without considering the matter thoroughly. As a result, she regretted afterwards shortly.

她在沒有全面考慮這個問題前就下了決定，結果，她之後很快就後悔。

38. Karen's father adores everything she does. As a result, she becomes

a very spoiled child.

凱倫的爸爸喜愛她所做的每件事，結果，她變成一個非常被寵壞的孩子。

39. The boy grew up threatened by his brother all the time. As a result, he became very shy and reserved.

這男孩成長時一直常受哥哥威脅，結果，他變得很害羞又保守。

40. She was very active in advocating for same- sex marriage in this conservative country. As a result, she lost the election.

在這個保守的國家裡，她很積極在代言同性婚姻，結果，她輸了這場選舉。

41. He misled us with his conflicted comments last time. As a result, we don't trust him anymore.

他以他矛盾的評論誤導了我們，結果，我們不再相信他了。

42. I did not have enough experience when I directed my first film. As a result, it was done poorly.

當我導演我的第一部影片時，我沒有足夠的經驗，結果拍得很不好。

43. People respected Dr. Sun Yat-sen very much. As a result, he was called the "national father" of the Republic of China.

人們非常尊重孫中山先生，結果，他被稱為是中華民國的國父。

44. John revealed the know-how of the company to its opponent. As a result, he was fired by his boss.

約翰把公司的技術洩露給對手，結果他被老闆開除。

45. He reacted to the everything negatively. As a result, he doesn't have many friends.

他因為對事情的反應都很負面，結果他並沒有很多朋友。

46. The disease spread out quickly as a result of the poor sanitation in the region.

因為這個地區很差的衛生，疾病迅速地擴散。

47. Nelson was sent into prison as a result of smuggling heroin across borders.

尼爾森因為走私海洛因過邊境的原因而被送進監獄。

48. He disappeared from our town as a result of the scandal.

他因為這個醜聞的關係，消失在我們的鎮上。

49. She begins to imagine how her Mr. right will look like all the time as a result of reading too many romance novels.

她因為看了太多羅曼史小說，開始一直想著她的白馬王子會長得怎麼樣。

50. I ended the relationship with my boyfriend as a result of his betrayal.

因為他的背叛，我終止了我和我男友的關係。

51. The song repeats in her head as a result of her listening to it so many times.

因為聽了這麼多次，這首歌在她的腦子裡重複。

52. He cannot swallow anything as a result of the surgery.

他因為手術的關係什麼東西都不能吞嚥。

53. The equipment performs better than usual as a result of the maintenance work done yesterday.

因為昨天所做維修工作的關係，這個設備表現得比平常好。

54. He refines his manner as a result of Nancy's criticism.

他因為南西批評的關係，因而改進了他的態度。

55. The company quickly fixes the problem as a result of everyone's complaint.

因為每個人的抱怨，公司很快地修正了這個問題。

56. I accomplished my goal as a result of your help.

因為你的幫助的關係，我達成了我的目標。

TOEIC篇

【句型 41】 Enough to

必考字彙表 Adj 1～Adj 28

1. friendly	8. reliable	15. relaxing	22. foggy
2. generous	9. loyal	16. joyful	23. nasty
3. compassionate	10. faithful	17. enriching	24. stormy
4. gentle	11. sunny	18. scary	25. windy
5. caring	12. pleasant	19. horrible	26. evil
6. cheerful	13. magnificent	20. traumatic	27. summery
7. patient	14. productive	21. boring	28. healthy

必考 句型與解析

【句型 41】enough to。

【結構】 The smart phone（主詞）+ is（動詞）+ user-friendly（形容詞）+ enough to（足夠）+ be used by any old person（達成、做某項動作）The smart phone ⇨ 主詞表示智慧型手機，user-friendly ⇨ 形容詞，表示友善的，enough to ⇨ 足夠…而可以發生某樣事或結果。

【句子】 The smart phone is user-friendly enough to be used by any old person.

【中譯】 這個智慧型手機對使用者足夠友善，可以讓任何老人使用。

由句型 41【Adj + enough to + V】此句型可得知，enough 有足夠…的意思，在本句裡，主詞 The smart phone 是智慧型手機，動詞第三人稱單數為 is，user- friendly 中間用連字符號相連是形容詞，對使用者友善的意思，The smart phone is user-friendly enough to...，到此意思是 " 這個智慧型手機足夠對使用者友善… "，這樣的特質滿足到會產生什麼樣的結果呢？在 to 之後，便設想可能發生的結果，在本句中，to 後是加 be used，被使用的意思，by any old person 被任何老年人使用。意指本台智慧型手機在設計上足夠對使用者友善、便利，以至於任何老人家能夠使用，完成本句子。

在構思【Adj + enough to + V】的句型時，可思考主詞句有什麼樣的形容詞特質，以致於能從事什麼行為、動作，寫作上，可用可採用不同的主詞，以表格上的形容詞設想不同的特質，構思不同的結果，變化演繹出不同的句子。

【1】 "enough" 在此作副詞，用於修飾形容詞，代表有足夠程度的某項特質，得以作某個動作，或達成某項結果。

如：

He is strong enough to move the rock.

他強壯到足以搬動這顆石頭。

如果要表示為某人／某事／某物做這件事，可加 "for"

如：

The room is large enough for four people to sleep in.

如要變化句型，也可以用 "Adj + enough for N"：

如：

He is experienced enough for the job.

他對於這個工作來說有足夠的經驗。

【2】 也可以用 "S V + Adv. + enough to V" 的變化句型，意指：enough 也可以修飾副詞，表示主詞從事某動作有足夠的特性，可以達到某項結果：

He uns fast enough to catch the thief.

他跑得夠快足以抓到小偷。

She sings well enough to be invited to perform on stage.

她唱歌唱得夠好足以被邀請到舞台上表演。

就是這樣寫

2. The philanthropist is generous enough to give us a large sum of donation.

   這位慈善家很慷慨，可以給我們這一大筆捐款。

3. Mother Theresa is compassionate enough to leave her family and serve the poor in India.

   德勒莎修女有足夠的愛心，讓她離開家人到印度侍奉窮人。

4. Her words are gentle enough to lift the burden on my heart.

   她的言語夠輕柔，除去了我心裡的負擔。

5. If you are caring enough to be a nurse, maybe it will be a suitable career for you.

   如果你有足夠的關懷可以當一名護士，也許這對你會是適合的職業。

6. The movie is cheerful enough to be taken as a comedy, but it also discusses serious issues.

   這部電影夠令人振奮到可以被當成一部喜劇，但它也探討很多嚴肅的議題。

7. Joe's brother opened the gift on Christmas Eve, but Joe is patient enough to wait till Christmas Day.

   喬的哥哥在聖誕夜就拆開了禮物，可是喬有足夠的耐心等待星期天早上。

8. The jeep is reliable enough for such a journey.

   這台吉普車對這樣的旅程來說是足夠被信任的。

9. All the employees left, but Victor was loyal enough to stay with his boss, despite the bankruptcy of the company.

   所有的員工都離開了，但維多有足夠的忠誠還跟他的老闆待在一起，即使公司已經破產了。

10. Abraham was faithful enough to follow the God's word, but his wife had doubts.

亞伯拉罕有足夠的信心去追隨上帝的話，但他的太太有疑慮。

11. The weather is sunny enough to dry out the clothes now.

天氣現在已經夠晴朗可以曬乾衣服了。

12. Their first date was pleasant enough that both of them wanted to meet again.

他們的第一次約會夠愉快，讓他們都想再見面。

13. The power of love is magnificent enough to overcome any hatred among people.

愛的力量很強大，足以對抗抗人們間的任何仇恨。

14. The farm is productive enough to provide food for an entire family.

這座農場有足夠的生產力為一整個家庭提供食物。

15. The music was relaxing enough to make anyone fall asleep.

這個音樂夠放鬆，足以讓任何人睡著。

16. The song is joyful enough to make everyone want to dance.

這首歌充滿喜悅，足以讓每個人想跟著一起跳舞。

17. The experience of volunteering for the organization is enriching enough to make Maggie continue to do it for five years.

為這個組織志工服務的經驗感覺夠豐富，讓梅姬可以持續做了五年。

18. The movie is scary enough to let any five year old cry.

這部電影夠嚇人，可以讓任何五歲小孩哭。

19. The situation is horrible enough to stop anyone from trying, but Tom went into the fire and saved the little boy.

情況很惡劣足以阻止任何人嘗試，但是湯姆走進火堆救了這個小男孩。

20. The memory is traumatic enough to make me never want to think about it again.

    記憶是如此的傷痛，足以讓我再也不要想起它。

21. The documentary is boring enough to put anyone into sleep.

    這部紀錄片無聊到可以讓任何人睡著。

22. It is foggy enough to block the view of the pilot, we had better not fly.

    天氣霧大到足以擋住駕駛的視線，我們最好不要飛了。

23. I believe his personality is nasty enough to do such a terrible thing.

    我相信他的人格惡劣，足以做出這樣糟糕的事。

24. The weather is stormy enough to destroy our rooftop garden.

    暴風雨大到足以摧毀我們的屋頂花園。

25. It is windy enough to open our sail now.

    風大到可以張開我們的帆了。

26. Nobody would be evil enough to hurt her.

    沒有人會邪惡到要傷害她。

27. It is summery enough to wear my skirt.

    天氣夠夏天到我可以穿我的裙子了。

28. My grandfather is healthy enough to run a marathon at the age of seventy.

    我祖父在七十歲還健康的足以跑馬拉松。

【句型42】More...than

1. purchase	8. feel	15. solve	22. hurt
2. earn	9. cut	16. wash	23. spread
3. write	10. plant	17. draw	24. steal
4. sing	11. bring	18. suffer	25. reduce
5. spend	12. buy	19. export	26. point
6. bake	13. build	20. upset	27. arrange
7. kill	14. donate	21. save	28. paint

必考 句型與解析

【句型42】More...than。

【結構】 I（主詞1）+ purchased（購買）+ more bread（名詞，麵包，指購買更多的事物）+ than you did（比起主詞2所購買的數量的數量）.
I ⇨ 主詞1 purchase ⇨ 購買，動詞 more ⇨ 比較多的，bread ⇨ 麵包，購買的物品，受詞 you ⇨ 主詞2。

【句子】 I purchased more bread than you did.

【中譯】 我比你買更多麵包。

解　析

由句型 42【S1 + V + more + N + than + S2】此句型可得知，此句型裡利用比較級，有第一個主詞與第二個主詞在從事某行為時，跟某個名詞關係 " 相比 " 的意味，在本句裡，第一個主詞 I，是我的意思，在過去的時候從事某個行為，動詞採用 purchase 購買，因為為過去式，改為 purchased，之後接受詞麵包 bread，"more bread" 就意味著更多麵包，接續用 than 跟主詞二相比，主詞二為 you，你的購買動作可以用 did 助動詞取代 purchased，所以 I purchased more bread than you did. 我比你購買了更多麵包，便完成此造句。

在構思【S1 + V + more + N + than + S2】的句型時，可先思考兩個主詞從事某動作時，跟某名詞之間的比較關係，在大小、數量多少、程度上有何不同，寫作上，可用不同的主詞，以表格上的動詞設想不同的動作，搭配不同的名詞，變化演繹出不同的句子。

新多益篇

【新多益】V29～V56

【1】 "S1 + V + more + N + than + S2" 此句型用以描述主詞 1 比主詞 2 從事
　　 某項事物數量更多、程度更大、或範圍更廣,如買更多東西、賺更多
　　 錢、唱更多歌、花更多時間等等…。

　　 ◆ buy more things 買更多東西

　　 ◆ earn more money 賺更多錢

　　 ◆ sing more songs 唱更多歌

　　 ◆ spend more time 花更多時間

　　 其中的名詞可以是可數或是不可數名詞,但都是以 "more" 來代表
　　 "更多"。

【2】 可依據情境改變動詞的形態,如成為過去式、完成式,句尾主詞 2 的
　　 助動詞必須與前面主詞 1 的動詞一致,在口語時常常省略。

　　 Mark caught more butterflies than I did yesterday.

　　 馬克在昨天比我抓了更多蝴蝶。

　　 Tina has won more points than Helen throughout the competition.

　　 蒂娜已經在整個比賽裡比海倫得到更多分數。

【3】 若在比較的第二句中的主詞、動詞和第一句一樣,則可省略第二個子
　　 句中的主詞和動詞。

　　 He earned more money than last year.

　　 他比去年賺更多錢。

就是這樣寫

2. She earns more money than her husband does.

   她比她丈夫賺更多錢。

3. I write more articles for the school newspaper than you do.

   我比你為校刊寫更多文章。

4. She sings more folk songs than most of the other female singers do.

   她比其他女性歌手唱更多的民俗歌曲。

5. I spend more time studying than you do.

   我比你花更多時間唸書。

6. She can bake more cookies than anybody.

   她可以比任何人多做出更多的餅乾。

7. Air pollution from the cars may kill more people than smoking does.

   汽車所造成的空氣污染所致死的人也許比吸煙所致死的還多。

8. She must have felt more pain than I have.

   她一定比我還感到更多的傷痛。

9. The new prime minister even cut more budget welfare than the previous on did.

   這位新首相甚至比前一任砍除了更多福利預算。

10. Betty plants more roses than her neighbor does.

    貝蒂比她鄰居種更多玫瑰。

11. He brought more enthusiasm to work than most of his colleagues do.

    他比他大多數的同事們帶更多的熱情去工作。

12. I bought more clothes than my sister did when we went shopping last weekend.

    上週末當我和我姊姊一起去買東西時，我比她買了更多衣服。

13. The architect built more houses than other architects did in his time.

這位建築師比起同時代的其他建築師蓋了更多房屋。

14. Jeff donated more books than I did to the library.

傑夫比我捐給圖書館更多書。

15. The mathematician solved more problems than anybody did.

這位數學家比起任何人解決了更多問題。

16. Grace washed more clothes than Fanny did in one hour.

葛瑞斯比起芬妮在一小時中洗更多的衣服。

17. Mike drew more paintings than Joe did in the art class.

在藝術課上麥克比喬畫更多畫。

18. She suffered from more pain than I did because she did not have anyone support her.

她比我受更多痛苦因為她沒有任何人支持她。

19. China began to export more industrial goods than Taiwan did in the 90s.

中國大陸在九零年代開始比台灣出口更多的工業產品。

20. The revised version of the policy even upset more people than the previous one did.

修正過的政策甚至比之前的版本讓更多人生氣。

21. I saved more money than my sister did during the past year.

過去這年我比我姊姊存更多錢。

22. A nuclear bomb will hurt more people than all the other traditional weapons will.

一顆原子彈將會比所有傳統武器傷害更多人。

23. Jessica spreads more rumors than Lisa does.

潔西卡比麗莎傳播了更多謠言。

24. Charlie stole more money from the company than Paul did.

查理比保羅從公司偷走了更多錢。

25. Sue reduced more weight than Tracy after the fitness program.

在健身課後，蘇比崔西減輕更多體重。

26. The new coach pointed out more mistakes that I made than the old one did.

新的教練比起舊的指出更多我所犯的錯誤。

27. My new agent arranged more work for me than my previous one did.

我新的經紀人比前一位為我安排更多工作。

28. Lucy painted more paintings than anyone else in her class did.

露西比她班上的任何人畫更多的畫。

【句型 43】 As...as

1. historical	8. responsible	15. pleasant	22. complex
2. scared	9. cute	16. embarrased	23. outstanding
3. traditional	10. political	17. guilty	24. negative
4. strong	11. healthy	18. lonely	25. straight
5. expensive	12. dangerous	19. mad	26. excellent
6. intelligent	13. famous	20. individualistic	27. perfect
7. poor	14. ugly	21. positive	28. valuable

必考 句型與解析

【句型 43】as + 原級（形容詞）+ as...（和…一樣）。

【結構】 The monument（主詞）+ is + as + historical（歷史悠久的）+ as + the pyramid in Cairo（比較的事物）The monument ⇨ 主詞 as historical as ⇨ 一樣歷史悠久，the pyramid in Cairo ⇨ 開羅的金字塔，比較的對象。

【句子】 The monument is as historical as the pyramid in Cairo.

【中譯】 這個紀念碑就像開羅的金字塔一樣歷史悠久。

解　析

由句型 43【as + 原級（形容詞）+ as...（和…一樣）】此句型可得知，此句型有第一個主詞跟第二個的主詞，在某特性（以形容詞為代表）上一樣、程度相等、內容類似的意思。在本句裡，第一個主詞為 The monument，代表一個紀念碑，因為第三人稱單數，用 is，as... as 之間的形容詞，用 historical，代表歷史悠久的意思，而 as 後就接比較的對象，在此句裡，設想此紀念碑比較的對象為開羅的金字塔，即 the pyramid in Cairo，所以整句的意涵為 " 這個紀念碑跟開羅的金字塔歷史一樣悠久 "，用 The monument is as historical as the pyramid in Cairo 代表。

在構思【as + 原級（形容詞）+ as...（和…一樣）】句型時，須先思考主詞與其欲比較的對象，確認兩者在某特質上，的確可類比，再嵌入 as..as 的句型。寫作上，可採用不同的主詞，依據表格上的形容詞，搭配不同類比的主詞作比較，變化演繹出不同的句子。

必考文法概念

【1】 "as + 原級形容詞 + as...(和…一樣)" 主要是描述主詞跟某事物有一樣的特質，其特質就用其間的形容詞來描述，請注意 as... as 間的形容詞要用原級，不可用比較級、最高級，才意味兩者之間的關係為平等。

【2】 第一個 as 為副詞，修飾形容詞，第二個 as 則為連接詞，其後連接子

句，所以在之後子句中的動詞往往省略。

如：He is as strong as a rock (is). 這男孩跟岩石一樣強壯。

【3】 在句型的變化上，也可作 "as + 原級副詞 + as...(和⋯⋯一樣)"，"as..as" 間可用副詞，代表第一個主詞執行某動作的情形，跟 B 主詞一樣，第二個 as 後的動詞常用助動詞代替，但注意時態要跟第一個主詞的動詞一致，如：

Mary runs as fast as John does.

瑪麗像約翰跑得一樣快。(fast 為副詞)

【4】 否定句的結構為 "not so (as) 形容詞 / 副詞 as" 不如，代表不如的意思：

Frank is not as tall as his brother.

法蘭克不像他哥哥一樣高。

Jane does not work as hard as her sister.

珍不像她姊姊一樣努力。

【5】 as...as 主詞的使用：通常在 "as..as" 句型裡，第二個 as 之後如果使用人稱代名詞，用主格或是受格都可以，但是用主格較正式，

如：

John is as old as I.

John is as old as me.

也可以用所有代名詞，如：

Your house is as old as mine.(= my house)

你的房子跟我的一樣老。

就是這樣寫

2. He is as scared as me.

他跟我一樣害怕。

3. Your mother is as traditional as mine.

你的母親跟我的母親一樣傳統。

4. The boy is short but he is as strong as a rock.

這個男孩很矮但他就像岩石那麼強壯。

5. The living expenses in Taipei are almost as expensive as New York.

在台北的生活費幾乎跟紐約一樣高了。

6. Helen is as intelligent as a PhD student although she is only twelve years old.

海倫像一個博士生班聰明,雖然她只有十二歲。

7. I am as poor as you. Sorry I cannot lend you any money.

我跟你一樣窮,抱歉我不能借你任何錢。

8. Louis is just as responsible as Jeff, why don't you let him do the project?

路易斯就像傑夫一樣有責任感,你為什麼不讓他做這個計劃?

9. Mary is as cute as Debby, and even with more character.

瑪麗就像黛比一樣可愛,甚至更有個性。

10. Joe was disappointed to find that his new department is as political as the old one.

喬很失望的發現他的新部門跟他舊的一樣政治化。

11. I am as healthy as a twenty-year-old although I will turn eighty next year.

我就跟二十歲的人一樣健康,即使我明年就要八十歲了。

12. He is as dangerous as a snake.

他跟蛇一樣危險。

13. During the actress's prime time she was as famous as Marilyn Monroe.

在這位女星的全盛時期她跟瑪麗蓮夢露一樣有名。

14. Your heart is as ugly as a criminal's.

你的心就跟罪犯的一樣醜陋。

15. His voice is as pleasant as the sound of the waves.

他的聲音就像海浪聲一樣令人喜歡。

16. Do not say sorry. I am just as embarrassed as you are.

不要說抱歉，我就跟你一樣尷尬。

17. It's both of our fault. I am as guilty as you.

這是我們兩個人的錯。我跟你一樣有罪。

18. I felt as lonely as a wandering cloud.

我覺得像漂泊的雲一樣孤單。

19. He is as mad as hell.

他像地獄一樣瘋狂。

20. Nowadays young people in Asia are as individualistic as the young people in the West.

最近亞洲的年輕人就像西方的年輕人一樣崇尚個人主義。

21. She is as positive as sunshine. She always cheers me up.

她就像陽光一樣正面，她永遠使我振奮。

22. The building is as complex as a maze. I can't get out.

這建築就像迷宮一樣複雜，我出不去。

23. Jessie is as outstanding as her sister.

潔西跟她的姊姊一樣傑出。

24. The way you talk is as negative as your father!

你的說話方式跟你的父親一樣負面！

25. Truth is as straight as an arrow.

真理就像箭一樣直。

26. The result is as excellent as I have expected.

結果就像我預期的一樣棒。

27. Men can never be as perfect as God.

人永遠不可能像神一樣完美。

28. Your remarks are as valuable as gold to me.

你的評論對我來講就像黃金一般珍貴。

【句型 44】關係副詞

1. adapt	8. flee	15. grind	22. forgive
2. stink	9. finish	16. break	23. forbid
3. seek	10. speed	17. choose	24. dive
4. weep	11. deal	18. freeze	25. blow
5. prevent	12. kneel	19. steal	26. throw
6. breed	13. dream	20. bite	27. draw
7. feed	14. hold	21. slide	28. withdraw

必考 句型與解析

【句型 44】關係副詞。

【結構】 This is the center（名詞）+ where（關係副詞）+ I（主詞）+ Adopted（領養）+ my dog（領養的事物），動物養護所 ⇨ 地點，Where ⇨ 指描述該地點，I adopted my dog ⇨ 在該地點做的事。

【句子】 This is the animal shelter where I adopted my dog.

【中譯】 這是我領養我的狗的動物養護所。

由句型 44【This is + 關係副詞 where / when / why / how】可得知，This is 開頭後，加上定冠詞 the 和名詞，本句為 the animal shelter，"This is the animal shelter" 代表這間特定的動物養護所，然後再用關係副詞引導的子句，來描述這間動物養護所的特性。

在本句裡，關係副詞採用 where，之後的子句為 I adopted my dog. 可以知道這就是我領養我的狗的地點，而時態發生在過去。

關係副詞後所引導的子句，是用來修飾主要子句的某一名詞。
如：
This is the animal shelter ⇨ 主要子句
where I adopted my dog ⇨ 關係副詞所引導的子句。
關係副詞所引導的子句用於修飾前一句裡的 animal shelter。加在一起就成為 " 這是我領養我的狗的動物養護所 "。

在構思【This is + 關係副詞 where / when / why / how】句型時，可以先想想在這個地方 / 時間發生了什麼事，或這就是主詞為什麼 / 如何從事某項動作的原因 / 方法，再依據表格上的動詞，變化演繹出不同的句子。

【1】 關係副詞有副詞與連接詞兩個作用，最常用的是 where / when / why / how，where 指地點，when 指時間，why 指原因，how 指方法。

通常結構為 "This is + 先行詞 + where / when / why / how"，關係副詞所引導的子句是形容詞子句，用來形容先行詞，如：

This is the day when she had the accident.

這就是她出車禍的那一天。

先行詞 day，是跟時間有關，所以關係副詞用 when，引導形容詞子句 " she had the accident" 並可依 where / when / why / how 語意作變化，如：

This is the place where I met my girlfriend.

這就是我遇見我女朋友的地方。

【2】 在關係副詞子句裡也常常省略先行詞，如：

This is (the reason) why I like her.

這是我喜歡她的原意。

This is (the situation) how the story happened.

這就是故事發生的情形。

【3】 "This is + 關係副詞 where / when / why / how" 當然也可以根據所需要表達的語意、時態，改為 It is、That is、This was

It is how we persuaded her.

我們是如此說服她的。

That is why people moved out of the neighborhood.

那是人們搬離那個社區的原因。

就是這樣寫

2. This is the reason why the socks stink.
   這是這雙襪子發臭的原因。

3. This is the place where I seek my inspiration.
   這是我尋求靈感的地方。

4. This is the true reason why she weeps so much.
   這是她哭泣這麼多的真正原因。

5. This is how you can prevent yourself from nose bleeding.
   這是你預防流鼻血的方法。

6. This is how people breed their cattle.
   這是人們繁衍下一代牛隻的做法。

7. This is the place where we feed our cows.
   這是我們餵乳牛的地方。

8. This is where the prisoners fled.
   這是囚犯逃走的地方。

9. This is how you lead people to finish a difficult job together.
   這是你領導人們完成一件困難工作的方法。

10. This is how to speed up the work.
    這是加快工作速度的方法。

11. This is why I do not like to deal with him.
    這是我不喜歡跟他接觸的原因。

12. This is where we kneel down to pray.
    這是我們跪下來禱告的地方。

13. This is when dreams occur.

這是夢發生的時候。

14. This is how you hold a sword.

這是你如何握一柄劍的方式。

15. This is how you grind the spices.

這是你如何磨香料的方式。

16. This is how you break a brick with your fists.

這是用拳頭如何打破磚頭的方式。

17. This is how you choose your husband.

這是妳選丈夫的方法。

18. This is the reason why you are freezing - you did not wear a hat to keep your head warm.

這是你這麼冷的原因─你沒有戴一頂帽子讓你的頭部保持溫暖。

19. This is how the thief stole the painting from the museum.

這就是小偷從博物館偷走畫作的方式。

20. This is why the dog bit you.

這是狗為什麼咬你的原因。

21. This is where the car slid down the hill.

這是車子滑下山丘的地方。

22. This is the reason why I cannot forgive him.

這是我不能原諒他的原因。

23. This is why his name is forbidden to be mentioned ever again.

這是為什麼他的名字永遠不准再被提起的原因。

24. This is the spot where we will dive down to find the shipwreck.

這就是我們會潛下去找到沈船的地點。

25. This is how you blow a trombone.

這是你吹法國號的方式。

26. This is how to throw a ball with the strength of your body.

這是如何以身體力量投球的方法。

27. This is the reason why the artist drew dots on every painting.

這是為什麼藝術家在每幅畫上都畫點點的原因。

28. The judge was unfair this is the reason why we withdrew from the competition.

裁判不公正,這是我們退出競賽的原因。

【句型 45】Until

1. witness	8. harm	15. block	22. contact
2. crack	9. lecture	16. limit	23. issue
3. comfort	10. marry	17. mix	24. punch
4. switch	11. schedule	18. register	25. resist
5. ship	12. tip	19. refer	26. quit
6. slice	13. implement	20. correct	27. dare
7. please	14. guarantee	21. post	28. refuse

必考 句型與解析

【句型 45】Until...（直到）。

【結構】 I will not tell anyone that I witnessed the crime ⇨ 我不會做某件事，until ⇨ 直到，I am certain it is safe to do so ⇨ 某項條件發生或成熟。

【句子】 I will not tell anyone that I witnessed the crime until I am certain it is safe to do so.

【中譯】 我不會告訴任何人我見證了這項犯罪，直到我確認這麼做是安全的。

解　析

由句型 45【until】得知，until 的句型有 " 直到…時間 " 的意思，主詞 I 是我，will not 代表將不會，動詞 tell 為告訴，anyone 為受詞，因此完成 " 我將不會告訴任何人 " 的子句，不會告訴別人什麼呢？I witnessed the crime 我見證了這項犯罪，之後再用 until 引導出前述內容要發生的情況或條件，"until I am certain it is safe to do so"，代表主詞一定要確認是這麼做是安全的，才會告訴別人 " 我見證了這項犯罪 "。

"until..." 通常使用在一個否定句型裡，代表 " 主詞不會從事什麼行為，直到 / 除非什麼時間條件或情況發生… "，因此在寫作時，可以構思主詞所執行動作的時間條件，再用 until 加以串連，可依照表格裡的不同動詞，加以造出多變的句子。

必考文法概念

【1】 "until" 是連接詞，用於否定句內，代表的意思是 " 直到某個時間，某動作才發生 "，如：

I didn't finish writing the paper until 2 o'clock in the morning.

我一直到早上兩點才寫完這篇論文。

在肯定句內，代表的意思是 " 直到某時間某個動作停止了 "，如：

He kept running until he exhausted himself.

他一直跑步跑到筋疲力竭才停。

She was awake until 3 o'clock in the morning.

她一直到早上三點都是醒著的。

因此，在肯定句中使用 until 時，主詞的動作應該要有延續、持續性的特質，才能表示 "持續地做某事一直到某個時間"。

【2】 until 與 unless 的分別：until 與 unless 都是從屬連接詞，until 表示有時間上的從屬關係、先後順序，unless 則有 "除非" 的意思，代表除非某情況發生，否則主詞還是會做某件事，或者在強調只有當某條件發生時，主詞才會採取某行動。如：

Unless it rains, we will go for a picnic by the river tomorrow.

我們明天會到河邊野餐，除非下雨。

Unless you apologize to me, I will not invite you to the party.

除非你跟我道歉，我不會邀請你到派對。

就是這樣寫

2. Nobody was able to eat the walnuts until he found a tool to crack the shell.

   沒有人能吃得到核桃，直到他找到了一個工具去打開殼。

3. The girl was not able to sleep until her mother came to her room to comfort her.

   一直要到她媽媽來到她房間安撫他，這女孩才有辦法入睡。

4. I couldn't see anything on the screen until I switched the seat with him.

   直到跟他換座位，我才能看得到螢幕上的東西。

5. There will be nothing we can eat on the island, until the boat ships us supplies next week.

   一直要到下週船把補給運給我們，我們在島上才會有東西可吃。

6. We cannot eat the cake until Nancy slices it.

   要等到南西切蛋糕，我們才能吃。

7. The teacher does not allow to the students to go out and play until she is pleased with their behavior.

   一直到老師對學生的行為感到滿意，他才准學生們出去玩。

8. The child will not think of fire as dangerous until he is harmed by it.

   一直要到被火燒傷，這孩子才會知道火是危險的。

9. I was never interested in this topic until I was lectured by an expert.

   一直要到專家跟我講課，我才對這個題目有興趣。

10. Ted never wore a tie until the day he got married.

    在結婚那天之前，泰德從來不曾打領帶。

11. I will not leave until you schedule an appointment for me with the doctor.

直到你為我跟醫生預約時間前，我都不會離開

12. The boy did not want to help us until we tipped him.

一直到我們付他小費，這男孩才願意幫我們。

13. The company was in a mess until the manager implemented the new policy.

一直到經理實施新措施，公司才停止一團混亂。

14. The client was very angry until the salesman guaranteed to give her money back.

一直到售貨員保證退還她錢，這位客戶才沒那麼生氣。

15. She did not feel anything wrong until her car was blocked by the gangsters.

一直到她的車被幫派份子堵住後，她才覺得有些不對。

16. He was fooling around everywhere until his parents started to limit his behavior.

一直到他的父母開始限制他的行為，他才沒有到處胡鬧。

17. The drink does not taste good until I mix it with honey.

這杯飲料很難喝，直到我把它跟蜂蜜混在一起。

18. You cannot join the class until you register at the counter.

直到你在櫃檯註冊前，你不能上課。

19. I did not know what to do until my friend referred me to a good doctor.

我不知道該怎麼做，直到我的朋友介紹我一個好醫生。

20. We should not hand in the report until all the mistakes get corrected.

直到所有的錯誤被修正前，我們不應該交出這份報告。

21. Nobody knows about the event until it was posted on the website yesterday.

一直到昨天被公佈在網站上，才有人知道這個活動。

22. We could not contact him until someone told us his phone number.

一直到有人告訴我們他的電話，我們才能聯絡他。

23. We could not get into the venue until someone issued us a ticket.

一直到有人把票發給我們，我們才能進入會場。

24. He thought he was winning the flight until his opponent punched him right on the face.

一直到他的對手在他臉上打一拳之前，他以為他會贏得這場打鬥。

25. The boy resisted cleaning up his room until his mother became very mad at him.

一直到他母親對他非常生氣前，這男孩都抗拒打掃他的房間。

26. You will not be hired as a driver until you quit drinking heavily.

在你戒除大量飲酒前，你不會被聘用為駕駛員的。

27. I dare not try the food until you tell me what it is.

直到你告訴我它是什麼前，我不敢試這個食物。

28. He refused to go to the concert with us until he found out his favoritesinger will be on stage.

一直到他發現他最喜歡的歌星會上台之前，他都拒絕跟我們去這個音樂會。

【句型 46】所有格代名詞

1. condo	8. invention	15. scent	22. pet
2. drug	9. linen	16. underwear	23. property
3. alarm	10. memory	17. visitor	24. reward
4. goldfish	11. receipt	18. volleyball	25. scarf
5. instrument	12. passenger	19. playground	26. mattress
6. jewel	13. shame	20. vacuum	27. wallet
7. necklace	14. racket	21. fan	28. company

必考 句型與解析

【句型 46】所有格代名詞

【結構】 The condo（公寓房子）+ is（動詞）+ theirs（屬於誰的）. Condo ⇨ 公寓，theirs ⇨ 他們的。

【句子】 The condo is theirs.

【中譯】 這間公寓是他們的。

解　析

由句型 46【N + V + 所有格代名詞】此句型可得知，主詞是 The condo，condo 是公寓房、房子的意思，因為第三人稱單數，採用 is，這個公寓套房是他們的，即可以簡潔的以 "The condo is theirs" 表示，取代 The condo is their condo. 的重複，其中的 theirs，就是 their 的所有格代名詞，用在句型中，可使句子較為簡潔。

在構思【所有格代名詞】的句型時，主詞可以是單數複數、可數或不可數，也可以有不同時態，可參考表格上的不同名詞，搭配不同的動詞，再加上不同的人稱代名詞，以完成 " 某物品是某人的 " 的表達。

必考文法概念

【1】

人稱代名詞（第一人稱 單數／複數）	
主格	I / we
受格	Me / us
所有格	My / our
所有格代名詞	Mine / ours
反身代名詞	Myself / ourselves

人稱代名詞（第二人稱 單數／複數）	
主格	you / you
受格	you / you
所有格	your / your
所有格代名詞	yours / yours
反身代名詞	yourself / yourselves

人稱代名詞（第三人稱 單數／男）	
主格	he
受格	him
所有格	his
所有格代名詞	his
反身代名詞	himself

人稱代名詞（第三人稱 單數／女）	
主格	she
受格	her
所有格	her
所有格代名詞	hers
反身代名詞	herself

人稱代名詞（第三人稱 單數／中性）	
主格	it
受格	it
所有格	its
所有格代名詞	X
反身代名詞	itself

【6】

人稱代名詞（第三人稱 複數）	
主格	they
受格	them
所有格	their
所有格代名詞	theirs
反身代名詞	themselves

【7】 所有格代名詞包含 mine（我們的）, yours（你們的、你的）, his（他的）,
hers（她的）, its（它的、牠的）, ours（我們的）, theirs（他們的）。在
此句型裡，乃是宣稱某物為某人所擁有，可設想不同名詞（N），動詞的
單複數、時態可作變化，搭配不同所有格代名詞，即完成句型。

⇨ The cup is his. 這是他的杯子。（單數）

⇨ These cups are his. 這些杯子都是他的。（複數）

⇨ The car was his. 這曾是他的車。（過去式）

⇨ The house has been ours for the past ten years.（完成式）

就是這樣寫

2. The drug is his.
   這是他的藥。

3. The broken alarm is mine.
   這壞掉的鬧鐘是我的。

4. The goldfish is hers.
   那是她的金魚。

5. The musical instrument is his.
   那是他的樂器。

6. The jewel is hers.

   那珠寶是她的。

7. The beautiful necklace is mine.

   這條美麗的項鍊是我的。

8. The crazy invention is his.

   這是他的瘋狂發明。

9. The white linen is theirs.

   這白布是他們的。

10. The memory is ours.

    這是我們記憶。

11. The receipt is his.

    這是他的收據。

12. The passenger is his.

    這是他的乘客。

13. The shame is mine.

    這是我的羞恥。

14. The tennis racket is mine.

    這網球拍是我的。

15. The scent is distinctively hers.

    這香味獨屬於她。

16. The underwear is not mine.

    這內衣不是我的。

17. The visitor is his.

    這是他的訪客。

18. The volleyball is hers.

    這是她的排球。

19. The playground is his.

這是他的遊樂場。

20. The vacuum is theirs.

這是他們的吸塵器。

21. The fan is his.

這是他的扇子。

22. The pet is hers.

這是她的寵物。

23. The property is theirs.

這是他們的財產。

24. The reward is theirs.

這是他們的獎賞。

25. The scarf is mine.

這是我的圍巾。

26. The mattress is ours.

這床墊是我們的。

27. The wallet is hers.

這是她的皮夾。

28. The company is his.

這是他的公司。

【句型47】分詞構句

1. ensure	8. seek	15. accept	22. throw
2. invest	9. become	16. depend	23. arrive
3. reduce	10. develop	17. differ	24. ignore
4. involve	11. achieve	18. recognize	25. admire
5. tend	12. prefer	19. reflect	26. approve
6. indentify	13. explain	20. intend	27. commit
7. continue	14. agree	21. settle	28. suppose

必考 句型與解析

【句型47】分詞構句

【結構】 分詞構句 V-ing / V-p.p..., S + V...。Sensing（感覺到）+（感覺到的事物）, +（主詞）+（動詞）...。Sensing our nervousness ⇨ 由 When he sensed our nervousness 改變而來，the taxi driver ⇨ 主詞，ensure ⇨ 動詞。

【句子】 Sensing our nervousness, the taxi driver ensured us we will get the station in time.

【中譯】 當感覺到我們的緊張，計程車司機跟我們確認我們會及時到車站。

 解 析

由句型 47【分詞構句 V-ing / V-p.p.., S + V...】此句型可得知，以分詞開始的片語…, 主要子句是由以下句型變換而來的：

When the taxi driver sensed our nervousness, he ensured us we will get the station in time.

省略主詞 ⇨ When sensing our nervousness, the taxi driver ensured us we will get the station in time.

動詞變分詞 ⇨ Sensing our nervousness, the taxi driver ensured us we will get the station in time.

因此第一個子句省略了主詞，動詞變分詞，由 sensing 開頭，代表真主詞 "the taxi driver" 感覺到了某樣事物，"our nervousness" 即為受詞，計程車司機感覺到的是我們的緊張。在逗號之後，繼續設想主詞在感覺到我們的緊張後的行為，於是計程車司機確保我們會準時抵達車站，用 "the taxi driver ensured us we will get the station in time." 作代表，完成了句子。

在構思【分詞構句 V-ing / V-p.p..., S + V...】的句型時，若兩個子句前後主詞一樣，可省略主詞，動詞做 Ving 或 V-pp，完成分詞構句後，逗點後再接主要子句，主要目的也是使文意顯得精簡、有力，可參考表格上的不同動詞，設想出各種多變的句子。

【1】 " 分詞構句 V-ing / V-p.p.., S + V..." 句型裡，逗點前的分詞構句主要是當副詞修飾主要子句，在某種狀態下，S + V... 所產生的行為。

如果是主詞主動執行某種動作，則由原形動詞 V 改為 Ving，作為分詞構句：

Ellen exercises two hours a day.

Ellen reduces her weight quickly.

可整併為：

Exercising two hours a day, Ellen reduces her weight quickly.

每天運動兩小時，依蓮很快地減輕了她的體重。

【2】 如果主詞是動作的接受者，或是被動的被給予某條件，則原形動詞 V 改為 V- p.p.，過去分詞的分詞構句則有被動含義，如：

Given the circumstances, I accept your offer.

被給予這樣的情況條件下，我接受你的出價。

是由 I was given the circumstances, I accept your offer. 轉變而來。

Given ⇨ 被動含義

主詞 I 是 given 的接受者。（被給予）

Hit by a car, I was in a hospital for a week.

被車撞到，我住院了一個禮拜。（被撞到）

就是這樣寫

2. Trusting the financial analyst's advice, Mark invested all his money on the stock.

   因為信任財務分析師的建議，馬克把他所有的錢投資在股票上。

3. Running out of money, Helen was forced to reduce her spending.

   因為快把錢用光了，海倫被迫降低她的花費。

4. Not knowing how to get out, he continued to involve himself in illegal activities.

   因為不知如何脫身，他繼續參與在非法活動中。

5. Needing someone's affirmation, children who grow up without enough care from the parents tend to feel a lack of security.

   由於需要別人的肯定，缺乏父母關愛的孩子通常覺得缺少安全感。

6. Having a confident smile, Gordon makes people identify with him right away.

   因為有自信的笑容，葛登讓人們很容易馬上認同他。

7. Determined to pass the exam, he continued to study as hard as he can.

   下定決心通過考試，他繼續盡他所能努力唸書。

8. Lacking enough confidence about my decision, I seek approval from my parents.

   因為對我的決定缺乏足夠信心，我向我父母尋求許可。

9. Exercising more than four hours a day, Debbie becomes very healthy and slim in two months.

   因為每天運動超過四小時，黛比在兩個月內變得非常健康又苗條。

10. Traveling together for more than three months, I developed a strong friendship with Ted.

在一起旅行超過三個月後，我跟泰德培養了堅強的友情。

11. Working as hard as he can, he finally achieved his goal of buying a house.

在盡他所能的努力工作後，他終於達成他買一棟房子的目標。

12. Tired of being in the crowd, I prefer to go home and spend the night alone.

厭倦在人群裡，我寧可回家自己一個人度過夜晚。

13. Seeing the confusion on his face, the teacher explained this math problem to Mark one more time.

在看到他臉上的困惑後，老師再跟馬克解釋這個數學問題一次。

14. Seeing how much you love my daughter, I agree that you marry her.

看到你有多愛我的女兒，我同意你娶她。

15. Given the circumstances, I accept your offer.

在這樣的情況下，我接受你的出價。

16. Losing his parents, the child can only depend on his grandmother.

由於失去雙親，這個孩子只能依靠他的奶奶。

17. Brought up in different families, the brothers differ from each other in personality.

由於由不同的家庭養大，這對兄弟彼此的個性不同。

18. Hearing her voice, I recognize the woman is Mary right away.

一聽到她的聲音，我馬上認出這個女人就是瑪麗。

19. Isolated in his cell in the prison, David reflected what he had done in the past.

當在他的獄房中孤立獨處，大衛反省他過去所做的事。

20. Knowing what had happened, I intended to help this poor man.

知道發生了什麼事以後，我意圖幫助這位可憐的男人。

21. Traveling all around the world, Ellen settled down in her hometown in the end.

旅行過全世界之後，艾倫最後在她的家鄉定居下來。

22. Irritated by John's remark, Lucy threw a pen at him.

被約翰的評論所惹怒，露西向他丟了一支筆。

23. Delayed by the traffic, we arrived twenty minutes late.

受到交通所延誤，我們晚了二十分鐘到。

24. Occupied by her own work, Helen ignored her son's strange behavior.

因為被她自己的工作所佔據，海倫忽略了她兒子奇怪的行為。

25. Hearing what the pilot had done to save the airplane from crushing, everybody admired him for his courage.

聽到這個飛行員為了拯救飛機不墜毀所做的事後，每個人都崇尚他的勇氣。

26. Touched by his determination, the committee finally approves of Bill's proposal.

被他的決心所感動，委員會終於提議比爾的提案。

27. Moved by Nancy's continuous devotion, Hank finally commits to help her finish the project.

受到南希持續投入的感動，漢克終於承諾幫助她完成這項計劃。

28. Tired of his behavior, I suppose I will not talk to Mark for a while.

因為厭倦他的行為，我想我有一陣子不會跟馬克談話了。

【句型 48】 Instead of 除了…之外

 必考字彙表 V1～V28

1. regret	8. divide	15. persuade	22. throw
2. quote	9. charge	16. attach	23. arrive
3. resolve	10. support	17. ignore	24. believe
4. roll	11. purchase	18. consult	25. realize
5. miss	12. submit	19. calculate	26. confirm
6. split	13. translate	20. distribute	27. follow
7. combine	14. illustrate	21. recommend	28. retire

必考 句型與解析

【句型 48】Instead of 除了…之外

【結構】 Instead of（與其）+ regretting（後悔）+ the mistakes in the past（某事）+ 你為什麼不做…。Instead of ⇨ 與其，regretting the mistake in the past ⇨ 懊悔過去的錯誤，（後悔的某事，A 動作）why don't you seize opportunity at the present moment? ⇨ 為什麼不把握現在的時刻，（倒不如做另外一事，B 動作），在此例句裡，意指與其做 instead of 後面的 A 動作，主詞不如做逗點之後

分句的 B 動作。

【句子】　Instead of regretting the mistake in the past, why don't you seize the opportunity at the present moment?

【中譯】　與其後悔過去的錯誤，為什麼你不把握在當下時刻的機會？

 解　析　

由句型 48【Instead of】句型可得知，Instead of 有 "與其⋯倒不如" 的意思，之後省略主詞，因為 instead of 是介系詞，後方動詞需改為動名詞，regret 改為 regretting，代表後悔的意思，"Instead of regretting the mistake in the past" 有與其後悔過去的錯誤的意思，而本範例 "倒不如" 所提出的另一個建議，則是用問句的方式呈現："why don't you seize opportunity at the present moment?"，"seize the opportunity" 為一片語，為把握機會的意思。

在構思【Instead of】的句型時，主要是要掌握兩個子句之間的內在關係，句意上要有 "與其⋯倒不如" 的關係，然後再套入句型結構中，可依據表格上的不同動詞，推演出各種變化的句子。

新多益篇

【新多益】V1～V28

【1】 "Instead of" 是介系詞，後方需搭配名詞，或省略主詞後動詞改為動名詞 Ving，放在句首之後要加逗點，有 " 替代 "、" 而不 " 的意思，或是整個句子若較長，有 " 與其…倒不如 " 的否定意涵，如：

Instead of Japan, she decided to go to Canada for vacation.

她決定去加拿大而不去日本度假。

Instead of taking a bus, I took a train to Taipei.

我搭火車而不搭公車去台北。

【2】 "instead of" 也可以放在句中，如：

I'll have coffee instead of tea, please.

我要咖啡，不要茶。

David wants to go traveling by himself, instead of joining a group tour.

大衛想要自助旅行，而不是參加團體旅遊。

✎ 就是這樣寫

2. Instead of quoting from others, I would like to hear your own opinion.

與其引用別人的話，我想要聽到你自己的意見。

3. Instead of resolving the conflict by violence, I suggest we all calm down and take a step back.

與其用暴力解決衝突，我建議我們都冷靜下來退後一步。

4. Instead of rolling the dough with your hands, you can also try to use

a rolling pin.

除了用你的手桿麵外,你可以試著用桿麵棍。

5. Instead of missing him terribly for the next three years, you can go to the United States to reunite with him.

    與其在接下來的三年痛苦的思念他,你可以到美國去與他重聚。

6. Instead of splitting up with Jack, Karen worked out problems with him and married to him.

    不但沒有跟傑克分手,凱倫解決了跟他之間的問題,並嫁給他。

7. Instead of combining our resources, my partner and I are always fighting.

    不但沒有結合我們的資源,我的夥伴跟我永遠在吵架。

8. Instead of dividing the cake into half, Jeff ate all the cake by himself.

    不但沒有把蛋糕分成兩半,傑克把所有的蛋糕自己吃掉。

9. Instead of charging me, the company transferred money to my account by mistake.

    不但沒有讓我付錢,這個公司還誤把錢匯到我的戶頭。

10. Instead of supporting her two children, I would like to see Jane live for herself.

    除了支持她的兩個小孩以外,我想看到珍為她自己而活。

11. Instead of purchasing all the mountain climbing equipment, why don't we borrow them from John?

    與其購買所有的登山設備,我們為什麼不向約翰借?

12. Instead of submitting your old manuscript to the publisher, I think you should write something new.

    與其把你舊的文稿交給出版者,我想你應該寫些新的東西。

13. Instead of translating all the Spanish poems into English, why don't you ask your students to pick up some Spanish vocabulary in the poems in tomorrow's class?

    與其把所有的西班牙詩翻譯成英文，你為什麼不請你的學生在明天的課上在詩中學一些西班牙單字？

14. Instead of illustrating for the newspaper, I prefer drawing for the storybook much more.

    與其為報紙插畫，我喜歡為故事書畫畫多了。

15. Instead of persuading him to go to the party, I'd rather and go to the party by myself.

    與其說服他參加派對，我寧可自己去派對。

16. Instead of attaching the file through an email, you can transfer the file to me using a USB.

    與其把檔案用 email 加載，你可以用 USB 把檔案傳給我。

17. Instead of ignoring Simon's mistake, the teacher pointed it out and made everyone know about it.

    不但沒有忽略賽門的錯誤，這個老師還指出它來讓每個人都知道。

18. Instead of consulting with her parents, Jessica went to a fortune teller to ask about which college she should apply.

    與其諮詢她的父母，潔西卡向一位算命師詢問她該申請哪一所大學。

19. Instead of calculating the gain and loss, Helen always makes decisions by her instincts.

    與其計算得與失，海倫總是以她的直覺做決定。

20. Instead of distributing the profits equally, the boss monopolizes all the money.

    不但沒有平等的分配利潤，老闆獨佔了所有的錢。

21. Instead of recommending a good restaurant for us to go, Ken suggested a lousy place to us.

不但沒有推薦我們去一個好餐館，肯給我們建議了一個很糟的地方。

22. Instead of throwing her old furnitures away, Martha rented a warehouse to store them.

瑪莎不但沒有把她的舊傢俱丟掉，還租了一個倉庫去存放他們。

23. Instead of arriving on time for the appointment, Jane was late for forty minutes.

不但沒有準時赴約，珍晚到了四十分鐘。

24. Instead of believing that he would come to save us, I suggest we find a way out by ourselves.

與其相信他會來救我們，我建議我們自己找到一條路出去。

25. Instead of realizing that John had lied to her all through the time, May was still in the fantasy that someday she would get her money back.

與其理解到約翰在過去一直在騙她，梅還是陷在有天她會把錢拿回來的幻想裡。

26. Instead of confirming the booking for me, the staff at the airline company had cancelled my booking by mistake.

不但沒有為我確認機位，航空公司的職員錯把我的訂位取消了。

27. Instead of following the crowd, you should develop your own style.

與其追隨群眾，你應該培養自己的風格。

28. Instead of retiring at the age of sixty-five, he continued to work till he was eighty.

不但沒有在六十五歲退休，他一直到八十歲還在繼續工作。

【句型 49】How + adj + S + V!

1. accurate	8. precious	15. polite	22. mischievous
2. adorable	9. stiff	16. rude	23. outrageous
3. boring	10. unthankful	17. concise	24. philosophical
4. logical	11. vulnerable	18. massive	25. secretive
5. irratating	12. galmorous	19. innovative	26. spontanenous
6. narrow	13. flexible	20. smooth	27. isolated
7. perfect	14. hospitable	21. sharp	28. treacherous

必考 句型與解析

【句型 49】How + adj + S + V（多麼）。

【結構】 How + accurate（精確的）+ your prediction（主詞）is!，how ⇨ 多麼的，accurate ⇨ 準確的，your prediction ⇨ 真正的主詞，is⇨ 動詞。

【句子】 How accurate your prediction is!

【中譯】 你的預測多麼準確！

解　析

由句型 49【How + adj. + S + V! 多麼】句型可得知，How 為句首的感嘆句有 “ 主詞多麼… ” 的意思，在本句裡，主詞為 your prediction，你的預測，而 accurate 來形容你預測是準確的，而由於主詞是第三人稱單數，就用 is 作動詞，完成了 How accurate your prediction is 的句子。

在構思【How + adj. + S + V! 多麼】的句型時，有倒裝的成分，將 Your prediction is accurate. 倒裝為 How accurate your prediction is! 動詞亦移到最後。在寫作時，可以將各個平述句改為感嘆句，產生驚訝、驚歎的意味，可以不同的主詞，搭配表格上的不同形容詞，演繹出各種變化的句子。

必考文法概念

【1】 “How + adj. + S + V!” 屬於感嘆句，how 是副詞，用於加強形容詞，因此在此句構裡，可以依據主詞設想不同的形容詞，然後之後的動詞依據主詞的單複數、時態作變化。

如：

How wonderful this book is! 這本書有多棒！ ⇨ 一本書

How wonderful those books are! 這些書有多棒 ⇨ 這些書

How lovely the party was yesterday! 昨天的派對有多美好！

⇨ 昨天的派對，發生於昨天，故用過去式 was。

【2】 替代用法可用："What + a adj. + N. + S. + V.!"，同樣依單複數、時態
變化，如：

What a beautiful girl she is! 她是個多麼美麗的女孩！

What sweet apples you have grown! 你種出多麼甜的蘋果！

【3】 常見的形容詞字尾

字尾	意義	範例
-ABLE	可以；可能	agree – agreeable; remark – remarkable
-IBLE	可以；可能	access – accessible; flex – flexible force – forcible; sense – sensible
-ANT	表現…動作	please – pleasant; rely – reliant
-ENT	表現…動作	differ – different; depend – dependent; confide – confident; urge – urgent
-IVE	造成…動作	attract – attractive; create – creative
-ING	造成…動作	amuse – amusing; excite – exciting; confuse – confusing; surprise –surprising
-AL	相關	accident – accidental; person – personal; region – regional; universe –universal
-ARY	相關	compliment – complimentary
-FUL	充滿	beauty – beautiful; delight – delightful; skill – skillful; success – successful
-IC	具有…本質	base – basic; photograph – photographic;
-ICAL	具有…本質	history – historical; magic – magical; logic – logical; practice – practical
-ISH	狀態	fool – foolish; child – childish; girl – girlish; self – selfish

-LESS	沒有；相反	use – useless; hope – hopeless
-LIKE	相似	life – lifelike; child – childlike
-LY	相似	friend – friendly; cost – costly
-OUS	狀態	danger – dangerous; mystery – mysterious
-Y	相似	dirt – dirty; mess – messy; rain – rainy
-ED	接受…動作	amuse – amused; excite – excited

就是這樣寫

2. How adorable the little doll is!

   這個小洋娃娃多麼令人喜愛！

3. How boring the lecture is ！

   這個演講多麼無聊！

4. How logical your reasoning is!

   你的論理多麼的有邏輯性！

5. How irritating his comments are ！

   他的評論多麼的讓人惱怒！

6. How narrow the road is!

   這條道路有多小！

7. How perfect the plan is!

   這個計劃有多麼完美！

8. How precious the antique is!

   這個古董有多麼珍貴！

9. How stiff my body is!

   我的身體有多麼僵硬！

10. How unthankful the boy is!
這個男孩多麼不懂得感謝！

11. How vulnerable our security system is!
我們的安全系統多麼脆弱！

12. How glamorous the gown is!
這件禮服有多麼華麗！

13. How flexible the company's policy is!
這個公司的政策多麼有彈性！

14. How hospitable the villagers are!
這些村民多麼好客！

15. How polite the Japanese people are!
日本人多麼有禮貌！

16. How rude the little boy is!
這個男孩多麼粗魯！

17. How concise this report is!
這份報告多麼簡潔！

18. How massive the rock is!
這塊岩石多麼巨大！

19. How innovative Steve Jobs was!
史提夫賈伯斯多麼創新！

20. How smooth your skin is!
你的皮膚有多麼滑順！

21. How sharp the knife is!
這把刀有多鋒利！

22. How mischievous your behavior is!
你的行為有多麼調皮！

23. How outrageous the poem is!

這首詩有多麼驚世駭俗！

24. How philosophical his thoughts are!

他的思想多麼有哲學性！

25. How secretive his behavior is!

他的行為有多麼神秘！

26. How spontaneous this performance is!

這場表演有多麼自然隨性！

27. How isolated this town is!

這個鎮有多麼孤立！

28. How treacherous the road is!

這條路有多麼崎嶇難行！

【句型 50】 Had better + 原 V

【新多益】必考字彙表 Adj 1～Adj 28

1. access	8. decrease	15. estimate	22. abandon
2. asisst	9. correspond	16. admit	23. expand
3. concentrate	10. prohibit	17. request	24. write
4. require	11. clarify	18. design	25. prioritize
5. analyze	12. construct	19. respond	26. reconsider
6. demonstrate	13. select	20. explain	27. fasten
7. unplug	14. throw	21. improve	28. swallow

必考 句型與解析

【句型 50】had better + 原 V（最好…）。

【結構】 had better + 原形 V。S + had better + access（進入）+（進入的地方）...。You ⇨ 主詞，had better ⇨ 最好，access ⇨ 進入，through the back door ⇨ 從後門。

【句子】 You had better access the building through back door, so nobody can see you.

【中譯】 你最好從後門進入這棟建築才不會有人看到你。

解　析

由句型 50【had better + 原形 V】句型可得知，"had better" 有最好的建議意味，在本句裡，主詞為 you，加上 had better 後，有 "你最好…" 的意思，之後的原形動詞接 access，代表進入，the building 為受詞，所以是你最好進入這棟建築…，用什麼方式呢？本句設想為 "through the back door" 的預測，從後門進來，才能達成 "so nobody will see you" 不會有人看到你的目的，完成本句。

在構思【had better + 原形 V】的句型時，主要是在設想主詞為了達成什麼目的，最好從事什麼行為，讓句意是合理通順的，可依據不同的主詞，搭配表格上的不同動詞，演繹出各種變化的句子。

必考文法概念

【1】 "had better" 中 had 為助動詞，而 better 為副詞，因此一般學生 看到 had 會認為是過去式，殊不知 "had better" 連用時，跟 should 的用法類似，是針對某種狀況下提出的建議，had better 之後一般接原形動詞，指主詞現在最好應該做某件事。

對第二及第三人稱使用時，具有告知或建議對方 " 有義務去做某事 " 的告知或建議的意思，所以 had better 並不適用於對上輩（如老闆、父母）使用。

【2】 "had better" 否定形式為 "had better not"，

如：

We had better not be late. 我們最好不要遲到。

You had better not miss the class. 你最好不要錯過這堂課。

【3】 "had better" 後，若接動詞的進行式 "had better + be + V-ing"，是表示最好馬上做某事，在口語中很常見，如：I had better get going. 我最好快走了。

如：

We had better not be late. 我們最好不要遲到。

You had better not miss the class. 你最好不要錯過這堂課。

就是這樣寫

2. You had better assist him in this project.
   你最好在這項專案中協助他。

3. You had better concentrate on your study before the exam.
   你在考試前最好專注於你的課業。

4. We had better require all the applicants to fill the forms immediately.
   我們最好要求所有的申請者立刻填完表格。

5. You had better analyze the data carefully before you make a statement.
   在你提出言論前，你最好小心地分析資料。

6. You had better demonstrate to the boy how to do the job before you ask him to do it.
   在你要求男孩做這工作前，你最好先示範給他看。

7. You had better unplug the TV when you go to sleep.
   你在睡覺前最好把電視插頭拔掉。

8. You had better decrease the amount of cigarettes you smoke to protect your health.
   你最好減少你抽煙的數量以維護你的健康。

9. We had better start to correspond with the reporter to know what is going on in the field.
   我們最好開始跟報導者通訊去知道當地發生了什麼事。

10. We had better prohibit the students from going out of the dormitory after eleven o'clock in the night.
    我們最好禁止學生在十一點以前從宿舍出去。

11. You had better clarify what you mean.
    你最好釐清你的意義是什麼。

12. We had better construct a tool shed to store all our tools.
    我們最好建造一個工具間以存放我們所有的工具。

13. I had better select some photos to send to him tonight.
    我最好選擇一些照片今晚寄給他。

14. You had better throw the ball with more strength.
    你最好用更多力量丟球。

15. You had better estimate how much the trip will cost you before you decide to go.
    你在決定出發前，最好計算這趟旅行會花你多少錢。

16. You had better admit your mistakes before it is too late.
    在太晚之前，你最好承認你的錯誤。

17. We had better request his help on this matter.
    在這件事上我們最好請他幫忙。

18. You had better design the dress with a different piece of cloth.

你最好用不同的布料設計這件衣服。

19. You had better respond to our questions immediately.

你最好立即回應我們的問題。

20. You had better explain what has happened.

你最好解釋發生了什麼事。

21. You had better improve your language ability if you want to be a flight attendant.

如果你要當一名空服員的話，你最好增進你的語言能力。

22. We had better abandon the car and start to walk to the next village before it gets dark.

我們最好拋棄這台車，在天黑之前開始走向下一個村莊。

23. We had better expand our customer base if we want to increase our business.

如果我們要增加生意的話，我們最好擴大客群。

24. I had better write it down because I don't think I can memorize his telephone number.

我最好把它寫下來，因為我想我應該記不起來他的電話號碼。

25. You had better prioritize what you want to do for this week.

你最好排定你這個禮拜想做的事的優先順序。

26. You had better reconsider your decision given all the circumstances.

在這種情況下，你最好重新考慮你的決定。

27. You had better fasten the seatbelt as we are going through a turbulence.

我們正在通過亂流，你最好繫緊安全帶。

28. You had better swallow the food more slowly; otherwise, you will choke yourself.

你最好吞嚥食物慢一點，不然你會噎到你自己。

英語學習 —職場系列—

定價：新台幣349元
規格：336頁 / 18K / 雙色印刷

定價：新台幣349元
規格：336頁 / 18K / 雙色印刷

定價：新台幣450元
規格：272頁 / 18K / 全彩印刷/MP3

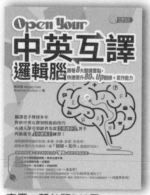

定價：新台幣349元
規格：328頁 / 18K / 雙色印刷

定價：新台幣299元
規格：320頁 / 18K / 雙色印刷

定價：新台幣349元
規格：304頁 / 18K / 雙色印刷

定價：新台幣349元
規格：304頁 / 18K / 雙色印刷

定價：新台幣349元
規格：304頁 / 18K / 雙色印刷

定價：新台幣360元
規格：288頁 / 18K / 雙色印刷/MP3

英語學習 —生活·文法·考用—

定價：NT$369元/K$115元
規格：320頁/17＊23cm/MP3

定價：NT$380元/HK$119元
規格：320頁/17＊23cm/MP3

定價：NT$349元/HK$109元
規格：352頁/17＊23cm

定價：NT$380元/HK$119元
規格：288頁/17＊23cm/MP3

定價：NT$329元/HK$103元
規格：352頁/17＊23cm

定價：NT$349元/HK$109元
規格：304頁/17＊23cm

定價：NT$380元/HK$119元
規格：352頁/17＊23cm

定價：NT$369元/HK$115元
規格：304頁/17＊23cm/MP3

定價：NT$380元/HK$119元
規格：304頁/17＊23cm/MP3

Leader 040

哈佛高材生的英語寫作筆記

作　　者	Nipa Wu
發 行 人	周瑞德
執行總監	齊心瑪
企劃編輯	陳韋佑
校　　對	編輯部
封面構成	高鍾琪

內頁構成	華漢電腦排版有限公司
印　　製	大亞彩色印刷製版股份有限公司
初　　版	2016 年 3 月
定　　價	新台幣 380 元
出　　版	力得文化
電　　話	(02) 2351-2007
傳　　真	(02) 2351-0887
地　　址	100 台北市中正區福州街 1 號 10 樓之 2
E - m a i l	best.books.service@gmail.com
網　　址	www.bestbookstw.com

港澳地區總經銷	泛華發行代理有限公司
地　　　　址	香港新界將軍澳工業邨駿昌街 7 號 2 樓
電　　　　話	(852) 2798-2323
傳　　　　真	(852) 2796-5471

國家圖書館出版品預行編目資料

哈佛高材生的英語寫作筆記 / Nipa Wu
著. -- 初版. -- 臺北市 : 力得文化,
2016.03 面 ； 公分. -- (Leader ;
40)ISBN 978-986-92398-9-9(平裝)
1.英語 2.寫作法 3.句法

805.17　　　　　105002274